THE FAIRY GUNMOTH

DANIEL PENNAC, was born in Casablanca in 1944, his father being in the French colonial service. He travelled widely in his youth, in Europe, Asia and Africa, and has been employed in a number of capacities, including woodcutter, Paris cab driver, illustrator and schoolteacher. He has written stories for children and for adults, and a highly successful book on the art of reading, *Reads like a Novel*, as well as the four humorous crime novels set in the Belleville quarter of Paris, of which *The Fairy Gunmother* is the second volume. He is married, with one child.

IAN MONK is one of the most resourceful translators from French. He made his own translation of Georges Perec's e-less novel *La Disparition* before Harvill published Gilbert Adair's version, and went on to translate Perec's novella that uses no vowel but e, *Les Revenentes*, the latter in a volume with two other Perec translations by his hand, *Three by Perec*, also published by Harvill. He has also translated Corto Maltese cartoon strips by Hugo Pratt. A long-time resident of Paris, he is well acquainted with the local idiom.

Daniel Pennac

THE FAIRY GUNMOTHER

Translated from the French
by Ian Monk

THE HARVILL PRESS
LONDON

First published in France by Editions Gallimard
with the title *La Fée carabine*, in 1987

First published in Great Britain in 1997
by The Harvill Press
84 Thornhill Road
London N1 1RD

1 3 5 7 9 8 6 4 2

© Editions Gallimard, 1987
English translation © Ian Monk, 1997

Daniel Pennac asserts the moral right to be
identified as the author of this work

A CIP catalogue record for this book
is available from the British Library

This edition has been translated with the financial
assistance of the French Ministry of Culture

ISBN 1 86046 325 8 (hbk)
ISBN 1 86046 326 6 (pbk)

Designed and typeset in Minion at
Libanus Press, Marlborough, Wiltshire

Printed and bound in Great Britain by Butler & Tanner Ltd
at Selwood Printing, Burgess Hill

"And no-one ever saved anyone by the sword.
That changed the dog and me."

ROBERT SOULAT (*L'Avant-Printemps*)

"Isn't growing old a shame?" my father used to say.
"But it's the only way I've found to avoid dying young."

To the French NHS

For Igor, for André Vers,
Nicole Schneegans, Alain Léger
and Jean-François Carrez-Corral.
And each word in memory of
Jean and Germaine.

The City One Night

A CITY IS A DOG'S
FAVOURITE DINNER

Chapter 1

IT WAS WINTER over Paris's Belleville quarter and there were five characters. Six, including the sheet of black ice. Or even seven, if you count the dog that had gone along with Half Pint to the baker's. An epileptic dog, with its tongue dangling out the corner of its mouth.

The sheet of black ice looked like a map of Africa, covering the whole of the junction which the old lady had started to cross. That's right, there on the ice walked an ancient, wobbly old biddy, gingerly inching one slippered foot in front of the other. A cast-off leek stuck out of her shopping bag, an old shawl was wrapped round her shoulders and a hearing aid sat in the shell of her ear. Across that Africa-shaped sheet of ice, her slippers' inching progress had now taken her as far as, say, the middle of the Sahara. There was still all of the south left, the land of apartheid and what not. Unless she took a short cut via Eritrea or Somalia; but the Red Sea was frozen solid in the gutter. These speculations were streaming through the consciousness of a blond head belonging to a man in a green overcoat, who was watching the old dear from the pavement. And it made him think that he had one hell of an imagination. Then the old dear's shawl suddenly spread out, like it was a bat taking off, and everything came to a standstill. She'd lost her balance. Then she got it back again. The disappointed blond cursed between his teeth. Watching people fall flat on their faces always made him laugh. That was one of the nasty things about this blond head. Though it looked as neat as can be from the outside, with its dense, evenly barbered crewcut. But its owner didn't like oldsters much. He found them a bit disgusting. He imagined them from their insides out, so to speak. So there he was, wondering whether the old biddy was going to take a dive or not on that African pack-ice, when he spotted two other characters on the pavement opposite, who were, in fact, not unrelated to things African: Arabs. Two of them. North Africans, if you want. Or Maghrebins, or whatever. He'd often racked his blond brains to know what to call them so as he wouldn't sound racist. It was very important for him not to sound racist, what with the opinions he held. He was Nationally Frontal and made no bones about it. And that's just why he didn't want people to say he was NF *because* he was racist. No, like he'd once learnt at school, this was not a case of cause and effect. It was a case of consequences. That blond head of his had become Nationally Frontal as a *consequence* of having objectively thought through the dangers of uncontrolled immigration. And he had quite sensibly made up his mind that all that scum should be chucked out of the country as soon as possible. Firstly, with a view to saving the purity of the French livestock, secondly because of unemployment and, finally, to uphold law and order. (When you've got that many good reasons for your healthy opinions, it wouldn't do to have them marked down as being racist.)

So there we are, with the old dear, the Africa-shaped ice, the two Arabs on the pavement opposite, Half Pint with his epileptic dog and the blond noddle thinking away to itself . . . It belonged to Vanini, Inspector Vanini, and it was particularly the law and order angle that was bothering it just then. That was what it was doing there in Belleville, alongside the heads belonging to various other plain-clothes inspectors. That was what the pair of chrome-plated handcuffs was doing there, bouncing up and down on his right buttock. And the revolver too, strapped up in its holster under his armpit. As well as the knuckleduster in his pocket and the CS gas canister in his sleeve, these being Vanini's own personal additions to the official armoury. First use the latter, so as to get in a nice easy beating with the former. It was his own tried and tested technique. That's right, the lack of law and order was a serious problem. Those four old dears who'd been cut up in Belleville in the last month obviously hadn't slit their own throats!

Violence . . .

Ah, yes, violence . . .

Vanini's blond head glanced across at the Arabs. We weren't just going to let them stick our old dears like pigs, were we? Suddenly, he felt like a real hero: there they were, the two Arabs on the pavement opposite, casually chatting away in their lingo, and then him, Inspector Vanini on this side, with his blond head and his heart full of that lovely warm feeling you get when you're just about to dive into the Seine towards an outstretched hand. Get to the old dear before they did. Act as a deterrent. And do it at once. So, the young inspector set foot on the African continent (just imagine if anyone'd told him he'd wind up going there!). He confidently strode off towards the old dear. His feet didn't slip on the ice. He had his metal-studded boots on, the same ones he always wore, ever since his army training days. So off he goes across the ice to help this senior, or even senile, citizen, while keeping an eye on the Arabs opposite. Out of the goodness of his heart. That heart is now swollen with goodness. For the old lady's frail shoulders suddenly remind him of his old beloved grandmother's. Beloved after her death, unfortunately. Yes, the old often die too soon, without waiting for our love to arrive. Vanini'd really held that against his grandmother, the way she hadn't given him the chance to love her while she was alive. But still, loving our dead ones is better than not loving anyone. That was what Vanini reckoned as he neared the wobbly old woman. Even her shopping bag was touching. And her hearing aid . . . Vanini's grandmother too had been deaf during the last years of her life and, in just the same way, she'd used to fiddle constantly with the volume button on her hearing aid, lodged between her ear and the few grey hairs left scattered on her scalp. That familiar movement of her index finger was a dead spit of Vanini's grandmother. The blond inspector was now melting with affection. It had almost made him forget about the Arabs. He was getting his little speech ready: "Would you like me to give you a hand, grandma?", that's what he'd say, sweetly, with almost grandson-like devotion, in a whisper so that the sudden burst of sound in the hearing aid wouldn't make the poor old dear jump out of her skin. Burning with love, he was now only one step behind her and that's when she turned round. All of a sudden. With her arm stretched out towards him. Like she was pointing at him. Except that, instead of an index finger, there was the barrel of an ancient

P.38, the German model, a gun that had come down through the century without aging, an ever-modern antique, an old traditional killing machine, with its hypnotic eye.

And she pulled the trigger.

Every idea in that blond head was blown to smithereens. Against the winter sky, it became a beautiful flower. Before the first petal had fallen, the old dear'd put her gun back into her shopping bag and set off again. The recoil had even given her a good yard's start across the ice.

Chapter 2

S O, THERE WAS a murder. And three witnesses. Except Arabs don't see anything when they don't want to. It's a funny thing about them. It must come from their culture. Or from something they've copped onto about ours. So these Arabs of ours saw nothing. They probably didn't even hear the "bang".

There's the kid and the dog left. But all that Half Pint saw through his round, rose-tinted glasses was a blond head turning into a heavenly flower. And that knocked him out so much that he legged it back home to tell us. That's to say me, Benjamin Malaussène, my brothers and sisters, our four granddads, my mother and my old mate Stojilkovicz who right now is massacring me at chess.

The door of the former hardware shop where we're living crashes open to reveal Half Pint bawling:

"Hey! I've seen a fairy godmother!"

But this doesn't stop the household in its tracks. My sister Clara, who's cooking a shoulder of lamb à la Montalban, just asks him sweetly:

"That's nice, Half Pint. Tell us all about it . . ."

And Julius the Dog goes straight over to check out his bowl.

"A real, nice, old fairy godmother!"

My brother Jeremy grabs the excuse to get his nose out of his exercise book.

"She did your homework for you?"

"No," says Half Pint. "She turned this bloke into a flower."

As no-one reacts, Half Pint comes over to Stojilkovicz and me.

"It's true, uncle Stojil. I saw a fairy godmother. She turned this bloke into a flower."

7

"Better that than the other way round," answers Stojil, staring at the chess board.

"Why?"

"Because if fairy godmothers started turning flowers into blokes, the countryside would become unvisitable."

Stojil's voice sounds like Big Ben chiming through a Victorian London fog. It's so deep it feels as if the air is reverberating around you.

"Check and mate, Ben, from a discovered check. I don't think your heart's in it this evening . . ."

It's not a question of my heart not being in it. I'm worried. I haven't really been following the game. What I've been following is the grand-dads. Twilight's their worst time. It's weird how dusk makes them itch for their smack. Their nerves crying out for their frigging fixes. They need to jack up. It's no time to let them out of my sight. The kids know that as well as I do and they're all doing their best to look after their official granddad. Clara goes to Granddad Kidney (an ex-butcher from Tlemcen, Algeria) to get some more tips concerning her shoulder of lamb à la Montalban. Jeremy (who's been put back into the second year again) makes out that he wants to know everything about Voltaire so that old Risson, his allotted granddad (and a retired bookseller), lays on some more juicy biographical details. Mum, stuck in her pregnant woman's armchair, lets Granddad Sweeney, an ex-hairdresser, curl then uncurl her hair, while Half Pint begs Verdun (at ninety-two years, the oldest of the granddads) to help him with his handwriting.

Every evening, it's the same ritual. Verdun's hand trembling like a leaf while Half Pint's hand steadies it from within, so that the oldster really thinks that his loops and curls are still as neat as they were before the First World War. But all the same, Verdun's sad. He's getting Half Pint to cover his exercise book with just one name: *Camille . . . Camille . . . Camille . . . Camille.* It's the name of his daughter who died sixty-seven years ago at the age of six, just at the end of the War to End All Wars, mowed down by that last fusillade of all, Spanish 'flu. When Verdun started getting smacked up, it was the image of Camille that he was reaching for. He saw himself, going over the top, dodging the bullets, cutting through barbed wire, steering clear of the mines and running, arms open, gunless, towards his Camille. He went right through the whole of the Great War only to find his Camille dead, mummified, more shrivelled up at six than he now is today. Double the dose of smack.

He hasn't been jacking up since I started hiding him. When the past gets to him he just looks at Half Pint with his bleary eyes and mumbles: "Why aren't you my little Camille?" Sometimes a tear drops on the exercise book and Half Pint says:

"You've smudged it again, Verdun."

Then it's too much even for Stojilkovicz, the ex-novice monk, ex-revolutionary, ex-victor over the armies of Vlasov and the hydra of Nazism, so that Stojil, now a coach driver for CCCP tourists and old ladies at weekends, clears his throat and groans:

"If God exists, I hope he's got a good excuse."

But my sister Thérèse is the one that works hardest at this crucial time of the evening.

Just now, in her witch's corner, she's patching up Granddad Sole. Old Sole isn't staying with us. He's our street's (Rue de la Folie Régnault) old shoemaker and he's got his own place next to ours. And he's never hit the smack. With him, we're taking preventive measures. He's old. He's lonely. He's childless. Retirement's doing his head in. He's a perfect target for the pushers. If we don't watch out, old Sole'll have more holes in him than a pub dartboard. Forgotten by everyone, after fifty years spent cobbling, Sole used to pace up and down to the rhythm of his depression. Luckily, Jeremy pressed the alarm bell: "Danger!" And Jeremy also sent a letter straight off to the town hall (in a perfect imitation of Sole's spidery handwriting) asking for a Civic Medal for the fifty years he'd spent at the same workbench. (That's right, in Paris you get decorated for that.) And wasn't Sole delighted when they answered yes! The very top mayor of all the mayors had remembered old Sole! Sole had a little place in the mayor of mayors' heart! Sole had been consecrated part of Paris's furniture. What glory and bliss!

But this evening, the eve of the great day, Sole is feeling down. He's frightened he won't be up to going through with the ceremony.

"Everything's going to be fine," Thérèse reassures the old man, holding his hand open in front of her.

"You're sure I won't do anything stupid?"

"I've told you I am. Have I ever been wrong?"

My sister Thérèse is as unbending as Science. She's got dry skin, a gangly, bony body and a primary schoolteacher's voice. All in all, about as charmless as you can get. She deals in a sort of magic I disapprove of, but all the same I never get tired of watching her in action. Every time an oldster turns up here, going to pieces from the insides out, sure that he's already worth less than zero before he's even dead, Thérèse drags him away into her corner, firmly takes his old palm in hers, opens his creaky fingers one by one, takes her time smoothing his palm out as if it was a sheet of crumpled paper and then, when she feels that the paw's perfectly relaxed, (hands that haven't been properly opened for years!) Thérèse starts talking. She doesn't smile. She doesn't butter them up. She just talks about their future. And the future's just about the most incredible thing that could happen to them. Thérèse gets her astral forces out for an airing: Saturn, Apollo, Venus, Jupiter and Mercury cook up the odd romantic encounter, sort out a few last-minute successes and open new horizons, all of which breathes new life into their old carcasses, showing them that they haven't come to the end of the road yet. And every time, a youngster reemerges from Thérèse's hands. Clara then gets out her camera to immortalize the transformation. And the photos of these rebirths decorate the walls of our flat. That's right. Our ageless Thérèse is a source of eternal youth.

"A woman? Are you sure?" old Sole splutters.

"A young brunette with blue eyes," Thérèse specifies.

Sole turns round towards us flashing a 3,000-watt grin.

"Did you hear that? Thérèse says that at the medal ceremony tomorrow I'm going to meet a young lady who'll transform my life!"

"Not just your life," Thérèse corrects him. "She's going to transform *all of our lives.*"

* * *

I'd dwell longer on the worried tone that breaks into Thérèse's voice, but the phone starts ringing and I recognize Louna, my third sister, on the other end of the line.

"Well then?"

Ever since mum's been pregnant again (for the seventh time, and for the seventh time by an unknown father), Louna's stopped saying "hello" and started saying "well then?"

"Well then?"

I glance over at mum. She's sitting in her armchair, perched motionless and serene above her belly.

"Well, nothing."

"What the hell's the sprog waiting for?"

"You're the qualified nurse, Louna, not me."

"But Ben, it's soon going to be ten months!"

That's quite true; the seventh happy event does seem to have gone pretty well over injury time.

"Maybe he's got a TV in there. He's seen what the outside world's like and he's in no hurry to take the plunge."

Louna chuckles, then asks:

"And the granddads?"

"At a low ebb."

"Laurent says you can double their doses of Valium if necessary."

(Laurent's our nursing sister's medic husband. They phone at the same time every evening to catch up on our atmospheric pressure.)

"Louna, I've already told Laurent that, from now on, we're their Valium."

"Whatever you say, Ben. You're the one in the firing line."

I've only just put the phone back on the hook when the postman (or whatever) rings a second time.

"Are you taking the piss, Malaussène?"

Oh dear, oh dear. I recognize that ferocious rattle. It's my boss, Queen Zabo, High Priestess of the Vendetta Press.

"You were supposed to be back at work two days ago!"

Quite true. Because of this business with the smacked-up granddads

I'd managed to wheedle two months' leave out of Queen Zabo by pretending I'd got viral hepatitis.

"I'm glad you called, your Highness," I reply, "I was just going to ask you for another month off."

"Out of the question. I'll expect you in at eight o'clock sharp tomorrow."

"Eight in the morning? No point your getting up so early for a month's wait."

"I'm not going to wait a month. If you're not in at eight, you'll be out and in the dole queue."

"You wouldn't do that."

"Oh, wouldn't I? You reckon you're that indispensable, do you, Malaussène?"

"Not a bit. You're the only indispensable one in the Vendetta Press, your Highness. But if you fire me, I'll have to put my sisters on the game, and my youngest brother too. He's a lovely little kid who wears rose-tinted glasses. You'd never forgive yourself for such immoral behaviour."

She chortles. (A threatening chortle which sounds like a gas leak.) Then carries straight on:

"Malaussène, I took you on as a scapegoat. You're paid to get your ear bent instead of mine. I miss you terribly."

(That's right, I'm employed as a goat. Officially, I'm a Literary Director, but in reality I'm a goat.) She presses brutally on:

"So why do you want this extra leave?"

In one sweeping glance I take in Clara at the cooker, Half Pint in Verdun's hand, Jeremy, Thérèse, the granddads and mum, who's presiding over the lot of them; a smooth, phosphorescent mum, like an Italian master's plump madonna.

"Let's just say my family needs me particularly badly at the moment."

"Exactly what sort of family do you have, Malaussène?"

Julius the Dog, lying with his dangling tongue at mum's feet, could easily pass for the ox and the ass. The photos of the granddads in their attractive frames seem to stare out into the future, like real Wise Men.

"A holy sort of family, your Highness . . ."

The phone goes silent for a moment, then that gravelly voice adds:

"I'll give you another fortnight and not a minute more."

She pauses.

"But listen up, Malaussène. *Just because you're on leave, don't think for a moment that you've stopped being a scapegoat* . You're a goat from your horns to your hooves. In fact, if anyone in Paris is looking for someone to blame for some immense foul-up, then that someone could well turn out to be you!"

Chapter 3

AND SURE ENOUGH, standing in his leather coat in Paris's minus twelve night-time weather, staring down at Vanini's corpse, Chief Superintendent Cercaria was looking for someone to blame.

"I'll murder whoever's responsible for this!"

With pinched grief picking out his black moustache, he was just the sort of copper to come out with something like that.

"Whoever's responsible for this, I'll murder him!"

(So he repeats it the other way round, staring at his reflection in the ice's dark mirror.)

At his feet, the uniformed officer who was chalking out Vanini's figure in the middle of the junction started belly-aching:

"Jesus, Cercaria, it's like a fucking ice-rink here!"

Cercaria was also the sort of copper who gets called by his surname. Not "Super", certainly not "Chief Superintendent", just his surname: "Cercaria". Cercaria liked his surname.

"Here, use this."

He handed him his flick-knife, which the officer used as an ice-pick before sketching out Vanini's tarmac suit. The blond head really did look like a broken flower – red in the middle, with yellow petals and, at the edges, a lingering purplish confusion. The officer hesitated for a moment.

"Trace it out as broadly as you like," Cercaria ordered.

Held at a distance by the blue police cordon, the eyes of the entire neighbourhood were fixed on the chalk's progress; like they were waiting for pennies from heaven.

"And not a single witness, then?"

Cercaria boomed out his question.

"Just onlookers!"

Silence from the small, well-wrapped-up crowd with their flurries of white breath: a shivering ball of lamb's wool unravelled just enough to allow through a TV camera.

"Listen, lady, this lad died for you!"

Cercaria addressed these words to a little old Vietnamese lady in the front row, wearing a straight Thai dress and thick hiker's socks stuck into a pair of wooden clogs. The old woman peered incredulously up at him then, realizing that it was really her this giant was talking to, she gravely announced:

"Hwas vely yun!"

"Yes, we pick them young for your protection."

Cercaria felt the muzzle of the lens start to lick his face. But this copper knew how to play to the camera.

"Plotekshen?" the old woman queried.

A quarter of an hour later, her long attentive face on the news would remind our most deserving viewers of Ho Chi Minh.

"That's right! For the protection of each and every old lady in the neighbourhood, without exception! So you can live in safety. SAFE-TY, you understand that?"

Then, suddenly, a sob broke Chief Superintendent Cercaria's voice as he addressed the camera:

"He was my finest officer."

The cameraman was immediately gobbled up by the network's car which then skidded him away round the corner. The crowd split up for home, leaving the coppers alone once more with the city. Only the old Vietnamese woman was still there, staring thoughtfully at Vanini's corpse which was being put into the ambulance.

"And you," Cercaria asked her, "why aren't you off home to admire yourself on TV like everyone else? The news will be on in ten minutes!"

She shook her head.

"Hi ghoing doan to Palis!"

She said "down to Paris", as opposed to "up to Belleville", like all the neighbourhood's oldest inhabitants.

"See tee family!" she added with a toothy grin.

Cercaria's interest in her died as quickly as it had been aroused. He snapped his fingers in order to get his flick-knife back from the uniformed officer, who'd pocketed it, then he barked:

"Bertholet! I want you to trawl over the whole of the east of Paris. Throw the net as wide as possible, then drag everything of interest down to the Station."

From the top of his frozen carcass, Inspector Bertholet pictured to himself a night spent waking up a hoard of bleary-eyed suspects.

"There'll be quite a crowd . . ."

Repocketing his knife, Cercaria swept away his objection.

"The more the merrier. Till we nail the right one."

He was staring fixedly at the flashing light of the ambulance that was taking Vanini away. Big Bertholet blew into his hands.

"And then there's the interrogation of Chabralle still to finish . . ."

Motionless in his leathers, Cercaria looked like a statue to Vanini, erected right there where he'd fallen.

"I want the bastard who did this."

He gulped down his stone tears and spoke with a leader's controlled grief.

"But Jesus, Cercaria, we can only hold Chabralle till eight. You want him to walk?"

Big Bertholet's voice had gone up a semitone. Since his squad had been working Chabralle over, the idea that this murderer might walk free one fine morning had been getting too much for him. Chabralle dunking a nice warm croissant in his coffee? Never!

"Chabralle's been giving us the run around for nearly forty-eight hours now. He's not going to crack at the last minute. You may as well let him go at once."

There was no answer to that. And revenge was in the air. Still, Bertholet made a last suggestion:

"And what if we called in Pastor to grill Chabralle?"

"Chief Superintendent Coudrier's little Pastor?"

This time Cercaria turned right round at once. In a flash, he imagined the Chabralle versus Pastor match. Chabralle, the mass murderer in his crocodile-skin coat, and the cherubic Pastor, Chief Superintendent Coudrier's little pet, lost in the baggy sweaters his mother always knitted for him. Chabralle against Pastor! What an excellent idea Bertholet'd had! Behind his mask of grief, Cercaria had a good giggle. For a full year now, Cercaria and Coudrier had been playing their little protégés, Vanini and Pastor, off against each other: Vanini the anti-riot ace and Pastor the crack interrogator . . . If you believed Coudrier, Pastor could make a gravestone confess! Vanini had been made of steel, and Vanini was dead. It was time to eliminate Coudrier's Little Prince Pastor – at least metaphorically.

"That's not a bad idea, Bertholet. If that bowl of mother's milk makes Chabralle crack, you can have my balls for breakfast."

Three hundred yards down the road, at the corner of Rue Faubourg du Temple and Avenue Parmentier, a tiny Vietnamese woman was doing her five-finger exercises in a cash point's gaping jaws. She was standing on tip-toe in her woollen socks and wooden clogs. It was eight-fifteen. Her picture had just flashed across every TV screen in the country, and every household had just been asked that disturbing, turn-of-the-century question:

"Plotekshen?"

But she was blithely getting this hole-in-the-wall piano to cough up its full load, at night, in the middle of the city, without taking the slightest precaution.

She didn't hear the big Black and the little thoroughbred Berber red-head come up behind her. She just smelt the former's cinnamon fragrance and the mint on the latter's breath. It made a slight wisp in the machine's mouth. Then there was a third odour: the impatient smell of youth. Pungent sweat, despite the cold. They'd been running. She didn't turn round. The notes piled up in front of her. When they reached 2,800 francs, the machine apologized for having to stop. She grabbed hold of the notes and stuffed them in a bundle through the slit of her Thai dress. One of them managed to make its escape and fluttered away under the red-head's nose. But the big Black's right foot stamped it flat onto the pavement. The escape bid was over. Meanwhile, the old woman got her credit card back and headed off towards métro Goncourt. She'd gently pushed her way between the two youths. All of William Tell's crossbow bolts would have snapped on the Black's stomach muscles and the Berber was broader than he was high. But she had slipped fearlessly between the two adolescents and was now walking calmly towards the métro.

"Hey, grandma!"

In two strides, the Black caught up with her.

"You lost some of your dosh, darling!"

He was a big third-generation Black African from Belleville. He waved the two-hundred franc note under her nose. She slowly pocketed it, thanked him politely then continued on her way.

"You've got to have a screw loose, getting all that dosh out round here."

The red-head had caught them up. The gap between his incisors made his grin broader than he was.

"Don't you read the papers? You dunno what smack-heads like us lot do to old wrinklies like you?"

Between the gap in his teeth, the wind of the Prophet was blowing.

"Linklees?" the old woman asked. "No hundastan 'linklees'."

"Oldsters," the big Black translated.

"You dunno all the tricks we get up to to get our hands on your dosh?"

"In just the last month in Belleville, we've done in three of you!"

"We grill your tits with Marlboros, wrench your nips off with pliers, crush your fingers one by one till you cough up your pin numbers, then we slit you in two. Just there."

The red-head's fat thumb traced the arc of a circle at the base of his neck.

"We've got our own consultant surgeon," the big Black added.

By now they were going down the métro steps.

"You're going to Paris?" the red-head asked.

"To myh doha-hin-lah's," the old woman answered.

"And you're taking the train with all that dosh on you?"

The red-head's right arm had wrapped itself like a shawl round the old woman's shoulders.

"Lheetle babee just bohn," she explained with a sudden smile. "Lotsa plezants!"

A train arrived at the same time they did in the Goncourt Brothers' natural grotto.

"We're going with you," the big Black decided.

He rapidly snapped up the catch of the door, which swished open.

"In case you bump into anyone nasty."

The carriage was empty. The three of them got in.

Chapter 4

MEANWHILE, BACK AT *the Malaussène residence*, as they say in my brother Jeremy's comic books, the granddads and the kids have had their dinner, cleared the table, crashed their way through the dishes, washed, got into their pyjamas and now they're sitting on the edges of their bunks, slippers dangling in midair with their eyes popping out their heads. For the small spherical object which is whistling and spinning horribly round the bedroom floor has frozen their very blood. It's black, compact, heavy, rotating at a mind-boggling speed and spitting like a nest of adders. I reckon that if the thing goes off, the whole family'll be blown away with it. Lumps of flesh and bits of bunk-bed will be found scattered from Place de la Nation to the Buttes Chaumont.

But it isn't the spherical object that's fascinating me, nor the icy terror that's gripping the kids and the granddads. What gets me is old Risson's mug, the way he *tells* it, his eyes staring, in a subdued voice, without making a single gesture, more concentrated than the explosive charge in that diabolical spinning-top. Old Risson tells a story every evening at the same time and, as soon as he gets going, it becomes more real than reality. When he sits himself down, bolt upright on the stool in the middle of the bedroom, with his burning eyes set in the middle of his incredible white mane, what becomes tinged with unreality are the bunks, the slippers, the pyjamas and the bedroom walls. Apart from what he's telling the kids and the granddads, nothing else exists. Right now, it's that black lump spinning round their feet and threatening to splatter them all over the shop. It's a French shell, fired on the 7th September, 1812, at the battle of Borodino (one hell of a slaughter, at which regiments of fairies turned regiments of blokes into flowers). The shell has landed at the feet of Prince Andrei Bolkonsky, who's standing there, motionless and indecisive, giving an excellent example to his men, while his orderly's got his nose buried in the mud. Prince Andrei is wondering whether what's spinning round in front of him has got his number on it or not, and old Risson, who's read *War and Peace* all the way through, knows that it has. He's just drawing out the pleasure in the half-light of the bedroom, with only one small lamp switched on, which Clara's covered with a blanket and which is shedding a mellow-yellow light across the floor.

Before Risson's arrival, it used to be me, Benjamin Malaussène, their irreplaceable big brother, who served them up their daily slice of bedtime fiction. It was the same thing every evening: "Tell us a story, Benjamin." I used to reckon myself the best act around. Even better than the box, when the box was already the best thing of all. Then along came Risson. (The new champ that always turns up to topple the old one . . .) It only took him one session to relegate me to the rank of a magic lantern and to give himself the dimensions of a cinemascopic-superpanavision and what have you. And he doesn't serve the kids up with your Mills and Boonses, but with the loftiest monuments of World Literature, huge novels that have been kept, still breathing, in his dedicated bookseller's memory. He then brings them to life again, in every detail, in front of an audience that has been metamorphosed into one gigantic ear.

I don't mind having been dethroned by Risson. First off, I was starting to run out of spit and to ogle second-hand TVs, and then, it's this visionary story-telling that's made Risson kick for good. He's found his brains again, his youth, his passion, his one and only reason to keep going.

It's a downright miracle, in fact! When I think back to the day he first appeared among us, it sends shivers down my soul.

It happened one evening, about a month ago. I was expecting Julie to call by, as she'd promised to bring us along another granddad. We were all eating. Clara and Grandpa Kidney had cooked us up some quails that were as chubby as a bent vicar's choirboys. We had raised our knives and forks ready to dig in, as they lay stark naked on their dishes, when suddenly: Ding dong!

"It's Julie!" I yell.

And my heart takes a leap towards the door.

It was my Corrençon, all right, with her hair, her curves, her smile and all that. But behind her . . . Behind her stood the most decrepit wrinkly she'd ever dragged along with her. He must have been pretty tall, once, but now he was so wasted that he'd lost all his dimensions. He must have been pretty handsome, but if corpses have their own special colour, then he had it too. A spiky skeleton swimming in its sagging skin. His every gesture was piercingly angular. His hair, his teeth, his nails and the whites of his eyes were yellow. His lips were gone. But the most striking thing of all was how, inside that carcass, behind his stare, a terrible vitality could be felt, something wilfully indestructible, that very image of living death which the yearning for heroin gives true smack-heads when they're hurting. Dracula in the flesh!

Julius the Dog slunk away growling to hide under a bed. The knives and forks dropped out of our hands and those little quails turned to cold turkey on our plates.

In the end, it was Thérèse who saved our skins. She got up, took hold of this ghoul by the hand and led him away to her table, where she got straight down to cooking up a future for him, just as she'd done with the other three granddads.

As for me, I dragged Julie into my room and did her a scene of whispered histrionics:

"You out of your tree, or what? Bringing us round a bloke in a state like that! You want him to croak here? You reckon my life's too straight-forward as it is?"

But Julie's got a gift. The gift of asking me questions which cut me in two. She asked:

"You don't recognize him?"

"So, I'm supposed to know who he is now, am I?"

"It's Risson."

"Risson?"

"Risson. The old bookseller from The Store."

The Store was my employer prior to the Vendetta Press, where I played just the same role of a scapegoat and where I got the sack after Julie'd written a long article in her magazine about the nature of my job. Now, there had indeed been an old bookseller there, tall and straight, white hair, proud as a peacock, crazy about literature, but with a ferocious nostalgia for nazidom. Risson? I brushed off the image of the little old wreck she was trying to shoulder off on us and made a comparison . . . Risson? Could be. So I said:

"Risson's an old cunt. His head's full of fermenting shit. I can't stand the man."

"Then what about the other granddads?" Julie slyly asked me.

"What about them?"

"What do you know about their pasts, about what they were like forty years back? Take Sweeney for example, a Gestapo informer, maybe? A barber gets to hear things, doesn't he? Then his tongue wags . . . And Verdun? still alive after the War to End All Wars, perhaps he hid behind his mates. And Kidney, the butcher from Algeria, just picture it: 'The Tlemcen Butcher'! Sounds just right for a mass-murderer . . .'"

Still murmuring, she popped open the first of our buttons and her lionness's purr slid smoothly into my ears.

"Believe you me, Benjamin, we'd best not delve into any of their pasts. Give them the right to remain silent."

"Right to silence, my arse! I can remember every word of my last little chat with old Risson. The man's got a swastika where his heart should be."

"So what?"

(The first time I saw Julie was when she was shoplifting a Shetland sweater in The Store. The way her fingers unfolded then snaffled it up made me want to be Julie's Shetland at once.)

"Benjamin, the important thing isn't to find out what Risson thought or did when his head was still functioning, but to get the fuckers that have turned it into a sump."

I don't know how she worked it, but this last sentence was spoken between our sheets and there didn't seem to be a stitch of clothing left around the place. But she still didn't let go of her point:

"Do you know why old Risson got junked out?"

"Don't give a toss."

This was true. I really didn't care. Not because of my anti-Risson position, but because Julie's nipples are my heart's resting place. While I was helping myself to them, she still went ahead with her explanations. And, with her fingers in my hair, she told me all about Risson's adventures.

TRAGEDY IN V ACTS.

ACT I: A year ago, when I got fired from The Store after Julie's article, the Work Inspectors got onto the management's case. They wanted to know what kind of outfit hires a scapegoat to sweep up everyone else's shit by bawling like a lamb to the slaughter whenever a customer gets nasty. And the ladies and gentlemen of the Inspectorate found out all sorts of things. Among others, that Risson had been keeping his book-selling business going illegally when he should have been pensioned off a good ten years since. Exit Risson. End of the First Act.

ACT II: Booted out, all on his tod in his little two-room flat on Rue Broca, Risson went to bed and went to pieces. The sort of apprentice corpse who's due to be found six months later as a large blob of fermenting jam by neighbours with a delicate sense of smell. But then, one morning . . .

ACT III: God in His kindness sees a nice young lady knock on Risson's door: a health visitor and home-help, presented as being all part of the Town Hall's service. A little brunette with azure eyes, as lively as a whippet and as sweet as a dream of womanhood. What a delightful last canoodle! The young lass gets our Risson going, works him up, then stuffs him full of tons of unmentionable drugs to patch over his down periods.

ACT IV: Risson spends all his pennies buying in more and more magic sweeties, escalates naturally from pills to the needle, takes off, starts going senile at a rate of knots until, one morning, as high as a kite after a good stab in the veins, he gets his kit off in the middle of Port-Royal Market. Just picture all those market gardeners gawping at his Methuselah strip-tease act!

ACT V: Being arrested, then sectioned in St Anne's should have been the logical finale of this horror show. But Julie'd been on the brunette's heels for some time, with the intention of getting Risson out of her needle-shaped clutches. So, when the old boy did his Sixties happening bit amid the fruit and veg, Julia, who'd been following him, threw her coat round his shoulders (a beautiful skunk-skin, as gleamingly black as a Buick's bonnet), stuffed him into a cab and, after two days and nights of enforced sleep, brought him round here, to the Malaussène residence, just as she'd done with the other three granddads, so that he could kick in peace. There we are. The rest's still to be written. It's the article Julie's working on for her magazine, with a view to nailing that pretty brunette, the jacker-up of wrinklies, and the rest of her gang.

Risson is retelling *War and Peace* and, in the sulphurous sizzling of that little bomb can be heard the revolving names of Natasha Rostov, Pierre Bezukhov, Andrei, Helena, Napoleon and Kutuzov . . .

My thoughts fly off towards Julie, my Corrençon, my journalist, my Ethics girl . . . Three weeks since we've seen each other. Be careful. The gang can't know where the oldsters are holed up. They wouldn't hesitate at blowing away such incriminating witnesses, not to mention their friends and relations . . .

Where are you, Julie? Please, be careful, I beg you. Don't fuck up, darling. Watch out for the city. Watch out for the night. Watch out for the killing truth.

With that in my mind, I wink discreetly at Julius the Dog, who gets to his legs to follow me out into Belleville for our daily snort of night air.

Chapter 5

WHILE PRINCE ANDREI BOLKONSKY was watching death swirl round a disused Belleville hardware shop, some girl or other was playing her violin by the river on Quai de la Mégisserie, behind her closed window. Dressed entirely in black, standing upright in front of the city, the girl was doing Handel's Sonata no.7 to death.

For the thousandth time, that sequence on the eight o'clock news played through her mind: the young policeman lying, with his green coat and exploded head, on the Belleville tarmac and that little Vietnamese lady, so old, frail and threatened, asking in close-up:

"Plotekshen?"

Overtopping the green coat, the young man's head was like a large bloody flower on its stalk. "How horrible!" her mum had said.

"Doesn't that Vietnamese woman look like Ho Chi Minh?" daddy had asked.

The girl had quietly left the family group and shut herself up in her room. With the light off. She'd picked up her violin and, standing in front of her closed double-glazed window, had started to play through her repertoire. She'd now been playing for four hours. She punctuated her night music with short sharp taps from her bow. The fingers of her left hand relaxed so quickly after the touch of the bowstrings that they damped out any hum. There was no sound but that of a series of chill, precise, glass-shivering notes. It was like she was bowing with a razorblade. That she was ripping her prettiest dresses to shreds . . . It was George Frideric Handel's turn now.

The city slits old ladies' throats . . .

The city blows blond heads away . . .

"Plotekshen?" asked a Vietnamese woman, all alone in the city . . .

"*Plotekshen*?" . . .

"Love doesn't exist," the girl muttered to herself.

That's when she saw the car. It was a big black car, whose bodywork gave off a faint gleam. The car had just come to a majestic stop right in the middle of Pont Neuf, above the Seine, like it was heaving to. The rear door opened. The girl saw a man get out. He was propping up a tottering woman.

"Drunk", was the girl's diagnosis.

(And the sweep of her bow made the strings jangle with one of those hideous shrieks that violins alone are capable of.)

The man and the woman staggered towards the parapet. The girl could feel the woman's head of red hair weighing down on her companion's shoulder.

"Unless she's pregnant," thought the girl. "There're loads of good reasons why people puke . . ."

Not this time. The woman didn't double up to chuck her maternal overflow into the Seine. No, in fact the couple looked like they were in a dream, the woman's head on the man's shoulder, his cheek in her hair. The woman's fur coat gleamed like the body of the car.

"No, they're in love," thought the girl.

(And George Frideric Handel got his first soft caress of the evening.)

"Her hair's just like mum's."

Her hair was in fact a wonderful shade of red, or perhaps Venetian gold, which trapped the light from the street lamps, giving the couple a russet sheen.

"So that's true love?"

Waiting patiently by the pavement, the car was giving off little white puffs of smoke into the chill night air. George Frideric Handel was dressing his wounds.

"True love!" the girl repeated.

It was just then that she heard the roar. It went straight through her window's double-glazing. A long metallic roar coming from the engine of the parked car, whose passenger door suddenly opened. Then the girl saw the man disappear behind the parapet and the woman drop from the bridge. It was as if she'd taken wing. She was still fluttering in midair when the man had already slipped back through the open door and the car screeched off. There had been the woman's white body in the darkness, the surge of the car, its rear wing smashing into a bollard, the metallic jolting of its rapid getaway along the riverside. The girl closed her eyes.

When she dared open them again – after a mere couple of seconds – the bridge was empty. But, between the gleaming banks of the river, the dark shape of a barge was going by. And there, on the ridge of a huge coal heap, the woman's naked body, broken like a dead bird, passed under the girl's eyes.

"At least he's still got the coat," she thought, "if nothing else."

Then, once again, she recognized the golden gleam surrounding the ashen face.

"Mummy," she muttered.

She dropped her violin and bow, threw open the window and screamed into the night.

Chapter 6

MINUS TWELVE WEATHER can freeze your balls off, but Belleville was still bubbling like a devil's cauldron. It was as if every copper in Paris was getting in on the act. They were crawling up from Place Voltaire, parachuting onto Place Gambetta, doing pincer movements from Nation and the Goutte d'Or. With sirens blaring, lights flashing, tyres screeching left, right and centre. The night was on fire. Belleville was vibrant. But Julius the Dog didn't give a damn. In the half-light that goes with doggyish pleasures, Julius was licking up a sheet of Africa-shaped black ice. It tasted delicious to his dangling tongue. A city is a dog's favourite dinner.

During this razor-sharp night, it was as though Belleville was settling all its old scores with the Law. Side alleys rang to truncheons. Information highways stretched through Black Marias to the Station. Pushers were having their sleeves pulled, the Arab hunting season was open, big mustachioed pigs were out for a barbecue. Apart from that, the neighbourhood was much the same as usual, that is to say, ever-changing. It's on its way to being clean, on its way to being smooth and on its way to being expensive. What's left of the old Belleville housing sticks out like fillings in a grinning set of Hollywood teeth. Belleville's on its way.

And it so happens that I, Benjamin Malaussène, know who's the guiding hand behind Belleville's being on its way. It's an architect. And he's called Ponthard-Delmaire. He squats in a glass-and-wood house perched up on Rue de la Mare, on the crest of the hill, between the trees. It's a classic heavenly retreat for one of God's blacksmith's shops. He's ever so famous, is Ponthard-Delmaire. What we owe him, among other things, is the rebuilding of Brest (the architectural equivalent in France of East Berlin). He's soon to publish (with the Vendetta Press, my employers) a fat book about his schemes for Paris: a sort of coffee-table door-stopper on glazed paper with colour photos, plus a fold-out map. The full works. A top-drawer deal. Full of lovely architectural jaw-wag: the sort of stuff that wings away in a flight of lyricism then flops down into breeze-blocks. The only reason I have the honour of knowing Ponthard-Delmaire, Belleville's gravedigger, is because Queen Zabo sent me to pick up his manuscript.

"Why me, your Highness?"

"Because if anything screws up during the book's publication, you'll be the one who gets the bollocking. This way, Ponthard will know your lovely little goat's face right from the word go."

Ponthard-Delmaire is a fat bastard who for once does not move "with an astonishing grace for his portliness". He's fat and moves like a fat man: heavily. Not much, in fact. After handing me the book, he didn't even get up to let me out. He just said:

"I hope for your sake there won't be any problems."

Then he sat there staring at me till the flunkey in the bumble-bee waistcoat had closed the office door behind me.

"Come on, Julius."

People think they take their dogs out for a piss every noon and night. How wrong they are. It's the dogs that beckon us out twice a day for a think.

Julius tears himself away from his iced-black Africa and we continue our stroll towards the Koutoubia, the restaurant which my mate Hadouch and his father Amar own. Belleville may be going into gastric fits, but nothing can change the round of the thinker and his dog. Just now, the thinker's dwelling on the woman he loves: "Julie, my Corrençon, where are you? If only you knew how much I fucking miss you!" Julie, or Julia as I called her at the time, stole into my existence about a year ago. She's a nomad and she asked me if I wouldn't mind being her aircraft carrier. "Touch down, my lovely, then take off as often as you want, from now on I'll be sailing in your coastal waters," is something like what I answered. (Sweet Jesus, how poetic . . .) Ever since, I've spent my life waiting for her. The snag is that brilliant journalists only screw you between articles. If she was a hackette for a daily rag, then, at least . . . , but she isn't, and my Corrençon's chosen to express her views in a monthly magazine. What's more, she only publishes something every three months. So I'm now doomed to quarterly love. "Julie, why are you bothering yourself with these ancient smack-heads? Are wrinkly junkies that much of a scoop?" I ought to be ashamed of myself, asking questions like that, but I don't have time to be. A hand shoots out from the darkness, grabs me by the collar and hoicks me up. I take off, then land again.

"Hi, Ben."

The corridor's dark, but I recognize the smile: startling white with a black gap between the incisors. If the lights came on, his hair would be red and curly on top of a pair of cat's eyes. It's Simon the Berber. I also recognize his minty breath.

"Hi, Simon, since when have you started collaring me like a copper?"

"Since the old bill's stopped us using the streets."

I know the second voice too. A supple voice which takes a step forward and then the darkness forms itself around Black Mo, Simon the Berber's huge shadowman.

"So what's happening, lads? Has another old dear been cut up?"

"No. This time it's an old dear who's blown away a copper."

Cinnamon and spearmint. Black Mo and Simon the Berber are the best double act running illegal games of chance between Rue de la Roquette and the Buttes Chaumont. They're the right-hand men of my mate Hadouch, Amar's son, and also my fellow pupil at Lycée Voltaire. (As far as I know the only University Challenge candidate to be reading the three-card trick.)

"An old dear turned cop-killer?"

(That's what's nice about Belleville – the little surprises you get.)

"Didn't Half Pint tell you? He was there with your dog. It happened on Timbaud junction. Me and Hadouch copped it all from the pavement opposite."

Frozen whispers, a piss-stinking corridor, but still Simon grins broadly.

"One of your real home-grown grannies, Ben. Shopping bag, slippers, the works. She plugged him with a P.38. On my mother's life."

(So it's true, fairies turn blokes into flowers. The old bitch. Coming out with the ultra-violence right under my Half Pint's rose-tinted glasses . . .)

"Ben, Hadouch wants you to do him a favour."

Simon undoes our jackets and a large brown envelope shifts discreetly from his body warmth to mine.

"It's some photos of the ex-copper, Ben. Take a gander and you'll see why Hadouch can't keep them round his place right now. And there's no way they're going to search yours."

"Come along, Julius."

The night's getting sharper and sharper.

"You coming or what?"

Pit-a-pat, pit-a-pat, he ambles along. He stinks so badly, does this dog, that his smell won't follow him. It goes on ahead.

"Shall we cut by Rue Spinoza or take a turn round Rue de la Roquette?" Why aren't you here, Julie? Why do I have to keep myself happy with Julius and Belleville? Because the way I look at journalism, Benjamin, why I write is the only reason why I keep going.

"I know that. I know that. Just try not to let it kill you."

Suddenly a car's headlights dazzle Julius and me. The revving of its engine can be heard from the other end of Rue de la Roquette. It must be doing a good ninety. (That's what I ought to do, in fact. Pass my test, buy myself a flash car and, when I'm hurting too much for my Corrençon, lap the ring road with my foot down.) Mesmerized by the car, Julius has slumped down onto his fat arse. He's staring back into the headlights like he's trying to hypnotize a dragon. What with all this black ice, it's a hundred-to-one on that the dragon's going to bury itself in Père Lachaise cemetery's gates.

"Want to bet, Julius?"

Julius wins. It revs and roars, changes down, nearly spins out on the curve, straightens up, then bombs up towards Menilmontant. The only thing is, when the black car was taking the bend, a door opened and something like a bird of ill omen fluttered out of it. My first thought was that it was a body, but it slumped to the ground like an empty skin. A coat, maybe, or a blanket. I step down into the gutter to take a look when a woman's long scream pitches into my blood. Then the police car which was following the speed freak throws me back onto the pavement. The unseen woman goes on screaming. I turn round. It isn't a woman. It's Julius.

"Shit, Julius, no. I can do without that!"

But Julius keeps on screaming, with his head screwed round towards where the car was, his mouth in a cartoon pout and his eyes alight with terror. A long feminine lamentation punctuated by short sobs. A lamentation which swells, fills the whole neighbourhood, until the lights come on in one window, then in another, having me leg it down Rue de la Folie Régnault, bent double like a child snatcher, my dog sitting in my arms and dribbling into the hand that's gagging him, my dog rolling his eyes in the red night-light of the city, my dog in the throes of an epileptic fit.

He's now lying on his side in my bedroom, but *still in a sitting position.* With his head screwed round, eyes fixed on the ceiling, as shaggy and as light as an empty coconut, he goes quiet. So quiet you'd think he was dead. But even though his breath stinks like he's waddling through hell, Julius the Dog is still very much alive. Epilepsy. It'll take some time. A few days, maybe. As long as whatever vision set off the fit is still stuck on his retina. I'm used to it.

"So, Dostoevsky, what did you see this time?"

Now, what I can see, when I've opened Hadouch's brown envelope, gives me pause for thought and my long-distant dinner rises slowly up towards my mouth. 'INSPECTOR VANINI' was written on the envelope and, in the photos laid out in front of me, a young man with a blond crewcut and a green overcoat is busy smashing in some brown heads with a knuckleduster. One of them has split open, an eye popped out of its socket. There isn't the slightest sign of pleasure on that blond head's face. Just a schoolboy's look of concentration. I understand why Hadouch doesn't want this lot to be found in his place. With Vanini dead, North Africa had better lie low for a while.

33

Suddenly the world makes me weary, but I don't feel sleepy. Too bad for the precautions. I pick up the phone and call Julie. I need to hear her voice. Julie's voice, please . . . Nothing. It rings on unanswered into the night.

Chapter 7

"IS SHE DEAD?" Pastor asked.

Kneeling in the coal, the medic was bending over the woman's body. He raised his eyes towards the young inspector in the baggy sweater, who was holding the torch.

"No, but near enough."

The blue and yellow of the police boat's flashing light lit up the body, the pitch blackness of the night followed, then the photographer's flash. One of her legs was broken at a ghastly angle. Two heavy lead bracelets had been welded round her ankles.

"She'd have stayed at the bottom for quite a while."

"Look."

The medic had gently taken hold of one of her elbows. He pointed at some bruising in the crook of her arm.

"Jacked up."

They conversed in frozen monosyllables. Between these snatches the deep panting of the diesel engines could be heard. The barge smelt of fuel and sweaty steel.

"Seen enough?"

Pastor ran the beam of the torch over the woman's body for a last look. There were needle marks, signs of beating and various burns. He paused for a moment when it reached her face. It was blue with bruises and the cold. A wide forehead, high cheekbones and an energetic, fleshy mouth. Then there was her golden mane. Her face looked as powerful as her body, sweetened by a kind of supple fullness. Pastor spoke to the photographer:

"Can you patch up her face a bit?"

"I know someone in the lab. He'll do a special print run for you. We'll get rid of the worst of it."

"An attractive woman," said the doctor, covering her with the blanket. Pastor's torch traced a semi-circle in the night air.

"Stretcher-bearers!"

He heard their steps crunch across the coal, like it was a heap of seashells.

"Multiple fractures," the medic summed up, "assorted burns, an indefinite amount of junk in her veins, not to mention probable chest problems. She's had it."

"She's tough," said Pastor.

"She's had it," the medic repeated.

"Want to bet?"

There was a playful tone in the young inspector's voice.

"Are you always so chirpy at this time of night, what with a mess like this?"

"I was on duty anyway," Pastor answered. "You're the one that got dragged out of bed."

Pastor, the medic and the photographer clambered back across the coal heap after the stretcher-bearers. There were lights flashing on the police boat, on the ambulance and on the Black Maria. What with Pastor's torch, plus the barge's mooring lights, the night was sparkling. Even more than the bargee's wit was sparkling between his chattering teeth.

"Ain't that just like me? Naked birds come dropping out of the blue into my coal heap and I don't even notice!" Like all bargees he looked like he worked in a fairground, brown and wrinkled from boredom and saloon bars.

"When girls start dropping out of the blue for you," said Pastor as he passed in front of him, "buy yourself a good mooring pole."

General laughter.

"She's dead, is she?" the bargee asked.

"Not far off," one of the stretcher-bearers answered.

"Where's our young violinist?" Pastor asked.

"In the van," one of the coppers answered. "That girl's stark raving, if you ask me. She reckoned it was her mum who was down in the coal heap."

Pastor took one step towards the Black Maria, then changed his mind. "Ah yes, I was forgetting . . ."

He turned back to the bargee.

"When you've made your delivery tomorrow, I suppose you'll go and have a drink in your local?"

"Or two," said the bargee, who was bouncing up and down on the spot.

"Not a word about all this," said Pastor.

He was still smiling. But his smile had become a fixed grin.

"What?"

"Not a whisper. You won't mention it to a soul. Not even to yourself. Nothing happened."

The bargee was flabbergasted. A minute ago, he'd been chatting to a funny little lad in an oversize sweater, arms gesticulating everywhere. Now he was up against a copper.

"And not a drop of drink for ten days," Pastor went on, as though he was dictating a course of treatment.

"Ay?"

"Drunks can't keep their mouths shut. Specially when it comes to telling the truth."

Pastor's eyes had become hollows, remote from his smile.

"You're on the wagon. Follow me?"

He suddenly looked tired.

"You're the Law," said the bargee sullenly. He'd just simultaneously been told to dry out and abandon a subject of conversation that would have lasted him a lifetime.

"There's a good lad," said Pastor slowly.

Then he added:

"Anyway, pretty girls don't drop out of the blue."

"Not often," the bargee agreed.

"Not ever," said Pastor.

The first person Pastor saw in the Black Maria was the uniformed officer. Hunched up at one end of the bench, he was sitting as far as possible away from the young violinist, an empty notepad open on his lap. The girl had dark brown hair, was very pale and extremely adolescent. She was dressed completely in black, with her hands chopped off at the first finger-joints by crocheted mittens. "I am in mourning for the World. Don't think for a moment you can make me smile." That's what this Sicilian-widow fancy dress seemed to be saying. The little uniformed copper greeted Pastor with a look like a dog has when it thinks it's going to be let off its lead. Pastor put his hand out towards the girl.

"Come along, Miss, it's all over. I'm taking you home."

In the squad car, sitting next to Pastor, who was driving slowly, the girl started to talk. The first thing she said was how upset she'd been by the face of an old Vietnamese woman on the eight o'clock news. "Plotekshen?" the old lady had asked, "and it was like the whole world lay threatening on her shoulders," the young violinist explained. Pastor drove on in silence. No flashing light. No siren. Wrapped up in his sweater and the girl wrapped up in her thoughts, they almost looked like brother and sister. The girl started to open up. She told him again about what she'd seen from her window, everything, to the slightest detail: the roar of the car, the naked woman in midair . . .

But, as far as she was concerned, the worst of it was that she'd thought it was her mother's body which had passed by "on its bier of coal". The fact that her mother had been fast asleep in the next room at the time apparently made no difference.

"It's just as if I'd killed my mum, Inspector. I tried to explain all this to your uniformed colleague, but he didn't seem to want to listen."

Indeed not. Pastor tried to imagine the expression on the young copper's face and nearly went through a red light.

After dropping the girl off home, Pastor found the Station in a state of chaos: the corridors were crammed with Arabs, squatting on the floor or squeezed onto the benches, there were doors slamming, people yelling, phones ringing, bursts of typewriter fire, furious coppers swarming this way and that with files stuck under their arms . . . It was Chief Superintendent Cercaria's homage to Inspector Vanini, who had fallen

38

that night, a victim to the city. It was Chief Superintendent Cercaria's spectacular mourning. Cells and charge sheets were filling up.

Pastor took refuge in the lift, thanking his lucky stars that he was one of Chief Superintendent Coudrier's men and not one of Cercaria's. Chief Superintendent Coudrier dealt discreetly with his business, in the half light of a comfortable office. Chief Superintendent Coudrier gave you coffee served in First Empire cups, stamped with a capital "N" for Napoleon. Chief Superintendent Coudrier kept himself to himself. He wasn't a man for the beat. If Pastor had just been gunned down in the street, Coudrier's mourning would have been a sober one. He would probably have drunk his coffee unsugared for a day or two.

Pastor opened his office door to reveal a tiny Vietnamese woman, perched on her wooden clogs, grinning sardonically while swallowing a tooth-glass-full of an off-white substance.

Chapter 8

WITHOUT BATTING AN eyelid, Pastor closed the office door behind him.

"What are you trying to kill yourself for, Thian? I heard you were a big hit on TV this evening."

With her head thrown back, the Vietnamese woman gestured for silence. This was a low-budget police office. Two tables, two typewriters, a telephone and metallic ring-binders. Pastor had installed a camp-bed. When he didn't have the strength to go home, he slept there. Pastor had inherited a large town house on Boulevard Maillot, close to the Bois de Boulogne. A large empty town house. Ever since the Councillor and Gabrielle had died, Pastor had slept in his office.

When she'd put down the glass and wiped her mouth with the back of her hand, the Vietnamese woman said:

"Get out of my face, kiddo. I can't stomach youngsters this evening."

There wasn't a trace left of her exotic, boat person's accent. It was the gravelly voice of a cop in a black and white movie, with the odd unmistakable tick from the twelfth arrondissement.

"What's got into you? Surely not Vanini's sad demise?" asked Pastor.

The Vietnamese lady wearily pulled off her sleek wig, revealing an ancient scalp with a closely cropped scattering of violent grey bristles.

"Vanini was a little fucker who must have got out of his league," she said. "Someone snuffed him, now let his soul rest in peace. That's not what's bugging me. Here, kiddo, give us a hand, will you?"

She turned her back to Pastor, who unhooked her silk Thai dress, then pulled its zip down to the foothills of her buttocks. The human form which emerged from the dress was entirely male and dressed in long johns. Pastor stopped breathing.

"What perfume are you wearing?"

"The Thousand Flowers of Asia. Like it?"

Pastor breathed out like he was emptying himself.

"It's amazing Cercaria didn't recognize you!"

"Even I don't recognize myself," Inspector Van Thian grumbled as he pulled out his service revolver, which was concealed between his scrawny thighs.

Then he added:

"You know what, kiddo, I feel like I've become my own relic."

Once he was out of his widow Ho weeds (he took it seriously enough to wear latex falsies, as flat as a pair of fried eggs), Inspector Van Thian was a chronically depressed, old, thin copper. He opened a pink box of Tranxene, flicked two pills into the hollow of his palm, then swallowed them, chasing them down with the glass of bourbon which Pastor handed him.

"My ulcers are all waking up at once."

Inspector Van Thian slumped back into the chair opposite Pastor's, his young partner. Pastor picked up the glass, filled it with water, dropped two soluble aspirins into it, placed it on the middle of the desk, then sat down as well. With their chins propped up on their clasped hands, the two of them silently watched the effervescent waltz. When old Thian had knocked back his aspirins, he said:

"I really reckoned I'd fingered two of them this evening."

"Two kids?" Pastor asked.

"If you say so. Simon the Berber and Black Mo. They run Hadouch Ben Tayeb's three-card trick business for him. They haven't got forty years between them. Compared with me they're babes in arms, but they've been around a bit, believe you me."

Pastor liked this time of the night when Inspector Van Thian would come back down from Belleville to type out his nightly reports at the Station. He didn't really know why, but old Thian's being there reminded Pastor of the Councillor. Maybe because Thian told him stories (of widow Ho's trials and tribulations), just like the Councillor had done when Pastor was young. Or maybe it was just old age coming on . . .

"Listen to this, kiddo. The two of them got their hooks into me by the cashpoint at the Rue Faubourg du Temple/Avenue Parmentier cross-roads. Imagine it. A cast-iron Black and a reinforced concrete Berber versus little widow Ho. I gave them a good sniff at nearly 3,000 francs. I even let a couple of hundred float away on purpose. And you know what? Up dashes Black Mo after me to *give it me back*. Right, so I reckon they're keeping me for later, so as to get their hands on the whole stash, nice and easy somewhere, down the métro for instance. So off I go down the métro. And down they go with me, grinning like silly cunts and whispering horror stories to me, how they're going to fry my tits, wrench off my nips and you get the picture . . . They get me into an empty carriage, sit me down between them and, instead of unburdening me of my finances, just carry on with their Gestapo torture bullshit. We change at République and head down towards Chinatown. (I'd told them I was going to see my daughter-in-law, who'd just had a kid.) And still they go on with their spiel till I reckon what they're after is screwing my daughter-in-law as a bonus then doing me the business in her bed. And then what? Fuck all! They took me along to the door of the block where my imaginary daughter-in-law was supposed to be living then pissed off without a word when we were about to get into the lift."

"So what do you reckon?"

"It's depressing, kiddo. Our two kids just didn't want to rob widow Ho. They even *protected* her. Turned out to be her bodyguards. They not only didn't lift a finger against her, but all the video-nasty scenarios they came out with were meant to put the shits so far up her that she wouldn't go for any more midnight strolls with the contents of a Saudi Arabian bank account in her handbag. And that, kiddo, is what gets me down more than the rest."

"Does this mean Cercaria's wrong about the Belleville youth?"

"It means everyone's got it arse-about, at least as far as this business with the old dears is concerned. Me included, just as much as that steaming shit-head of a Cercaria."

They thought it over in silence. There was also something about Thian which was reminiscent of Gabrielle, the Councillor's wife, when she had her thinking cap on. The Councillor would then say to Pastor: "Gabrielle's thinking, Jean-Baptiste. In a minute or two we'll be all the wiser." Gabrielle and the Councillor were both dead now.

"You know what, kiddo? Dragging myself up in Belleville for the last month's at least taught me one thing: wrinklies can wander the streets at night, stark naked, with diamond studs in their navels and the family silver hanging round their necks and not one smackhead'll so much as touch them. The word's gone round. And even the most bombed-out freak among them would rather get a good hiding any day than rip off a Belleville granny. I don't mean the kids in the neighbourhood are mending their ways, mind you, it's just they've got their heads screwed on. The streets are crawling with crafty little coppers like Vanini, the kids have twigged on and they're keeping their noses clean. That's all. And I wouldn't be at all surprised if they didn't wind up nailing the loony with the cut-throat themselves. See what I mean, kiddo . . . ?"

Thian's face, full of world-weary wisdom, stared across at Pastor.

"See what life's like? I says to myself that I'm going to blow away our old-ladykiller before Cercaria's boys get to him, just so as to bow out nicely before retiring and give old Coudrier a good-bye present and what happens? I find myself in the running against a load of street arabs."

Inspector Van Thian eased his thirty-nine years of service off the chair and sat them back down again behind his desk. He made himself a thick sandwich of typewriter paper and carbon, then fed it into his machine.

"What about you, kiddo? Did you come up with anything this evening?"

At that very moment, the door was opened by a lab messenger bearing the answer.

"That's what I came up with," answered Pastor, thanking the officer and throwing over a handful of still-clammy photos to Thian.

Thian took a long look at the naked body of the woman, whitened by the flash and standing out against the coal.

"Whoever threw her into the Seine revved up their car to drown out the splash," Pastor explained. "That's why they didn't hear the barge."

"Silly cunts . . ."

"Then they skidded and lost their bumper. I found it in their wake. It belongs to a BMW which should be easily traceable."

"Why the big hurry?"

"They were amateurs, maybe. Or else speeding out of their minds. The woman had been drugged."

"Any witnesses?"

"A girl who was giving the night a violin concert two floors up. By the way, she saw you on telly. You completely got her down. Hence the violin . . ."

Thian didn't move. One by one, he slowly examined the photos.

"What do you think?" asked Pastor. "A whore who's been over-disciplined?"

"No, this isn't a whore."

Still in his depressed-Asian-wisdom tone of voice, Inspector Van Thian sounded certain.

"What makes you say that?"

"I got two of my brothers-in-law and three of their cousins banged up for pimping. Before we got wed, my missus used to work the pavements in Toulon and now my daughter's working in a home in Nanterre for streetwalkers who've come in from the cold. We know about whores in my family."

Then, shaking his head again:

"No, this isn't a whore."

"We'll check anyway," said Pastor, feeding paper into his own machine.

The fact that he worked quickly and accurately, and checked everything out, was one among many things that appealed to Thian about Pastor. All the same, he wasn't much sold on youngsters. And especially not on kids from comfortable backgrounds. Pastor's father had been a State Councillor and one of the people behind the setting up of the French Public Health Service. As far as that great popper of pills, Inspector Van Thian, was concerned he was as remote as the Pappy of the Roman Priesthood. Thian also didn't much like the mannered ways, the pullovers, the posh talk and the resistance to slang which he'd inherited from his family. But still, Thian really loved Pastor, like an old peasant woman with no politics will love the Colonial Governor's son.

44

And, about this time of the night, when their two keyboards were chattering away, he'd end up telling him so:

"I really love you, kiddo. I hate saying it, but I really do."

That's when the telephone would start ringing, someone would burst into the office, one of their machines would jam or something else happen to snap him out of it. This evening was no exception. "Hello. Police. Inspector Van Thian speaking . . ."

Then:

"Yes, he's here, yes, I'll send him along, yes, right away."

And:

"Give your night music a break, kiddo. Coudrier wants to see you."

Chapter 9

EVEN IN THE middle of a summer's day Chief Superintendent Coudrier's office was a twilight zone. And in the middle of a winter night, even more so. His rheostat gave off the bare minimum of light necessary. The Napoleonic knick-knacks on the shelves stood out from the surrounding primordial gloom and the double-glazed windows peered out over the urban night. At the crack of dawn, he'd draw the curtains. Whatever the time of day or night, the room was diffused by that smell of coffee which has people slump into thought and chat in hushed voices.

Coudrier: You were not supposed to be on duty tonight, Pastor. Whom are you replacing?

Pastor: Inspector Caregga, Sir. He's fallen in love.

Coudrier: Coffee?

Pastor: Please.

Coudrier: I make it myself at this time of night. It won't be up to Elisabeth's standards. So, Caregga's in love.

Pastor: Yes, Sir, with a beautician.

Coudrier: And how many of your fellow officers have you replaced this week, Pastor?

Pastor: Three, Sir.

Coudrier: When do you sleep?

Pastor: Now and then, in dribs and drabs.

Coudrier: That is certainly one way of doing it.

Pastor: That's your way of doing it, Sir. And I've adopted it.

Coudrier: You are as fawning and aloof as a British butler, Pastor.

Pastor: Your coffee's very good, Sir.

Coudrier: Did anything of importance happen this evening?

Pastor: Attempted murder by drowning, on Quai de la Mégisserie, just in front of the Station.

Coudrier: A failed attempt?

Pastor: The body fell into a barge which happened to be passing under the bridge at that very moment.

Coudrier: Just in front of the Station, you say. Does that surprise you?

Pastor: It does, Sir.

Coudrier: Well, it shouldn't. If the Seine were dragged around Pont Neuf then half the missing persons on our files would turn up.

Pastor: And why is that, Sir?

Coudrier: Provocation, the thrill of the risk, a raised finger at the forces of law and order. Disposing of a corpse right under the coppers' noses is more of a 'turn on', as the young people of your generation might put it. Murderers' arrogance . . .

Pastor: May I ask you a favour, Sir?

Coudrier: Please do.

Pastor: I'd like to lead the investigation myself, instead of handing it over to Caregga.

Coudrier: What are you working on at present?

Pastor: I've just sewn up the SKAM warehouse case.

Coudrier: The case of arson? So, was it the owner trying to get the insurance money?

Pastor: No, Sir. It was the insurance broker himself.

Coudrier: That's original.

Pastor: He was going to share the pay-out with the owner.

Coudrier: Not so original. Do you have proof?

Pastor: I have confessions.

Coudrier: Ah yes, confessions . . . More coffee?

Pastor: Yes please, Sir.

Coudrier: I must say I like the way you say "Sir".

Pastor: I always spell it with a capital "S", Sir.

Coudrier: And that's just the way it comes across. By the way, Pastor, talking about confessions, do you know anything about the Avenue Foch bank job?

Pastor: Three deaths, forty million francs gone with the wind, and the arrest of Paul Chabralle by Chief Superintendent Cercaria's squad. Van Thian helped them out with some of the investigation.

Coudrier: Well, I've just received a phone call from my colleague Cercaria.

Pastor: . . .

Coudrier: All his men are busy after Vanini's death. Now, Chabralle can be kept in custody only until eight o'clock this morning. And he's still pleading his innocence.

Pastor: He shouldn't do that, Sir.

Coudrier: Why?

Pastor: Because he's lying.

Coudrier: Don't play the fool, Pastor.

Pastor: No, Sir. Is there any hard evidence?

Coudrier: A mass of circumstantial evidence.

Pastor: But not enough to charge him with?

Coudrier: Ample. But Chabralle is a past master at getting cases thrown out of court.

Pastor: I see.

Coudrier: And I have had it up to here with Chabralle, my lad. He's behind the shooting of a good thirty people, at the very least.

Pastor: Some of whom are no doubt decomposing under Pont Neuf.

Coudrier: Perhaps. I have therefore offered your services to my colleague Cercaria.

Pastor: Very good, Sir.

Coudrier: Pastor, you have got five hours to make Chabralle crack. If he hasn't signed by eight o'clock, you will have a few more killings of security guards and cash girls to look into.

Pastor: I think he'll sign.

Coudrier: Let us hope so.

Pastor: I'll go along straightaway, Sir. Thank you for the coffee.

Coudrier: Pastor?

Pastor: Yes, Sir?

Coudrier: I have a feeling that, in this case, my colleague Cercaria wants above all to test your abilities as an interrogator.

Pastor: Then let's test them, Sir.

"Thian, tell me about Chabralle. Give me some dirt on him, something to bring him alive for me. Take your time."

"'Bringing people alive', as you put it, isn't really Chabralle's ball game, kiddo."

But Inspector Van Thian couldn't resist telling a story. He remembered investigating a double murder committed eleven years ago, of which they'd suspected Chabralle. A tax consultant and his lover. Thian had been the first on the scene of the crime.

"It was a bijou loft in a done-up warehouse near Les Halles. The place was as massive as an aircraft hangar and as high as a cathedral, with old pink roughcast walls, white gloss furniture, frosted-glass windows and metal girders full of fat round rivets. The sort of thing Ponthard-Delmaire did loads of in the seventies."

The first, and for that matter, the only thing Thian had seen when he'd smashed down the door was a novel sort of chandelier.

"The man and the woman were hanging from the same rope, which'd been thrown over the flat's main supporting beam. As the woman was seventeen pounds lighter than the man, which happened to be the exact weight of their dog, they'd hung it round the woman's ankle. It made a perfect balance."

A fortnight later, Van Thian had gone to Chabralle's residence with Superintendent, not yet Chief Superintendent, Cercaria.

"And guess what Chabralle had on his bedside table, kiddo? A little golden balance. Identical. With the man, the woman, and the dog. Course, it didn't prove anything . . ."

"Now, can you sum up the last bank job for me?"

At about four in the morning, Pastor bounded into Cercaria's office.

"One of my boys was gunned down tonight in Belleville and, what with all these grasses we've got in, I haven't got a man left available, you know the score . . . Chabralle's in Bertholet's office, the third on the left."

The coffee machines were empty, the ashtrays full, fingers yellow, eyes baggy from lack of sleep and shirts crumpled up around hips. There were bursts of rage, the walls were dazzling with white light. Pastor took the atmospheric pressure. He could hear his fellow officers' brains ticking over: so that's Pastor? the midwife of confessions, the murderer's gynæcologist, Chief Superintendent Coudrier's Spanish inquisitor? Looks like a mummy's boy. Had strings pulled for him. Scrabbling up the ladder while we, Cercaria's lads, are in the frontline facing a hoard of pushers and getting our heads blown away into the bargain. A few steps more and Pastor will find himself face to face with the accused, Chabralle. And Cercaria's men knew a bit about Chabralle! He'd just been leading them by their noses for the last forty-two hours. Even aces like them! Pastor sensed that not one of them, with their chain bracelets and leather jackets, would have put a penny on his old home-knitted sweater when it came up against Paul Chabralle's stainless-steel grin.

Pastor went into the office, politely threw out the man who was guarding Chabralle then carefully locked the door.

"Come to tidy up a bit, have we, deary?" asked Chabralle.

Twenty minutes later, an attentive pair of ears that happened to be passing heard the clacking of a typewriter coming through the locked door. Their owner beckoned over to another pair, which also stuck itself to the door. In the office, a voice was murmuring, accompanied by the tapping of the machine. Other ears attached themselves to the door. Then, there was a pause.

The door at last opened. Chabralle had signed. He admitted taking part not only in the last bank job, but also in six of the other seven cases which he'd got thrown out of court.

When their initial surprise was over, Chief Superintendent Cercaria's hard nuts would have picked Pastor up onto their shoulders in triumph. But something in the young Inspector's gaze put them off. It looked like he'd just contracted some terminal disease. His old pullover hung off him like dead skin. He went by without noticing them.

"Want to hear a joke, kiddo?"

Inspector Van Thian was well acquainted with the state his young partner was in. Interrogations always got him this way. Pastor never failed to get his confession. But after each session, Van Thian got his kiddo back more dead than alive. His boyish face looked thirty years older. He was a dying shadow of himself. He needed reviving. Van Thian insisted on telling him funny stories.

"How about a Taoist proverb, kiddo? It'll stop the success you've just had going to your head."

Thian sat Pastor down on a stool. He then crouched in front of him and tried to make eye-contact with his young partner, though his stare had retreated back inside his head. Their gazes at last met. And he started his story. No beating about the bush, he went straight for it:

"A Taoist proverb, kiddo: *If tomorrow, after tonight's victory, you look at yourself naked in the mirror and see that you have a second pair of testicles, do not, oh my son, puff yourself up in pride, all it means is someone's buggering you.*"

Whenever the story was over, a spasm would cross Pastor's face, which Thian took for a short burst of laughter. Then the young inspector's features would start to knit themselves back together. He loosened up. He looked human again.

The Goat

CRY, MY OLD CHAP.
CRY LIKE YOU MEAN IT.
THERE'S A GOOD GOAT

Chapter 10

THE NEXT DAY, a Saturday, the City of Paris is due to decorate our old Sole in the Town Hall of the 11th arrondissement for the fifty years he'd spent shodding Belleville's trotters. A little fat man in a blue, white and red sash officially declares that this is wonderful. Sole is a bit sad that the speech isn't being delivered by the Mayor of Mayors himself, but the Mayor of Mayors is paying his last respects to the corpse of a young police inspector who was gunned down last night, in the same neighbourhood, just a few hundred yards from Sole's old workshop.

"It was for the worthy men and women of your generation that this young hero sacrificed his life . . ."

But old Sole's not thinking about the young inspector. Old Sole's heart's set on the medal he's been promised. There it is, glittering in its little velvet-lined coffin on the long table, behind which are seated a massive Deputy and the Permanent Secretary for Senior Citizens, a well-groomed young fast-laner. As far as the crowd goes, my mate Stojilkovicz has crammed the room full, thanks to several toings and froings in his legendary coach. No sooner had Sole arrived than the assembled tender-foots proclaimed him Emperor of Tarmac, unanimously voted him King of the Clodhopper and Grand Vizier of the Doc! And now the fat tricoloured person behind the long table gets his compliments out for an airing:

"I know you well, my dear fellow . . ."

(A lie.)

"I have always admired . . ."

(Another one.)

"Whenever I think about you . . ."

55

(Oh yes?)

After that, it's our local member's turn. With his square face, just tailor-made for long-distance jawing, he shifts up a gear:

"Men like myself now have the arduous task, and the honour, of succeeding men of your stamp . . ."

And off he goes on about how the Powers That Be should always venerate the Venerable and how the Powers That Were hadn't venerated them enough. But be patient, my friends, we are back again, the ball's in our court and, in a few months' time, all those senior citizens who have made our wonderful country what it is today will be off to put their feet up in Majorca, free of charge, as they deserve, "to pay the debt the Nation owes them".

(To sum up.) Cheers, wagging of approving heads, our old Sole's ruddy cheeks; we narrowly avoid an encore and the Permanent Secretary for Senior Citizens rises to his feet. He's a young man in a three-piece whose blond head is split in two by an impeccable parting and who's less long-winded than the member, going in more for facts and figures than rhetorical flourishes. He's called Arnaud Le Capelier. As soon as he opens his mouth, everyone can see that Administration, not politics, is his ball game and that right from the cradle on he's been programmed for serving permanent public institutions. Mankind is a plantigrade adapted to ladder-climbing, and Arnaud Le Capelier's tootsies must still bear the traces of everyone he's clambered over from nursery school on up to his present job. He kicks off his discourse by praising "the medal winner's marvellous autonomy" (sic) (what this means is that if Sole is too old now for cobbling, he can still tie his own shoelaces), he "is delighted to see him with so many supporters" (bravo, Stojilkovicz!) and "can only deplore the fact that this vision of happiness will not be broadcast into every living room in the country."

"But the State and the Social Services are there to make up for human failings, to look after those senior citizens whom circumstances have left in desperate, and quite often degrading, loneliness." (Sic, again.)

Arnaud Le Capelier is certainly not a bundle of laughs. He's got an odd way of speaking. A sort of "attentive" delivery. Yes, that's it. He *talks like others listen,* he wants *to hear* what he comes out with seep into his

56

audience's brains. And what does he come out with for our oldsters? This is what he tells them: when you start to feel like you're losing it, or you're puffing too much on the stairs, don't wait around for your kids to come along and bail you out. No, my old dears, come straight along to me and I'll see you right. And if you can't work out how "autonomous" you are (he definitely seems to like this formaldehyde formula) you can leave that in the capable hands of our health visitors, who the State and Local Authorities lay on free of charge for senior citizens. They will then be able "to dispatch" (sic, sic!) you towards "the SCH which will be best suited to your particular requirements".

Once you suss out that SCH stands for Senior Citizens' Home, then you've also sussed out what our handsome Arnaud Le Capelier's up to. Touting for a bit of bed-ridden business, that's what. By chance, our eyes meet ("Hey, Arnie my lad, if you reckon we're going to let you get your hooks into our granddads, then you've got another think coming"). And it's like his eyes can hear me thinking. I've just about never seen such an attentive stare in my life before. And what a funny-looking bloke he is. His parting slices him in half like a knife through butter. It continues down his razor-sharp nose then ends up cutting his face in two by dropping onto a dimple in his chubby chin, like the dot of an exclamation mark. All in all, he's an odd mixture. A sort of sturdy limpness. A soft hide concealing a fashionable sportsman's muscular body. He's probably a good tennis player. And one for bridge nights too, a dab hand at crafty contracts. I don't like Arnaud Le Capelier, that's what. I don't like him. And the thought that he's our "Mr Wrinkly" gets my goat. All I want to do is get my oldsters out of here as soon as possible. I feel like a hen when she's sniffed out a fox. I shall never, my dear Arnie, ever let you into my yard. My oldsters are mine, right? The only health visitor they get is me. Got me?

While I let my paranoia run rife, the little spherical mayor's taken things in hand again. He pins the Fifty Years' Service Medal on Sole's beating breast. My little sister Clara starts snapping away, shooting Sole, the rapturous crowd, the officiating officials, reloading her Leica with Rambo-like precision, all a-glow at this chance to satisfy her photographic passion. Kisses. Handshakes. Tears in Sole's eyes (all this emotion might knock years off his life expectancy!). Congratulations . . .

Standing slightly back from all this carry-on, my little brother, Jeremy the Forger (the one who's actually behind this whole wonderful ceremony) is silently meditating on Power and Glory.

Chapter 11

STOJILKOVICZ PACKED UP the Bellevillian and Malaussènian widows and widowers in his coach and the party ended up in Amar's, our family eatery, amid pale dunes of couscous and a red sea of Sidi Brahim plonk. As soon as we got into the smoke-filled room, Hadouch, Amar's son and my old schoolmate, collared me.

"Benjamin, my brother, how's it going?"

His bird-like profile pecks at my ear.

"All right, Hadouch. How about yourself?"

"Fine, thanks be to God, my brother. Did you stash away nice and safe those snaps the Berber gave you?"

"They're under Julius's rug. Who was that copper?"

"Vanini, an inspector in the Drug Squad, but also a big NF man. He used to go in for beatings. He killed a few of our boys, one of my cousins included. Those snaps might well come in handy. Guard them well, Benjamin . . ."

When he'd finished his whisper, Hadouch went off to do the serving. At the end of the table, the conversation was already in full swing.

"As for me, I was a barber in the same neighbourhood for twenty-five years," Granddad Sweeney confides to the widow next to him. "But, do you know what? Shaving chins was what I really liked. Razors, real cut-throats!"

The widow stares back in admiration under her whipped-cream perm.

"When the guild decided that chins were no longer worth shaving, I let it all go. My vocation had passed away."

Sweeney is now in full flight.

"A razor every morning reshapes the face. Do you see what I mean?"

The widow nods. She sees.

"So I got myself a job as an undertaker's barber."

"An undertaker's barber?"

"In all the posh parts of town. I used to shave all the big-wigs. Your hair keeps growing after you die. You could keep on shaving it till kingdom comes."

"Talking about hair," Granddad Kidney, the Tlemcen butcher, butts in, "I'm almost seventy-two, and just look at me, my hair's still black but my beard's gone white, can you explain that, Sweeney?"

"I can," Stojil booms out. "It's like anything else. You wear out what you use. You've been stuffing your face all your life, and now your beard's white. As for your grey matter . . . your hair's still black. You've chosen the path of wisdom, Kidney."

There is a simultaneous translation into Arabic and general amusement. Widow Dolgorouki has the prettiest laugh. She's sitting next to Stojil. And she's Clara's and Mum's favourite widow.

"The trouble is," says Risson seriously, "there are no real *trades* anymore. The idea of having a trade is going down the drain. All of us here had a real *trade*."

Jeremy doesn't agree.

"An ex-bookseller, an ex-butcher, an ex-barber, what does all that mean? When you're an ex-something, you must turn into a new something else!"

"Oh really? And you are an ex-what, my lad?"

"If you're an ex-barber," the kid answers back, "then I'm an ex-pupil at Pierre Brossolette! Ain't that right, Benjamin?"

(Quite right. Last year, the little bugger burnt his school down and he was an ex-pupil before the ashes had had time to settle.) But Verdun tring-tring-trings with his fork to get our attention. Those among us who know what our oldest oldster's going to say bury our noses in our plates. The red carpet of silence is rolled out.

"Sole," Verdun declares solemnly, "Sole, I'm going to crack a bottle in your honour."

And he plonks a pint bottle full of a see-through liquid down in front of him.

"Summer 1976," he announces, getting out his pocket-knife.

It's just what we were afraid of. Water that's been stagnating in its blown-glass prison for the last six years. That's right, Verdun collects bottles of rain water. This obsession goes back to the summer of 1915. His little girl, Camille, had read in the papers that our brave boys at the front were in dire need of water and had started filling bottles up with rain "so that daddy won't be thirsty anymore". And, as a homage to Camille, Verdun kept it up after the Spanish 'flu had taken his child away. When we took him in, the only possessions Verdun wanted to bring with him was his collection of bottles. 284 of them! One for each season since summer 1915! All very poetic . . . just that Verdun's been treating us a bit too often of late. For Thérèse's birthday, Half Pint's first fairy tooth, someone's party, someone else's special event, any excuse to crack another bottle . . . we've been overdosed on stagnant water.

"Summer 1976," says widow Dolgorouki kindly. "That was a particularly dry one, wasn't it?"

"Ah yes, a very good year," sighs Kidney, ogling the Sidi Brahim.

Upon which, old Amar dumps down the couscous between the silent guests and bends his ancient white sheep's fleece over me.

"All right, my son?"

"All right, Amar, thanks."

But is it really as all right as all that? Frankly speaking, it should be. Around the white table cloth, we form a united family group of grandchildren and granddads partaking of the most catholic of communions. (OK, the granddads are fakes and the dads have all gone AWOL, but no-one's perfect.) No, it should be all right. So what's wrong, Malaussène? Julius the Dog's had one of his attacks, that's what. This business with the wrinkly junkies is starting to drag on and I'm getting the creeps, that's what. Julie, are you watching out for yourself at least? You're not screwing up? The drug business is no bundle of laughs, you know that . . . watch it, Julia, watch it.

The jukebox starts playing a song by Umm Kulthum.

The warm semolina and the exotic herbs are beginning to smell good.

"Did you see that? It isn't made of bronze, it's only brass!" Sole suddenly bursts out, brandishing his medal. "They've given me a brass medallion!"

"Just like our old colonists' tea-spoons," grins Hadouch, setting down the kebabs.

"And they also gave me an ashtray shoe."

The laced-up butt receiver gets passed round the guests. Its heel bears the Town Hall hallmark. Very classy.

"And some anti-depressants."

"What?"

Sole hands me a plastic bag crammed full of multi-coloured pills.

"The health visitor told me to take one every time I feel down in the dumps."

"What health visitor?"

"A little brunette, just like the one Thérèse saw in my palm."

(The pills are all bundled together, with no instructions for use and no prescription.)

"Rinse them down with a good shot of Pernod, that's what she told me."

"Let's have a look-see."

Hadouch's tanned fingers wrap themselves around the packet. His hand weighs it for a moment.

"She told me she'd bring round some more when I've finished this lot."

Hadouch opens the packet, bites into one of the pills, makes a face then spits out.

"They're amphetamines, Ben. That on top of a Pernod and he'll be flying to the moon. What's the Town Hall up to?"

I don't have time to answer this interesting question. The door of the Koutoubia flies open and the little restaurant fills up with coppers – at least two per customer.

"Nobody move! This is a raid! Nobody move!"

The cop who's doing the yelling is large, mustachioed and in a leather coat. His smile says how much he'd like someone to move, just so he'd have the pleasure of running him in. The old dears and boys open their eyes wide in fright. The children look at me and go still. Hadouch is quick enough to slip the bag of pills into a bread basket, but someone even quicker catches him at it.

"Hey, Cercaria! Take a look at this!"

The coat with the moustache catches the bag. At the back of the restaurant, on the jukebox, Umm Kulthum's voice accompanies her own coffin on its way to Allah's gardens. The crowd rends its garments as she passes by.

"Shut that racket up!"

Someone rips the lead out of the machine and, as silence suddenly descends, the mustachioed mouth murmurs:

"So, then, Ben Tayeb, we're dealing the latest stuff now, are we?"

I open my mouth, but Hadouch darts a glance at me that shuts it up again before a word can escape.

Silence.

Chapter 12

THEY TOOK AWAY two knives, a razor, the bag, Hadouch and two other Arabs. A rosy-faced copper, who's as socially aware as I am, in a nice tone of voice advises the kids and the oldsters not to come to places like this anymore. Despite all of Amar's pleading, lunch is over before it's begun. The copper with the moustache has the place closed down for the rest of the day; for a search. Stojil has now gone off to take the old dears out in his coach. The rest of the tribe has gone home with their heads drooping on their chests. As for me, I'm still with the big man and his moustache.

We're having a chat.

In a Black Maria.

A lovely little chat.

Just so there won't be any misunderstanding, Mr Leather-Tache tells me straight out that he's not some two-bit drug squaddie, but one of the big brass, Chief Superintendent Cercaria in person, the Lord High Executioner of Dope. The way he tells me this makes me feel like I'm supposed to wag my head in dumb adoration. Sorry, Cercaria, but I don't watch the box.

"And, by the way, what's your name?"

(Ain't that life? There are the knowns and the unknowns. The knowns always want to be recognized and the unknowns want to stay that way. But still it fucks up.)

"Malaussène," I say. "Benjamin Malaussène."

"You from Nice?"

"My name is, that's all."

"I have family there. It's a lovely town."

(So it is. Smells of mimosas, apparently.)

"Well, my lad, I suppose you can imagine that I am not here in Belleville on a Saturday just to give out parking tickets."

('My lad'! He's trying the nice angle, is our Cercaria. Thanks to my long-lost cousin in Nice.)

"How long have you been living in this neighbourhood?"

(He's a colossal fifty-year-old, with muscles bulging out of his leather coat in places where most people don't even have places, a signet ring and chain bracelet of the same gold, shoes for face-shaving and, probably, shooting trophies lined up on his mantelpiece.)

"Since I was a kid."

"You know it well, then."

(I'm on the slippery slope, I can feel it.)

"Better than Nice, anyway."

"And you often eat out at Ben Tayeb's?"

"I take my family there once or twice a week."

"Those were your kids round the table?"

"My brothers and sisters."

"And I suppose you've got a job, have you?"

"I'm a Literary Director of the Vendetta Press."

"Oh, and how do you like it?"

(Now we're onto my job he's gone a bit more polite. He's a simple soul, is Cercaria. What did it look like I did before my title wiped out the first impressions? A plumber? A dole boy? A pimp? An alkie?)

"I mean, how do you like moving in literary circles? You must meet so many fascinating people!"

(So that they can give me a bollocking for the most part. Imagine Mr Butch Moustache's face if he knew that behind the Literary Director really lurked a rampant scapegoat.)

"That's right. All sorts of wonderful people."

"I've got one or two ideas for a book myself . . ."

(No, really?)

"In the police force, we've got ringside seats. We see all sorts of things."

(Literary Directors with faces like fuck-heads, for instance.)

"But I've decided to keep the writing in reserve for my retirement."

(Wrong. When you're retired, buy a lawn-mower, not a pen.)

Then, all of a sudden:

"Your friend, Ben Tayeb, could well be in all sorts of trouble."

"He isn't my friend."

(As lies go, this is a white one. I have to be careful. With this ogre in front of me, the best way of helping out Hadouch is pretending I've got nothing to do with him.)

"That's better. We'll be able to help each other out more easily. Was he peddling you those pills when we arrived?"

"No, he'd just put the kebabs down on the table."

"With that big bag in his hand?"

"I hadn't noticed it till you lot arrived."

A pause follows which lets me sniff out this Black Maria's personal perfume. A mixture of leather, feet and stale tobacco. Coppers whiling away their time playing poker till they get the chance to have a poke at something better. Cercaria resumes in confidential register:

"Do you know why I'm playing at cowboys and Indians in the Drug Squad?"

(There's no answer to that.)

"Because you have brothers and sisters, Malaussène. And I can't bear for a moment the idea of a needle sticking into a young kid's arm. That's why."

He's put so much conviction into what he's just said that I suddenly think to myself: "Oh, if only it was true!" Really I do. I even want to believe it for a minute or two. I get a glimpse of a society in which the forces of order work for the well-being of one and all. A wonderful world where wrinklies would only jack themselves up if they really wanted to. Where nice fairies don't turn blond heads into crushed pumpkins in the middle of the road. Where blond heads don't crack open brown heads. Where no-one needs to be socially aware. Where Julia, my lovely Corrençon, would at last swap her reasons for writing for reasons for screwing me. Jesus, wouldn't that be nice!

66

"And while I have lots of respect for intellectuals like yourself, Malaussène, I won't have them standing in my way when it comes to nailing a drug-dealing A-rab."

(And thus the dream comes to an end.)

"Cos that's what we're up to, in case you hadn't copped on. What Hadouch Ben Tayeb was trying to flog you, or about to try to flog you, was a load of amphetamines which our health inspectors threw on the scrap heap, but which he picked up cheap in some Algerian chemist's shop and is now trying to offload on us."

(If they can be bought over there, that means we export them, doesn't it? But I keep this neat observation to myself.) I say:

"Maybe they're old Amar's medicine. I know he's got terrible rheumatism."

"Bullshit."

There we are, then. If he won't believe that, then who's going to tell him it was the Town Hall that bunged old Sole the stuff? I'm starting to see just why Hadouch went mute.

"Well, Malaussène, our little chat is coming to an end."

(If you say so.) So I get to my feet, but an icy steel arm grips me as I go by.

"One of my men was killed yesterday in this dump of a neighbour-hood. A good lad who'd been sent out to protect the old ladies – from getting their throats slit by junkies. His death is going to be paid for, and dearly. So don't fuck me around, Malaussène. If you hear anything, keep on the straight and narrow and phone me right away. I can respect your penchant for things North African, but only up to a certain point. Get me?"

I walk back home half in a dream and nearly get run over by a red coach-load of ecstatic old dears. Stojil hoots at me and I answer him with a distracted kiss blown off the tips of my fingers. There are some as slit old dears' throats; then there's Stojil who resurrects them.

At Timbaud junction, I notice what I'd overlooked last night: a chalk outline of a body in the middle of the crossroads. Wrapped up in a dozen shawls, a little girl from the other side of the Mediterranean is playing a lonely game of hopscotch on it. Her two feet are firmly planted on the dead man's feet. The wide circle of his head makes a perfect target for her pebble.

Chapter 13

STOJILKOVICZ DROPPED WIDOW Dolgorouki off at the corner of Boulevard de Belleville and Rue de Pali-Kao. The coach had pulled off amid a roar of fresh laughter from the old dears and widow Dolgorouki was now strolling down Rue de Tourtille like a teenybopper. She was old. She was a widow. She had Russian roots. She was carrying a small crocodile-skin handbag, the last remaining trace of the good old days. But she was smiling. The future looked rosy to her. A copper in a leather jacket was watching her as she went by. He reckoned she should be more careful about wandering round Belleville in a daydream at this twilight hour. But he was sure about one thing, at least: no-one was going to kill her. He was watching over her. She was a lovely old dear, in fact, that's what he thought. And he was a good lad. He had Belleville in his sights.

Widow Dolgorouki was daydreaming about "Saint Stojilkovicz". That's what she always called him, "Saint Stojilkovicz", while smiling to herself. He and his coach had now made a social whirlpool of her loneliness. (She was a one for expressions like that "social whirlpool", with deep vowels and a roll of the "r".) Saint Stojilkovicz took the ladies out in his coach. There were the "Saturday outings" when she and her friends would do their weekly shopping under Stojilkovicz's direction, as he knew "the shops of their youth" like the back of his hand. Then there were the Sunday excursions when Stojil took them out into Paris just for the fun of it – into a forgotten Paris that would spring back to life in the soles of the boots they'd worn as young women. Last week, he'd taken them dancing on Rue de Lappe. They'd done the foxtrot, the Charleston and slower numbers too. The dancers' heads had traced the paths of a maze through the dense cigarette smoke.

Today, at the Montreuil flea-market, Saint Stojilkovicz had talked down the price of a small, Kiev-style fan for her. His booming papal voice had given the stall-holder a good preaching:

"Your job is a truly repellent one, young fellow my lad. An antique dealer robs people's souls. As this lady is from Russia, this fan is part of her cultural inheritance. If you don't want to turn into a real piece of shit, I'd give her a nice big mark down."

Yes, it had been a good day for widow Dolgorouki, even if a quarter of her monthly pension had been blown, so to speak, on the fan. And tomorrow was Sunday – another excursion . . . Then, like every Sunday afternoon, "Saint Stojilkovicz" would lead his troop of old dears down into the catacombs where, amid the piles of dusty old bones, they'd laughingly start up a session of "Active Resistance to Eternity", as he called it. (But they had all sworn not to say a word about this little game, and widow Dolgorouki would sooner have died than spill the beans.)

After the ceremony in the catacombs, they would all go off to have tea at the Malaussènes'. While the outings were just for the ladies, this is where widow Dolgorouki met "the gentlemen". There was the mother, nearly ten months' pregnant and radiant with it. She didn't seem worried at all. Her daughter Clara served tea and sometimes took photos. The mother and the daughter both had faces like icons. At the back of the hardware shop, which had been converted into a flat, a second, gawky daughter told people's fortunes. A little boy in rose-tinted glasses told wonderful stories. The calmness of the house soothed widow Dolgorouki.

Suddenly, widow Dolgorouki thought about widow Ho, her neighbour across the landing. Widow Ho was Vietnamese. She was very frail and felt very lonely. Yes, her mind was made up. Next Saturday, widow Dolgorouki would ask widow Ho to go with her in the coach. They would all have to shove up a bit, that's all.

That's what widow Dolgorouki was daydreaming about as she walked down Rue de Tourtille on her way home, tailed by the little copper in his leather jacket. The hardest part of the day was going to be the staircase. It was a dark staircase (the lighting had been cut off by the electricity board), cluttered with rubble and abandoned dustbins on each landing. Five floors! When she was twenty yards away from her front door, widow Dolgorouki started taking deep breaths, like she was getting ready to take a dive. The bulb in the last street lamp was dead (probably a victim of little Nourdine's sling). She opened the door. She went into the familiar darkness. The little copper didn't follow her into the building. He'd just cased all the landings. Two widows lived there: widow Ho, the one who'd been on TV last night, and widow Dolgorouki. The little copper was their invisible guardian angel. Widow Dolgorouki had just got home safe and sound. The little copper turned back. He didn't want to let Belleville out of his sight.

As soon as she was over the threshold, widow Dolgorouki sensed danger. Someone was there. Crouching under the stair-well of Staircase B. A yard away on her left. She could sense the warmth of his body. And his tensed nerves. She slowly opened her bag. Her hand slid inside and her fingers located the hazelwood grip. The revolver was a short, stocky model, especially designed for this sort of close combat. A Llama 27. She slipped the bag from her right hip till it was over her stomach. Now the gun was pointing towards the danger area. She took the safety-catch off as quietly as she could, feeling the cylinder turn inside her palm. She stood still. She turned her head towards the black hole of the stair-well and said:

"Who's there?"

No answer. He was going to spring her. She would shoot only at the last moment, when she saw the razor, without taking the gun out of her bag.

"Come on! Who's there?"

Her heart beat faster, but it was from the thrill of it. She pretended to clutch her handbag fearfully against herself.

"I've just taken out my pension," she said. "It's here, in my bag."

Silence.

"With a Kiev fan and the keys to my flat."

The shadow still didn't budge.

71

"Fifth floor, on the right," she added.

Still nothing.

"Very well," she said. "I'm going to call for help. There's a policeman just outside."

The shadow showed itself at last.

"Don't be daft, Missus Dolgo. This is an ambush."

She recognized the voice at once. She dropped the revolver as though it was red hot.

"Now then, Nourdine my lad, what on earth are you doing there?"

"I'm waiting for Leila," the kid whispered. "I want to give her a scare."

(Leila was one of the daughters of old Amar Ben Tayeb, the restaurateur. Every evening, Leila took up widows Dolgorouki and Ho their dinner.)

"To make her drop her tray, like you did last week?"

"No, Missus Dolgo, just to get a bit of a fondle."

"All right, little Nourdine. But only when she's on her way down."

"Okay, Missus Dolgo, when she's on her way down."

"Come in, Leila, it's open."

She had just put down her handbag and coat. She hadn't got her breath back yet.

"It isn't Leila, Madame Dolgorouki. It's only me."

She turned round, a surprised smile on her lips. She didn't have time to protect her throat. The blade of the razor swished in front of her. She felt how deep and clean the wound was. It was as though she was drowning in herself. It wasn't such a bad way to go, like a foaming headiness.

Chapter 14

THE YOUNG WOMAN who'd been found in the barge had now been fast asleep for the last four days.

"If you're not a whore, my lovely, then what are you?"

Pastor was kneeling by her bed, whispering in the silence of the hospital bedroom, hoping that she'd hear an echo of his murmuring in some corner of her coma.

"And who did this to you?"

She wasn't on police records as a prostitute, nor had she been reported missing. Apparently nobody was out looking for that sumptuous body. Nobody was worried about her as she swayed to and fro between life and death. Pastor had been through the computer records and the cardboard box-files.

"I'll get them. Don't worry about that. There were at least two of them."

Lying in the chemical stench of the hospital, she had tubes sticking out all over her.

"We've already found the car. A black BMW. It was just by Place Gambetta."

He leaned over her to tell her the good news. The sort of news that might make her break surface.

"We should learn a lot from the fingerprints."

The red beep on the metal casing showed that she was thinking, but far away. Her heart-beat was as erratic as anything. She'd been drugged up to the eyeballs.

"Even Thian, with all his pill-popping, couldn't cope with that amount of shit in his veins. But you're a strong lass. You'll pull through."

Her jaws hadn't taught them much either. One of her molars had been capped and a wisdom tooth had been extracted. But there wasn't a dentist in France who'd x-rayed those jaws or taken a mould of that molar.

"And what about your appendix? The doctor says the operation has only been done recently. Two years ago at the most. Who took out your appendix? Not a French surgeon, anyway. Your photo has been round every operating theatre in the country. One of your fans, maybe?"

Pastor smiled in the half-light of the room. He pulled a chair over to the bed and slowly sat down.

"Right. Now let's think logically."

He was murmuring into the sleeping woman's ear.

"You get your guts operated on and your teeth fixed abroad. With a bit of luck, the composition of the cap will tell us where it comes from. So, there are two possibilities."

(You can interrogate anyone, no matter what state they're in. The truth isn't usually got at by the answers, but by how the questions are sequenced. Pastor had learnt that from the Councillor, when little Jean-Baptiste had still been at school.)

"You're either a beautiful foreigner, who has been murdered on French territory, a spy perhaps, which would explain why they tortured you, in which case the investigation will be out of my hands, which makes me exclude that possibility at once."

"Or else you are a professional traveller."

Pastor let the metallic din of a trolley die down in the corridor. Then he asked:

"A teacher for the VSO?" (He pouted sceptically.) "No, this body is no teaching body. An embassy official? A business woman?"

Her curvaceous body, her powerful muscles and her strong, determined face made that seem possible.

"Not that either. Your men would have come looking for you."

Pastor had encountered a few such jet-setteresses. It was incredible how grown men fell to pieces whenever they were away.

"Tourism? Maybe you're in tourism? A patient guide for worried sheep?"

No. He wouldn't have been able to explain why, but Pastor was sure this wasn't right. She didn't look like someone who kept to the beaten track.

"A journalist then?"

He played around with the idea. A journalist . . . a reporter . . . a photographer . . . something along those lines . . .

"But why hasn't your newspaper been out looking for such a beautiful missing penwoman?"

He looked back over her body. A lovely woman. Lovely bone structure. Lovely face. Vigorous, supple fingers. A natural mane of hair.

"Because you're not a hackette slaving for a daily rag, nor a gossip columnist who phones in her prefabricated stories just after tea time."

No, he saw her rather as an investigative journalist. The sort who melted into the landscape. Who'd vanish for weeks on end then reemerge when her investigations were over. A historian of now, an ethnographer of here, just the sort of woman who'd dig out things that were supposed to stay hidden. And then want to talk about them. In the name of ethical transparency.

"Is that it?"

The door had opened without Pastor hearing it. Thian's gravelly voice burst ironically into his ear:

"That, or else a typist on holiday, or an heiress who got in the way . . ."

"Typists don't get medical treatment abroad and heiresses don't get tortured, Thian. They just get wrapped straight up in concrete overcoats. You're stubborn for an Annamese. That's a rare mix."

"A bit of a Frenchie, you mean. Come on, kiddo. Let's get out of here. Hospitals make me sick."

Inspector Van Thian was depressed. Days had gone by and he still hadn't found widow Dolgorouki's murderer.

"She was my neighbour, kiddo. The door just opposite mine."

Someone was going round Belleville with a razor. Someone was cutting up old ladies right under Inspector Van Thian's nose and Inspector Van Thian was incapable of nailing him.

"Why didn't that shit-head come to my place? Oh no. He has to do his business over the way."

Widow Ho was hurting inside. In Inspector Van Thian's breast. Compared with widow Dolgorouki, widow Ho was rolling in it. She went around Belleville waving wads of notes under paupers' noses and it was the other widows that got done. Widow Ho slept on a mattress stuffed full of dosh while other widows clung onto their tiny pensions. Pensions were poisonous. They killed off widows. Inspector Van Thian and widow Ho's relationship was on the rocks.

"Listen, kiddo, I'm fed up being an old prick disguised as an old cunt."

Pastor poured out bourbon after bourbon to wash down the antidepressants.

There was nothing else to be done.

"And to think I've been on the case night and day . . ."

This was true. Inspector Van Thian had tried everything he knew. Dressed in plain clothes, he'd quizzed every head likely to know anything. In his widow's weeds, he'd put temptation in every smack-head's way. Widow Ho had been seen ambling down the road side by side with junkies so full of holes that they were like watering cans. Their teeth chattered. Sweat bucketed out of them. But still they let widow Ho be. Widow Ho was like a huge forbidden bone under a salivating dog's nose. All that dosh! Jesus! Allah! All those spondulicks that would never chase a dragon! Widow Ho was like the Tree of Knowledge, planted right there in the middle of Belleville's brains: out of bounds! When she walked down the road, smack-heads would faint from frustration. Widow Ho didn't believe in herself anymore, and she'd gone right off her accent.

"I've had it up to here with chucking 'spling-lolls' into everything I come out with."

In fact, widow Ho couldn't speak a word of Vietnamese. Her accent was crap. Her working methods, too.

"I've had it up to here with doing the crafty Asian bit in my thick French bonce."

In the office every evening, an utterly disgusted Thian would slip out of his Thai dress with its silky black sheen. The Thousand Flowers of Asia would leap out of the dress and grab Pastor by the throat. When widow Ho was depressed, Inspector Van Thian would get into a confidential mood. He was a widower too. His wife, Janine the Giantess, was dead – had been dead for twelve years. She'd left him with a daughter, Gervaise. But Gervaise had married God. ("I'll pray for you, Thianie, but I just won't have the time to come and see you.") Inspector Van Thian felt lonely. In fact, he felt like he came from nowhere.

"During the 1920s, my mum was a primary schoolteacher in Tongkin. I've kept the first and only letter she ever wrote to her family. It's postmarked Mong Cai, where she'd been sent. Do you want to read it, kiddo?"

Pastor read the letter.

Dear Parents,

There is no point in insisting, our presence in this country will not last another twenty years. We are too greedy for them and they are too wily for us. As I am good at rape and pillage, I'm picking up anything valuable that I come across and shall be returning home on the first boat. Expect me back soon.

Louise.

"And what did she come across?" asked Pastor.

"My father. The smallest Tongkinese in all of Tongkin. She was a big girl from the twelfth arrondissement. Round Tolbiac way, you know. The Bercy warehouses. That's where I grew up."

"So to speak."

"In the plonk business, kiddo. A lovely little Gamay."

* * *

Pastor's investigations weren't going too well either. He'd drawn a blank with the fingerprints on the BMW's bodywork. It belonged to a meticulous bachelor dentist who hadn't taken his gloves off since the start of the great AIDS panic. And the two killers had been just as careful as him. So this car was the only one in Paris without a *single* fingerprint on it. The last mechanic that had serviced it had even wiped his off.

Following Thian's advice, Pastor had traced every emergency call which had been recorded by the police the night the girl had been thrown into the barge.

"There might have been a struggle when she was put into the car. She might have yelled out. Someone might have heard and phoned the police."

"Might have," Pastor nodded.

On that particular night, in the town and suburbs of Paris, three hundred and two women had screamed. The police had been called out two hundred and eight times. There had been premature births, cases of acute appendicitis, noisy love-making, beatings that had been forgiven as soon as the uniforms turned up. Nothing promising. Pastor decided to check out the rest of them.

Photos of the sleeping beauty didn't ring any bells. If certain businesswomen were absent, they were present and correct some-where else and doing very nicely thank you. Pastor also went round those parts of the press which employed special reporters or foreign correspondents. There were more of them than he had bargained for. Several more days would be needed before he'd checked them all out.

Then, one evening, Caregga, a broad-backed, bull-necked inspector who always wore the same fur-collared pilot's jacket come rain or shine, ran out of paper clips. Caregga was a slow, methodical worker who was in love with a young beautician. He'd just typed out a detailed report of a case of bag-snatching, aggravated by exhibitionism. The theft he could have pardoned, but now that he'd discovered the purity of true love he found the exhibitionism revolting. Caregga spent a full minute wondering from whom to borrow the paper clip which was needed to stick his report together. He plumped for his young colleague Pastor. Pastor was a good bloke, in a quiet but permanent state of jollity, who did all sorts of people all sorts of good turns without expecting anything in return. Pastor was always available. He slept in his office. It was thanks to Pastor, who had replaced him on duty, that Caregga had been able to spend his first night with Carole. (In fact, nothing had happened that night. All Carole and Caregga had done was talk about their future. It was only at six-thirty the next morning that their future had finally got going.) Pastor shared his office with a tiny Vietnamese who had a French mother and who spent his life filling in national health insurance reimbursement claims. Van Thian and Pastor's office was next door to Caregga's. It was for all of these reasons (professional, emotional and topographical) that Inspector Caregga went into Van Thian and Pastor's den that evening. Standing side by side, with their backs towards the door, the two inspectors were watching the winter night scatter its flakes through the city's neon lights. They didn't turn round. Borrowing a paper clip without asking permission first was the last thing Caregga would have done. On the other hand, he didn't like going straight to the point (by saying something like: "Hey, Pastor, lend me a paper clip, will you?"). So Caregga was looking for a way to make his presence felt when he spotted a photograph on Pastor's desk. This photograph, which had come from their lab, showed a beautiful naked girl on a coal heap. She was disfigured, but still beautiful. This was confirmed by a blow-up of her face. In his rough, strongman-of-few-words' voice, Inspector Caregga said:

"I know that girl."

Pastor turned slowly round. His face had gone tense.

"What did you say?"

Inspector Caregga repeated that he knew that girl.

"She's called Julie Corrençon. She's a journalist with *Actuel.*"

A downpour of pink pills splashed onto the floor. When Van Thian straightened his tube of Tranxene, it was empty.

The telephone rang.

"Pastor?"

At the other end of the line, a copper's voice, running over with professional enthusiasm, was saying:

"We've found out who she is at last!"

"So have I," said Pastor.

And he hung up.

Chapter 15

O N MY SIDE of the fence, I got my thinking cap on. A health
visitor working for the eleventh *arrondissement* had tried to
drug our old Sole and Hadouch had got nicked red-handed
with the pills. He'd stopped me speaking up for him because he was sure
no-one would believe me. He'd decided to get himself out of the shit.
But, one week later, Hadouch still hadn't broken surface. My conclusion
was that he needed help.

I decided to do the only thing that was feasible: nab the dope-visitor
and make her cough. So I sent old Sole off to the Town Hall to make a
date with the above-mentioned pedlaress by pretending that he'd run
out of his ration of happy pills. He'd dropped in his message and was
promised that the health visitor would call by to see him at half-past four
that afternoon, and I stashed myself in Sole's wardrobe. An ambush.
All in a dither about seeing her again, Sole was pacing up and down his
room.

"I've got that brunette under my skin, Benjamin, and that's the truth
of it!"

"Shut up, Sole. If she turns up, she'll hear us."

Said I, crouching amid the ancient two-pieces and handmade shoes.
Sole's wardrobe smelt of a wholesome past.

"A brilliant smile, and flashing eyes. You'll see!"

"I won't see anything at all if you keep on like that. If she twigs you're
not alone, she'll split!"

"I haven't stopped thinking about her since the moment I met her."

I can't see Sole, but I can hear him pacing around. He's got himself
dressed up to the nines. His shoes are doing a 1950s creak.

"And such a bright little thing! She stroked the palm of my hand when she was giving me my medicine . . ."

In fact, he's as nervy as he would have been if he'd really swallowed that bag of explosives. I start getting worried about my plan.

Knock! Knock! Here she is. The plan's in action.

Sole's soles stop creaking.

Another knock-knock. Sole is frozen to the spot. I start whispering furiously:

"Go and open the frigging door!"

Nothing doing. Old lover boy's petrified, frozen with fear. And from where I am, crouching in the wardrobe, I suddenly figure out why Sole wound up hitched to bachelorhood.

KNOCK! KNOCK! KNOCK! this time.

If I don't do something sharpish, our little brunette will piss off, just like all the other women in Sole's life once they'd been lured up to a door which was never to open. So I leapt out the wardrobe, crossed the room and flung the door open.

"About time!" a gargantuan blonde says, before shoving me to one side like I was a scrum-half and positioning herself in front of our paralyzed Sole.

"So, what's up, granddad?"

Sole's gone mute. The juggernaut turns back to me.

"What's the old feller's problem? You know I've got loads of other calls still to make today."

"He was expecting someone else," says I. "He's a bit taken aback."

"Someone else? He asked for the local health visitor didn't he?"

"That's right. But he was expecting the other one. The brunette."

"There isn't any brunette. There are only two of us in the neighbourhood and the other one's a red-head. And even uglier than I am. You're barking up the wrong tree."

"All the same, last time it was a lovely little brunette who gave him his medicine. It did him lots of good so he asked for one of you to come round and top him up."

"Have you got the prescription?"

"What prescription?"

Her big lardy face suddenly goes rock steady. Her eyes screw up.

"Don't play silly buggers with me, sonny. If he got some medicine, then he must have been given a prescription."

"Oh no he wasn't. It was just a batch of loose pills in a plastic bag. Against anxiety attacks . . ."

"Do you want me to call the police?"

The conversation comes to a halt. The giantess had slipped that in just like she was asking me out for a drink or something.

"You really are all as thick as shit in this neighbourhood. It's the third time this week that someone's tried to con a fake prescription out of me. In the first place, I'm against it, and in the second place, I couldn't do it anyway."

Then, suddenly, wily wrinkles start rumpling up her forehead. She points her thumb at Sole and says:

"And the dope isn't for that old wreck over there, is it? It's for you . . ."

(Oh deary me!) And then she goes sweet on me.

"Drugs aren't the answer, sonny jim. I know a far better solution."

She moves over to me as she speaks. How tall is she? If I hadn't instinctively backed off as she came forward my head would have ended up jammed between her mammaries. Without turning back, she gives Sole his marching orders:

"Go and wait in the kitchen, granddad."

No sooner said, than we're alone. Her ogress's head towering above mine, her granite breasts crushing me against the wall, her docker's fist inching intimately down (to my intimates) while her rapist's voice dictates my prescription:

"I don't have the time right now, lover boy, but you have to come round to my place for treatment this evening, at the latest, or else I'll call in the cops. Here's my address."

Sure enough, her fingers had glided to the other side of my belt and slipped an ice-cold calling card into my personal mail-box. Which senses that it's printed with embossed letters. Very classy.

In other words, if Sole's supplier is a health visitor, then I'm the Queen of England. She'd obviously got nothing to do with the Town Hall, which employed its own health visitors – who didn't drug their patients, but raped them.

So, if she isn't on the council payroll, that means she either works on her own, or else with a gang that goes around touting for business wherever oldsters get together. (She's already got three of them lined up in the neighbourhood.) And then, suddenly, eureka! I remember that little brunette who drugged Risson and who Julia's been tailing . . . What if they were quite simply one and the same?

The Malaussène investigations then proceed in a dark-room under my sister Clara's photographic fingers with a red light bulb dangling over our heads. (How sweet Clara's face looks in that light . . . Tell me, Clarinette, who's going to fall for you and when? And how will your big brother put up with him when he does?)

We decided to develop all the photos Clara took during the medal ceremony. With a bit of luck, our brunette might be in one of them.

"Look at the Deputy, Ben, he's a real laugh . . ."

And lo and behold, the people's elected representative starts to appear at the bottom of the dish's chemical soup.

"His jaws come out first. That's what having a vigorous face does for you."

Clara chuckles. Clara's a photographer and has been ever since her almond eyes first opened sixteen years ago. Julie hit on that at once when I introduced them. ("Ben, you wouldn't believe how that girl sees the world. It's as if she can take in the surface and the depths all at once.")

"Now for the Permanent Secretary for Senior Citizens . . ."

With Arnaud Le Capelier, it's his parting that comes out first, then the ridge of his nose and the dimple cleaving his chin. On either side of that dividing line, his face is as smooth and expressionless as a helmet. A bit soft for a helmet, of course, but rigid, with a staring slit for his eyes. (Jesus! he gives me the creeps.) Arnaud Le Capelier is leaning down from the rostrum. He's shaking our decorated and beaming Sole by the hand. In fact, he's only given him his fingertips. As though he found the whole thing disgusting. I reckon our Arnaud's allergic to oldsters. The Permanent Secretary for Senior Citizens! What a cruel fate!

We keep on working for a good couple of hours, with Clara's scent struggling against the stench of the development fluid. Then Clara finally says:

"The close-ups aren't going to be of any use, Benjamin. The girl must have been on her guard. I'm going to do some blow-ups of the crowd."

"We've got all the time in the world."

"Not you, you haven't. Uncle Stojil said he'd call by this evening."

(Stojil, I beg you, leave me in this red night with my favourite sister.)

"He needs you, Ben. He hasn't got over Madame Dolgorouki being murdered. Go on. If I find anything I'll give you a shout."

Stojil's already there. He's taken a chair and sat himself down in the room where the children and granddads are sleeping. He's waiting for me. We've both more or less got into the habit of listening to the oldsters and the kids as they sleep. The children take the top bunks, with their allotted granddads beneath them. (This was Thérèse's idea, with Clara's agreement, the wholehearted approval of the little ones and authorized by my own authority. The oldsters were all so shaken up when we took them in that they couldn't sleep anymore. "The children's breathing will soothe them," Thérèse declared. Children breathing, or the scent of young girls? Either way, since we made that decision, the granddads have been sleeping like Yuletide logs. And Stojil and I spend our evenings playing chess and talking softly through the merging streams of their sleep.)

"Today," says Stojil, "I took some Russians out around town."

Jeremy turns over in bed, just above Granddad Sweeney, who does likewise.

"All good communists, with their leave passes duly stamped and instructions to be on their guard."

Half Pint grumbles to himself. Thérèse coughs.

"The agency told me to take good care of them. There was an apparatchik with them. A Ukrainian. A jolly fellow. He laughed when he told me: 'No propaganda, comrade. We know all your lies off by heart.' They're always the same. When they talk to you, everything's a joke, but the joke is a killing one. Like you were getting bitten by a snake with the giggles."

"Remember Khrushchev, for example. He used to laugh a lot."

"He was a specialist, that one, till one fine day someone started doing the laughing for him."

The granddads' breathing has slowly fallen into pace with the children's.

"So I gave them their own version of Paris: memorials to communists and the trade union headquarters. That's all they saw. When I caught the apparatchik staring into the window of a charcuterie, I told him: 'Propaganda! Everything inside is fake! Those sausages are made of cardboard! If you look at them, Alexei Trophimovich, I'll have to report you!'"

Risson hiccups happily, like he was laughing in his sleep.

"At noon," Stojil went on, "I took them to lunch at the Renault factory's canteen. Then, in the afternoon, they wanted to see Versailles. They all want to see Versailles. I didn't fancy dragging myself all the way out there again, so I drove them up to Saint-Lazare railway station and told them: 'Here is Versailles. A tyrant's palace which the Revolution has converted for the use of the masses!' And they all flashed at it with their cameras."

He smiles. The sleepers are all breathing in time. All their lives in one sole breath. I say:

"They owe you a visit to Moscow now."

But Stojil has changed the subject.

"My widow Dolgorouki knew the pre-revolutionary authors perfectly. She was a communist when she was twenty, just like I was when I left the monastery. She was in the Resistance here, while I was a partisan in Croatia. She had Mayakovsky's poetry off by heart, we would recite entire scenes of *Revizor* to each other and she even knew Bely."

"I remember that old lady. She used to tell mum: 'Your Clara's face is as pure as an Old Believer's icon.'"

"The Dolgoroukis were princes, long ago, legendary princes even. Some of them chose the Revolution."

Stojil gets to his feet. He tucks Half Pint's arms back under his blanket.

"What did Risson tell them this evening?"

"*August 1914.* By Solzhenitsyn. As Jeremy wanted to know everything about the uniforms of '14, Verdun had to help Risson out. Apparently the army used up 700,000 metres of flannel per month at 3.50 francs a metre, 2,550,000 pairs of socks, 250,000 mufflers, 10,000 balaclavas, 2,400,000 metres of double sheets for uniforms, which works out at 77,000 tons of suint. Verdun knows all that, and all the prices down to the last centime because he was a tailor at the time. This flood of information had the kids even more agog than the taxis on the Marne did."

"Yes," said Stojil dreamily. "Youth loves death."

"What's that?"

"Youth loves death. At twelve, they read themselves to sleep with war stories and at twenty they go to war, just like widow Dolgorouki and I did. They dream of killing in a just fight, or of dying a glorious death, but either way, it's death they love. Nowadays in Belleville, they cut an old woman's throat then stick her life's savings into their veins in the quest for a resplendent death. That's what my widow died of: the love youth has for death. If she'd been run over by a young lunatic in a fast car, her death would have been the same. That's it."

Silence. The sleepers breathe regularly. And then:

"Hey, Clara's bed's empty!"

"Not for much longer, uncle Stojil," Clara's voice answers close by. (Even when far away, Clara's velvet voice sounds close by.) "Here I am."

Then, after giving Stojil a kiss:

"I think I've found our health visitor, Ben."

Lights up. And there's our little brunette. Her eyes swallow up her face ("with flashing eyes" said Sole). Her pallid looks are surrounded by her dark hair. In one of the photos, her handbag is open and she's taking a small bag out of it which could well be the packet of sweeties. The next blow-up is further confirmation. Yes, it could well be her . . .

"Well done, sweet heart, we'll get Julie to confirm it tomorrow."

Chapter 16

IT ONLY TOOK Inspector Caregga two seconds to tell Pastor what he'd been trying to find out for the last week. The barge's sleeping beauty was called Julie Corrençon, she was a reporter for *Actuel* magazine and she'd been questioned a year ago in connection with the series of bombs that had gone off in that big department store.

"As a suspect?"

"No, just as a witness. She happened to be there when one of the bombs exploded."

A visit to her magazine didn't tell Pastor much. No-one on the editorial staff knew where Julie Corrençon was and no-one thought that this was any cause for concern. She sometimes vanished for months on end, then reappeared with an article she'd researched at the other end of the world, or in the suburb down the road. There was never any sign of her in the meantime. She didn't mix much with her colleagues and even less with the world of journalism in general. In this realm of exuberant introverts, she was considered to be a lass who was secretive, rather than aloof, without any particular hang-ups or complexes, and totally foot-loose. The main point about her was that she wrote magnificent articles and never revealed the subjects in advance. They were always accepted. "Our super-girl's going to be famous some day." She didn't go in for drugs or drink. All her colleagues agreed that she was "a real good-looker", "one hell of a turn-on" and indestructible. As for her private life, she was not known to be going out with anyone. Attempts to find out if she was hetero, homo, onano, a sportswoman or a stamp collector received no precise answers and Pastor was soon to work out that such inquiries were considered to be old hat. One thing was sure, however. Julie Corrençon might arouse obsessive passions, but the idea that she had fallen into the clutches of a maniac was out of the question.

During the next few evenings, stretched out on his camp-bed, Pastor read his way through the journalist's complete works. The first thing that struck him was the collected way she wrote about explosive subjects. Her sentences were perfectly punctuated, the style neutrally subject-verb-object. It seemed to be saying: "Let the facts do the talking, they stand up fine on their own, without any frills." It was quite different from the style of her magazine and of turn-of-the-century journalism in general.

Julie Corrençon's curiosity had led her to the four corners of the world. She worked just as Pastor had imagined, by plunging herself into her subject matter, living each article out to the full, then starting again from scratch for the next one, while putting her life constantly on the line. When researching the cocaine trade she had got herself voluntarily imprisoned in a women's jail in Thailand, then escaped hidden under a heap of prisoners who'd died of cholera. She'd also spent an equally risky spell with a Turkish Minister of the Interior in order to plot out the top-secret route taken by locally grown poppies to the laboratories in Marseilles where they are turned into our twentieth-century heroin. Pastor made a mental note how much she'd written about drugs. But she'd also tackled other subjects. She'd done a world-wide survey of love, from which she'd concluded that the only love worth its name is enjoyed in the last of the world's primitive cultures and by revolutionaries on the eve of the final victory (but it then turns sour the next day). This made Pastor fall into a temporary day-dream in the half-light of his office. He thought of his father the Councillor and Gabrielle. If Gabrielle had read this article she would certainly have invited Julie Corrençon round to see her in action with her superb bald-headed lover, despite their advanced age. Pastor had barged in on them once: it was like the fauna of a rain forest in eruption.

La Corrençon's most recent article was a piece of photo-journalism composed in Paris six months before. It was about one of The Store's employees during the period when that huge shop was being hit by a series of bombs. This employee was a man of an unguessable age, who looked strangely transparent and who answered to the name of Benjamin Malaussène. His job in The Store was to act as a scapegoat. He had to take responsibility for whatever went wrong and, when customers started complaining, he'd pull such a pathetic face that their anger would turn to pity and they'd leave without demanding any compensation. Some of the photos showed Malaussène with the Human Resources Manager, both looking absolutely delighted at having duped their clientele. Next came an analysis of the money which The Store was saving (the game was certainly worth playing). Julie Corrençon also revealed Malaussène's salary (a decidedly handsome one). The rest of the report showed Malaussène at home. In this context he looked much younger and more distinct. As the eldest brother of a large family, he was shown in the midst of his brothers' and sisters' bunk-beds, telling them stories that literally lit up their eyes.

As in all of her other articles, Julie Corrençon refrained from making any value judgements. There was not a single exclamation mark. Subject, verb, object.

The Public Records Office revealed that Julie Corrençon was the only child of Jacques-Emile Corrençon – born on January 2, 1901 in a small village of the same name in the Dauphiné, near Villard-de-Lans – and of Emilia Mellini, an Italian citizen, born in Bologna on February 17, 1923. Despite the age difference, her mother had died first, in 1951, and the father in 1969.

Inspector Van Thian knew Jacques-Emile Corrençon's name.

"He was a bit like my mum," he announced.

(Old Thian liked taking Pastor by surprise. He sometimes succeeded.)

"Grew up in a wine cellar too, did he?" Pastor asked.

"No. He was a Colonial Governor who didn't believe in colonialism."

Thian explained how Corrençon's name had first hit the headlines in 1954 when, along with Mendès-France, he had negotiated with the Viet Minh. That same year he had also played an active part in obtaining an autonomous status for Tunisia. Under de Gaulle, Corrençon had gone on in this direction by entering into contact with all the pro-independence underground movements in Africa.

"And did you read this article by La Corrençon?" Pastor asked Thian.

Pastor didn't like letting Thian surprise him without getting his own back. He handed him an illustrated article which made old Thian turn from yellow to green.

The article told how, in her search for boat-people, Julie Corrençon had been tossed around in the China Sea on a raft hardly more sea-worthy than those belonging to the refugees (photo) and how she'd then been struck down by acute appendicitis (photo). They had had to operate without anaesthetic (photo) and, as all her mates started passing out one after the other (photo), she'd finished off the job they'd begun herself, holding the scalpel in one hand and a small mirror in the other (photo).

"That tells us at least one thing," said Pastor after Thian had gulped down a tranquillizer. "The lads that gave her the third degree before throwing her into the barge definitely didn't get anything out of her."

In the afternoon of the same day, Inspector Pastor tried for the tenth time to draw his service revolver faster than Van Thian, his team-mate. It snagged in his pullover, fell out of his hand and went off as it hit the floor. An official 7.65mm bullet whistled past Thian's shoulder-blades, ricocheted off the ceiling, tore a lump of polyester sound-proofing out of the wall and then went still.

"Let's start again," said Thian.

"Let's not," said Pastor.

In the practice gallery, four of Pastor's eight bullets scored good marks on Van Thian's target. Pastor's own target (which depicted a cardboard gunman in an aggressive stance) remained intact.

"How do you manage to shoot so badly?" Thian asked in admiration.

"If you have to shoot, it's already too late," Pastor replied philo-sophically.

Pastor was then called into Chief Superintendent Coudrier's office. As ever, his boss's office had its curtains drawn and was bathed in an imperial green light. A secretary, as tall as a copper's story and who answered (silently) to the name of Elisabeth, poured Pastor a cup of coffee. Elisabeth held Chief Superintendent Coudrier in unspoken admiration and he never took advantage of that fact. She came in and went out again without making the slightest noise. And she always left the coffee pot behind her.

Chapter 17

COUDRIER: THANK YOU, Elisabeth. Now, tell me, Pastor . . .

Pastor: Yes, Sir?

Coudrier: What is your opinion of Chief Superintendent Cercaria?

Pastor: The head of Narcotics? Um, well, Sir . . .

Coudrier: Yes?

Pastor: Let's just say I find him quite narcotic.

Coudrier: One lump or two?

Pastor: One and a half, please, Sir.

Coudrier: In what way?

Pastor: Sorry, Sir?

Coudrier: In what way do you find Cercaria narcotic?

Pastor: He's an archetype, Sir. An archetypal copper on the beat. And archetypes are rare and mysterious things.

Coudrier: Explain yourself.

Pastor: Well, when such a large amount of evidence has been amassed concerning any given person, then that person becomes unreal, as mysterious as a metaphor.

Coudrier: How interesting.

Pastor: The woman I'm investigating at the moment is another archetype: a militant-idealist-reporter. It wouldn't even wash in the movies.

Coudrier: She's *over the top*, as my grandsons would put it.

Pastor: You're a grandfather, Sir?

Coudrier: Twice over. It's almost a second career. And are your investigations bearing fruit?

Pastor: I have discovered the victim's identity, Sir.

Coudrier: And how did you manage that?

Pastor: Caregga recognized her.

Coudrier: How convenient.

Pastor: She's Jacques-Emile Corrençon's daughter.

Coudrier: The Mendès-France man? A good sort. He rather reminded me of Conrad. Except that he went in for decolonisation.

Pastor: The other side of the adventure.

Coudrier: That's one way of putting it. More coffee?

Pastor: Please, Sir.

Coudrier: Pastor, I'm afraid that my colleague Cercaria is once more in need of your services.

Pastor: Very good, Sir.

Coudrier: Or, rather, of your help.

Pastor: . . .

Coudrier: In so far as that is possible.

Pastor: Naturally, Sir.

Coudrier: During his investigations into the Vanini affair, Cercaria has arrested a certain Hadouch Ben Tayeb, who was caught *in flagrante delicto*. This Ben Tayeb of ours was trying to sell amphetamines to customers in his father's restaurant.

Pastor: In Belleville?

Coudrier: In Belleville. During the questioning, Cercaria has behaved in, how shall I put it . . . ?

Pastor: An archetypal way?

Coudrier: Quite. He is convinced that Ben Tayeb was involved in Vanini's murder, or is covering for someone who was.

Pastor: And Ben Tayeb hasn't cracked?

Coudrier: No. But the worst of the matter is that he's just spent a week in the infirmary.

Pastor: I see.

Coudrier: An unfortunate incident. Pastor, you are going to have to try to sort it all out before the press becomes involved.

Pastor: Very good, Sir.

Coudrier: Can you question Ben Tayeb today?

Pastor: Straightaway.

As soon as Pastor entered Cercaria's brightly-lit office, the huge mustachioed cop got to his feet with a grin of complicity on his lips and, even though he stood a good head taller than Pastor, wrapped an arm round his shoulders.

"I didn't have time to congratulate you for Chabralle, my lad, but I'm still flat on my arse in admiration."

He led Pastor round the room in a sort of slow dance.

"Now, as regards this Ben Tayeb, let me explain the set-up. This little mother-fucker . . ."

Cercaria's office was much larger and brighter than his colleague Coudrier's. There was aluminium and glass everywhere. The complete set of diplomas which Cercaria had received over his career in the force decorated the walls, alongside class photographs, and snaps of scout troops and shots of rag week in the law faculty. The Chief Super-intendent was also to be seen in the company of various tenors of the Bar, as well as big names in show biz and politics. Glass cases contained cups for marksmanship, while the opposite wall was decked with a fine collection of hand-guns, including a small four-barrelled pistol which caught Pastor's eye for an instant.

"A .32 annulus percussion Remington-Elliot Derringer," Cercaria explained. "The perfect weapon for wary poker aces."

Then, as they passed a small fridge, which was tucked in between two aluminium filing cabinets:

"Fancy a tinny?"

"Why not?"

Pastor had always got on well with hulks. His tiny build meant that he didn't get in their way, while his sharp wits drew them to him. From his nursery school days, the Councillor and Gabrielle had taught their little Jean-Baptiste not to be afraid of muscle. At secondary school, Pastor had often been a sort of pilot fish swimming in front of sharks who seemed to have short-sighted souls.

"As I was saying, that little Tayeb son of Tayeb fucker got me a bit wound up."

As a copper, Cercaria had really proved himself, won his street-cred by being wounded several times, and his interro-cred from the screams that came out of his office. (Many a delinquent had paid dearly for his deductive line of beating.)

"Tayeb whacked Vanini, I'd stake my balls on it!"

If Cercaria was that certain, then Pastor tended to believe him. But he asked:

"Any proof?"

"No, just a motive."

Pastor gave Cercaria time to find his words.

"Vanini beat up a bit hard on your A-rabs. He topped one of Tayeb's cousins during a demo. A public danger."

"I see."

"But there's a snag, my lad. Hadouch Ben Tayeb took some photos of Vanini in action. And we can't lay our hands on them. If we do Tayeb, then he'll get someone to publish them."

"Right. So what's the answer?"

"That's where you come in, my lad. First off, Tayeb's got to confess to murdering Vanini. Then, and especially then, we'll stitch him up a nice suit of grass so as his mates won't defend him by publishing those snaps of Vanini."

"Okay."

"Is it doable?"

"Sure."

Chapter 18

HADOUCH BEN TAYEB was in much the same state as Julie had been when Pastor had found her at the bottom of the barge. "Looks like you fell down quite a long staircase," said Pastor, when he'd closed the door behind him.

"Something like that."

But Ben Tayeb was far from being comatose. On the contrary, it was as if the beatings had sharpened his wits.

"You know what you're suspected of? There's no point trying to spin me a yarn."

"Don't worry about that, my memory's been knocked nicely into shape."

As usual, Pastor had insisted on being left alone with the suspect. He gazed thoughtfully round the room (a huge office stuffed with typewriters and telephones). Pastor walked round it, sliding his fingertips over the furniture. His face had become haggard.

"So what I suggest is that we both try to save each other's time."

Pastor noticed that one of the phones was off the hook. He nodded, put his finger to his lips for Ben Tayeb to stay quiet and took out the eraser which was propping the receiver a few millimeters off the cradle. Then he hung up.

"We're all on our own now."

At the other end of the line, Cercaria didn't hear this last observation. Nodding his head in approval, he hung up.

As usual, ears became glued to the door. As usual, the ears could soon hear a faint murmur over the sound of a typewriter.

Three quarters of an hour later, Pastor went back into Cercaria's office with four typed sheets of paper in his hand.

"Sorry about the phone, lad," Cercaria said with a laugh. "Just a bit of professional curiosity."

"It's not the first time someone's tried it," Pastor answered.

He looked very tired, but in less of a state than he had been in after grilling Chabralle.

Cercaria took no notice of how Pastor looked. He stared at once at Ben Tayeb's signature.

"He signed? You really are as good as they say you are, Pastor. Go and get yourself a beer. You've earned it."

Just then, it was as though the huge copper adored the little copper. Then Cercaria put on his glasses and started to read the confession. The smile that flickered round his lips stiffened from one paragraph to the next. In the middle of the third paragraph, he slowly lifted up his head. Beer in hand, Pastor calmly met his stare.

"What the fuck's this supposed to be?"

"The truth, probably," Pastor answered.

"So Vanini was whacked by a little old lady! You taking the fucking piss?"

"That's what Hadouch Ben Tayeb saw."

"And you believe him?"

"Since he told me, when I asked him nicely," Pastor quietly replied.

"So that's your famous method, is it?"

"You should read through to the end."

For a second, Cercaria stared silently back at Pastor, then he started reading again. The young inspector politely finished his beer. His features were filling out again. In the middle of page three, Cercaria lifted up his eyes once more. The expression on his face was the same as the one Pastor had already seen on others': a sort of bewildered brutality.

"And what's this crap about the Town Hall supposed to mean?"

"Well, Ben Tayeb says that the amphetamines you found on him when he was arrested had been given to an old lad by a health visitor during a medal ceremony."

"Okay, Pastor, and you want me to swallow that like a mogadon and wash it down with a glass of water do you?"

"That's up to you. But drugs aren't in Ben Tayeb's line of business."

Cercaria started to look at Pastor in a different light. A cub that was growing up in Coudrier's pack, ready to gobble down the whole set-up one day. He was already coming out with advice.

"So what is Ben Tayeb's business then?"

"Gambling. He runs every illegal lottery from Belleville to the Goutte d'Or. If you want to charge him, then you can on that score. I have the names of his two right-hand-men on page four. His second-in-command is a red-head who goes by the name of Simon the Berber. The next one down the chain is a large African called Black Mo. The evening Vanini was killed, the Berber and Ben Tayeb had just taken receipt of their three-card trick earnings outside Père Lachaise cemetery. They witnessed the murder on their way home, from the opposite pavement."

"What a coincidence."

"A coincidence which means they don't have an alibi, yes."

Cercaria's ears pricked up. Was this last observation pushing something his way? Was it a hint? Once again he felt a liking for this well-brought-up kid. He'd have to think about pinching him from Coudrier one of these days. Cercaria shut up for a moment, then asked:

"And would you care to know what I think about all this?"

"Of course I would."

"Right. First off, you're a good copper, Pastor. You'll go far."

"Thank you."

"And you take compliments from your superiors modestly."

Pastor managed to laugh in exactly the same way as Cercaria.

"Now, this is what I think," Cercaria said.

A hint of authority in his tone of voice made it clear that he was now the boss again.

"What I reckon is, Ben Tayeb's been taking the piss with his story about gun-toting grannies. I wonder how much you really believed him," he added, glancing meaningfully over to Pastor. "Anyway, I'm sorry, but old dears in Belleville don't go around blowing away coppers that have been sent out to protect them. Not on my patch they don't. The only reason Ben Tayeb came out with this porky is that it's such a whopper. Who'd believe that he'd lie *that much*? Get me? By increasing the lie, you make it sound true. Every smart-arsed kid knows that. And your A-rabs better than the rest. But where Ben Tayeb fucked up is when he admitted, in black and white, that he was on the scene of the crime and at the right time. That's what matters. And he's signed it. In the end, you managed to make him cough up a bit of the truth. The bloody bit. As for the story about the old dear with the P38 ('cos it was a P.38, you know that?), I reckon it would get laughed out of court."

He paused.

"So this is what I'm going to do. In the first place, I'm going to charge Ben Tayeb with the murder of a policeman, then I'm going to fit him out nicely as a grass as far as his two henchmen, Simon the Berber and Black Mo, are concerned. That way, they won't lift a finger to protect him and the photos that little shit Tayeb took will never get published. What do you reckon?"

"Ben Tayeb's your prisoner, not mine."

"Too right. And I reckon you've also got it wrong about the drug business. Ben Tayeb's up to his neck in that shit. But we need further information about that. I'll have to give that Malaussène character a bit of a working over now."

Julie Corrençon's article and the photos of Malaussène flashed through Pastor's mind. He made a mental note of the name.

Cercaria leant down over him. His voice was a semi-tone lower and had gone all paternal:

"You're not put out by what I just said?"

"No, not at all."

"You realize that even you can get it wrong sometimes?"

"That can happen."

"Ah, you know what? That's another part of being a top copper!"

In the squad car, Pastor told widow Ho about his interview with Cercaria. In his widow's weeds, Inspector Van Thian started to fidget horribly.

"What's the matter, Thian, something wrong?"

"No, nothing, just a bilharziosis relapse, that's all. I always get one whenever I hear someone mention Cercaria."

A thick layer of cloud blacked out the city sky. A winter sky as threatening as a tropical storm.

"Do you know what a cercaria is, kiddo?"

Thian was violently scratching at his fore-arm.

"Apart from our copper friend, no, I don't."

"It's a nasty little bastard of a short-tailed larva that lives in paddy fields. It gets under your skin, you start itching like fuck, then it rots inside you and you start pissing blood. That's bilharziosis. And that's what Cercaria does to me."

"Is all of this because your father was from Tongkin?"

"We South-Eastern Asians have our own ideas about medicine, kiddo. By the way, where are we going?"

"To Julie Corrençon's."

"The hospital?"

"No, her flat. 85–87 Rue du Temple."

Chapter 19

"JULIA?"

When I get to Julia's landing, clutching the photos of the pseudo health visitor in my hand, her door is half-open. So I murmur from the landing:

"Julia?"

Timidly, with my heart beating in double-time: one thump for love, one thump for panic.

"Julia . . ."

And then I have to take in what I don't want to take in: the lock's been forced. The bolt's broken.

"JULIA!"

I fling the door open. It's Verdun (the town). Or, what it looked like as a battlefield. It doesn't even look as though it could ever be put back together again. The wallpaper and carpet have been ripped to shreds, the bed, sofa and the cushions have been gutted. The furniture has been taken apart stick by stick, then smashed to splinters. All her books are lying spread-eagled in the middle of the carnage. Handfuls of their pages have been torn out. The TV's and the stereo's electronic innards have been cleaned out, the two halves of the phone have sprung across to opposite sides of the room, as though it had been axed in two. The bog-bowl has been uprooted, the hermetic shell of the fridge is lying flat on its back, the water-pipes have been laid bare then sawn apart into sections. The floorboards have been ripped up one by one; the skirting-boards, too.

No Julia.

No Julia?

Or no more Julia?

My heart beat's gone weird. It's a beat that's new to me. A solo beat. Hammering into nothingness. Beating for an answer that will never come. My heart's just been transplanted. It's a widower's heart now. Because whoever did *this* to her flat would be capable of doing anything to Julia herself. They've killed her. They've killed Julia. They've killed *my* Julia.

Some people break down under suffering. Some fall into a day-dream. Some chatter on about any old nonsense on the edge of the grave, then on into the car, any old nonsense, not even about the dead one, just daily chit-chat. Some of them will commit suicide later and you'd never guess it to look at them. Some of them cry a lot then heal up quickly. Some drown in their tears. Some people are pleased to be rid of someone else. Some can't see their dead ones any more, they try, but they can't. Their dead have taken their faces away with them. Some people see death everywhere, they try to wipe it out by selling off the clothes, burning photos, moving house, changing continents, starting up again with a living person, but that doesn't change anything: death is still there in the rear-view mirror. Some go picnicking in cemeteries and some avoid them like the plague – they already have their graves dug in their imaginations. Some stop eating. Some start drinking. Some wonder whether their grief is genuine or fake. Some turn into workaholics and some finally take a holiday. Some find death outrageous and some find it natural given the age, the way things were, war, sickness, a motorcycle, a brawl, modern times, life. Some think death is life.

And other people do the first thing that comes into their heads. Like start running, for instance. Start running like they're never going to stop. That's what I do. I leg it down the stairs. I'm not running away from anything. It's more like I'm running after something, something like Julia's death . . . but the only thing I run into is a tiny Vietnamese woman who's blocking the third-floor landing. I barge into her and she literally takes off, spraying out a shower of multi-coloured pills, bottles, tubes and tablets. It's like a chemist shop's just exploded. And a photo album, too, because on impact I drop the snaps of the drug visitor. Luckily for her, four steps down the Vietnamese woman lands in the arms of a young curly-headed bloke all wrapped up in a baggy sweater. I'm already much further down and don't even stop to say sorry. I keep on running and burst out of the building and into a cold shower. The heavens have opened and started to drop their load on the city. So through it I run, along Rue du Temple like I'm a skimming pebble, across the 33,677 square metres of the Place de la République, leaping over car bonnets, the hedges in the square and the urinating dogs, then head up the 2,850 metres of the Avenue of the same name. The torrent beats against me, but nothing can stop a man running when he no longer has an objective, because it's towards Père Lachaise cemetery that I'm running, which can hardly be called an objective, my objective, my lovely secret objective, was Julia, buried there under the weight of obligations, it was Julia, but I keep running and don't think about that, I run and don't suffer, the dark rain has given me the glittering fins of a flying fish, I run for miles when the very thought of doing a hundred metres used to leave me drained, I run and will never stop running, I run in the two swimming pools of my shoes where my thoughts are drowning, I run and in this new life as an underwater sprinter – it's amazing how quickly you get used to things – images start appearing, because while you can always run faster than an idea, images arise from the very rhythm of the race, the wrecked flat, Julia's broad face, the ripped-up cushions, Julia suddenly grimacing, the decapitated telephone, Julia suddenly screaming (so was *that* what you saw, Julius?), Julius wailing as well, a long tortured wail, the skirting-boards torn from the walls, Julia thrown to the floor, now I run from puddles to punches, from splashes to screams, but not only that, I spring over a gutter and Julie first comes into my life, the swaying of her hair and her hips, the torn-up books and Julie's firm breasts, too, punches, slaps and punches, but Julie's strong smile above me: "In Spanish slang, *comer* means 'to love'", running so that Julie can eat me, the gutted fridge – what were they trying to find? – and thoughts start catching up with the images, thoughts that are still rapid, despite the weight of terror, to know what Julie knew, that's what they wanted, "the less you know, Ben, the better it will be for everyone". That's true, Julie, don't let them get their hands on our oldsters, "don't phone me, Ben, don't come to see me, in fact I'm going to disappear for a while", but what if *they come round to me*, while I'm running like a silly bastard, what if finding out where the granddads are hiding is exactly what they wanted to know, and what if they now know that and what if they've headed straight round there and broken into the place while mum is alone with the children and the granddads? Puddles, punches, gutters, panic, I cross the avenue by the Lycée Voltaire, horns blaring, shouts, skidding, bodywork brushing against bodywork, but I've already dived like a stoned seagull down Rue Plichon, crossed Chemin-Vert and crashed into the hardware shop's door. Olympic runners must be all shit-scared, there's no other possible explanation. They smash records because they're shitting themselves.

One of the misty panes of glass breaks on impact and, when I open wide the door, a warm trickle of blood runs down my face, mingling itself with the cold soup from the heavens. The hardware shop is empty. But not with just any sort of emptiness. It's a hurried emptiness. An emptiness from having been torn away. A last-minute emptiness. An unexpected emptiness which leaves everything in place. An emptiness that should be full. Nobody. Nobody, except mum, sitting motionless in her armchair. Mum, who turns her tear-drenched face towards me and stares at me like she doesn't recognize me.

Chapter 20

"ARE YOU ALL right, Thian?"

Pastor had given up trying to salvage all the pills. Some of them had bounced all of the way down to the ground floor, one step after the other, carefully taking all the bends. Sitting doubled up on the third-floor landing in her strict Thai dress, widow Ho was gasping for breath.

"All right?" Pastor repeated.

"As right as someone who's just been massacred."

"Can you make it to the top?"

"The dead rise all on their own, so they say."

Pastor slid his arm under widow Ho's wings and helped her up until they were in front of Julie Corrençon's door.

"Phew."

Thian wasn't sure if his "phew" referred to the effort he'd just made or the scene which the flat's open door revealed. As Pastor made no response, Thian turned back to look at him. The expression on the kid's face frightened him. Pastor was staring at the disaster area like it was his own home. He was so shocked that he had slumped against the door frame. His face was ashen. His eyes fixed. His mouth agape.

"What's the matter, kiddo, never seen a burglary before?"

Pastor raised a leaden hand.

"On the contrary, I have. That's just the point. Don't worry about me, Thian, I'll be all right in a minute."

They stayed on the threshold for a long time, as if they were scared of adding to the chaos.

"Malaussène couldn't have done all that on his own," he said.

"Malaussène?"

"That's the name of the character who barged into you on the staircase."

"He left you his calling card on the way down?"

"Julie Corrençon wrote an article about him, a special report, with photos."

Pastor's voice sounded distant, as though buried inside him.

"Malaussène, you say? I'll remember that," said Thian.

They now walked into the flat, lifting their feet up high, as though they were walking through rubble and being belatedly cautious.

"There were at least two or three of them, I reckon."

"Yes," said Pastor. "Specialists. In the building trade. It's got that written all over it."

There was a sort of fury in his dreamy voice.

"Look," he added, "they've even been into the drains and through the wiring."

"Do you reckon they found anything?"

"No. They didn't find a thing."

"How do you know that?"

"Because they couldn't resist smashing things."

Thian gingerly picked his way through the debris.

"What do you think they were looking for?"

"What do you look for in a journalist's place?"

Crouching down, Pastor picked up a photo, still stuck under the shards of its shattered frame.

The photo showed a man, awash in a white uniform, convulsively clutching a cap decked with oak leaves. The man seemed to be gazing at Thian and Pastor ironically. He was standing among some hollyhocks that were taller than he was. His uniform was so immense that it looked like it belonged to someone else.

"That's Corrençon père," Thian explained. "He's wearing a colonial governor's uniform."

"Was he ill?" Pastor asked.

"Opium," Thian answered.

For the first time, Pastor understood the meaning of the expression

Gabrielle and the Councillor used to use when talking of old friends who were ill: "He's gone on us." In the photo, Julie Corrençon's father had definitely "gone". Something inside him had cast off. His skin and his bones no longer functioned together. And the fire in his eyes came from the dizziness of climbing a final peak. Pastor remembered something the Councillor had said about Gabrielle's last illness: "I don't want to see her go on us." Pastor made a superhuman effort to chase away the two images of Gabrielle and the Councillor.

"I wonder."

Scratching his head, Thian looked like a Thai peasant standing in the wreckage after a typhoon had hit.

"This Malaussène character . . ."

Pastor tried to sound light-hearted:

"A bad memory, is he?"

"As far as my ribs are concerned, he's not a memory yet. He was on his way down from here, just now, wasn't he?"

"Probably."

"I seem to remember he was holding some photos when he barged into me. Some photos, or a wad of paper."

"Some photos," said Pastor. "He dropped them on impact and now I've got them."

"Do you reckon he found them here?"

"We'll ask him."

Julie Corrençon lived above a relatively legal sweat-shop. The only one in the neighbourhood that didn't make its Turkish workforce stay on for more than two hours over the legal limit. In the workshop, nobody could remember hearing any noises from the flat upstairs.

"The only thing we sometimes hear," said the boss (a fine, solid-gold fellow), "is the sound of a typewriter."

"How long has it been since the last time you heard it?"

"Dunno. A fortnight maybe."

"What about the tenant, how long since you saw her?"

"We don't see her that often. Pity really. She's a knock-out."

* * *

It had started to rain. A real spring downpour in the middle of winter. Hard, icy rain. Pastor drove on in silence.

Thian asked him:

"Did you notice the body of a typewriter in the wreckage?"

"No."

"Maybe she takes it with her to work on."

"Maybe."

What rain! . . . it was the same rain Pastor had gone through on his way to his last appointment with Gabrielle and the Councillor. "Give us three days," the Councillor had asked him, "in three days' time you can come. Everything will be settled then."

"How about dropping in on The Store?" Pastor suddenly suggested.

"Why The Store?"

"It's the last place La Corrençon wrote about. And that's where Malaussène used to work, as Scapegoat."

"Scapegoat? What the fuck are you on about?"

"I'll explain on the way."

At The Store, the young Human Resources Manager, dressed up to the nines, and answering to the mediaeval name of Sinclair, couldn't tell them much.

"Whatever is all this about? I've already had to speak to some of your fellow officers concerning this matter and we *never* employed Malaussène as a Scapegoat. He worked for us as a Quality Controller. If he did have the absurd habit of bursting into tears in front of the clientele, then that was his own problem."

"All the same, if you gave him the boot, then that was down to the article Julie Corrençon wrote, wasn't it?" Thian asked.

The young manager almost jumped out of his skin. He hadn't been expecting this old Vietnamese woman to ask him that, least of all in a gravelly film-cop's voice.

Above their heads, the rain drummed down on The Store's plate-glass roof. Winter rain, with a monsoon-like persistence. I could never have gone into business, thought Pastor. You need an answer to everything. He remembered something Gabrielle used to say: "That child never answers anything. He only asks questions." "One day, he'll answer the lot in one go," the Councillor had predicted.

"Do you think Malaussène might have killed the journalist in revenge after he'd got sacked?" Pastor asked.

"Yes, that sounds just like him," the young manager answered.

Pastor looked worn out. Thian insisted on taking the wheel.

"Where the fuck's all this rain coming from? Anyone'd think we were in Vietnam."

Pastor stayed silent.

"How about a joke, kiddo?"

"No thanks, I'll be fine in a minute."

"I'll drop you off at the office, then head back up into the hills. Got a few things to check out. See you this evening for the report, okay?"

Pastor was welcomed back into his office by a ringing phone.

"Can I speak to Pastor?"

"Speaking."

"This is Cercaria, do you know what, lad?"

"No, but I soon will."

"Just after you'd left, I got a call from the Town Hall in the eleventh arrondissement."

"So?"

"From the Health Service. One of the health visitors. And apparently Malaussène uses oldsters to get amphetamines prescribed for him free of charge."

"Malaussène?" Pastor asked, as though he'd never heard the name before.

"Yes, he's the bloke Ben Tayeb was trying to flog his stash to when I nicked him. His name's Malaussène."

"So what are you going to do now?"

"Give them a bit more rope, my lad. It isn't hanging time yet."

" . . . "

"Pastor?"

"Yes?"

"Believe you me, if you're not one of the best yet, you're already one hell of a cop!"

Pastor gently hung up the phone, like it was made of bone china.

Chapter 21

THERE'S WATER BOILING on the stove and dinner sitting in the oven, but no Clara and no Kidney. Jeremy's history book's lying open on the table, but without Jeremy. Beside it, lies Half Pint's exercise book with a big ink blot in the middle of the page. But where's Half Pint? Thérèse's tarot pack is on her table, an open fan of the future, but what about Thérèse? And Sweeney? And Sole? And Risson?

Mother finally recognizes me and says:

"Oh, it's you, number one son. So you've heard the news. Who told you?"

She dries her tears with the back of her hand so slowly it's like watching the grass grow.

"Who told me about what, mum? What the Jesus in hell has happened here?"

She indicates the dinner-table with her chin and murmurs:

"It's Verdun."

What with the state I'm in, drenched with blood and rain, I start off by reckoning like a silly bugger that she's talking about the war. It's been trench warfare for me for quite some time now.

"He was getting Half Pint to do his letters, then he collapsed face down onto the exercise book."

The front door's still open behind me. A damp breeze flutters up a page of the said exercise book, which then flops down again like it had run out of puff. I say Verdun over to myself. Verdun, Fur Done, then in a German accent Verd Hun. And I can't make head nor tail of it.

"Look at yourself, son, you're bleeding. I'll get you a plaster. Close the door, will you?"

The obedient son closes the door, which stays open anyway since I've broken one of its panes of glass. There's an ink blot in the middle of the exercise book, like a blue explosion over Verdun.

"Did Verdun have an attack?"

That's it. The penny drops.

"Verdun's dying."

I twig what's going on, I finally twig it and still today I hear the relief in my voice as I ask:

"Is that all? Nothing else?"

And I can still see the expression on mum's face. She doesn't look shocked, like she would if she was thinking "My God, my eldest son's a monster!", no, it's a look that seems to be saying that I'm the one who's dying. She gets to her feet with that weird weightlessness she has, specially when she's pregnant, like she's a heavenly vision (one gesture from her and everything in the flat shifts silently back into place). She fetches a huge towel then dries me down while my clothes fall to my feet. The son stands naked before the mother.

"They left you all on your own?"

It's amazing how a plaster stuck on your forehead seems to have a life force of its own.

"They took him to Saint-Louis Hospital."

She rolls my clothes up into a ball of papier-mâché then comes back with the necessary dry and warm replacements.

"They all insisted on going with him and you ought to go along and join them. They'll need you there. Have you been running?"

Bovril. Essence of crushed carcasses. Brimming with life. And boiling hot.

Verdun, my old mate Verdun, it's true. Nothing else would have been such a relief to me than news of your impending death. I admit that to you straight out in the cab that's taking me to the hospital so that you can start working on my defence as soon as you're past the pearly gates. You wouldn't hold it against me that I'd rather you died than a certain other person, now, would you? You saw too many uniforms that weren't yours explode, didn't you? But Him up there, Sod almighty, He doesn't know about war, He's never made war, just watched it from way up yonder and seen brave souls go to it. He's never made love either, though He is supposed to be Love, and so knows nothing about the abject categories of our own loving, which makes me sooner see Verdun die than Julia . . .

But now, thanks to you, I know Julia's immortal! If they laid into her flat like that, it means they couldn't lay their hands on her, if they tortured her furniture, it's because she's slipped through their fingers and, given her experience as a wily adventurer, there's nothing particularly surprising about that. Even I can't trap her into my bed. Tell Him that, Verdun, from me, how this relief is going to cost Him dear the day we're weighed in the balance! And, while you're at it, tell Him your little Camille's Spanish 'flu's going to cost Him dear as well, the way He helped you through five years of raining steel only to fire off that last salvo (from his Salvation Army): Spanish 'flu. And kill your daughter, the little girl you'd worked so hard to stay alive for!

And so went my fervent revelations in the cab taking me to Verdun, my address to Him who, if He exists, is proof that shit is really and truly the world's fundament and who, if He doesn't exist, that is, if Innocence doesn't exist, is handier still since he's a goat like me, a Scapegoat at the origin of nothing and responsible for everything. On the windscreen, the wipers slice their way through the storm. It's as if they were our only means of propulsion. The driver's got it in for the Almighty too. According to him, such a downpour's unheard of at this time of year. He must be up to something big up there, Him and His angels!

"Stop!"

I yelled that out so loud that the cab's brakes screech and it does a little rain dance.

"What did you do that for, for Christ's sake?"

"Wait here a second!"

I leap out into the rain and head towards a tiny figure who is kneeling, as if in prayer, against a drainpipe which is pissing its liver out.

"Jeremy! what the hell are you doing here?"

On his knees in the torrent, drenched up to his eyeballs by the water that's pouring out like it's oil from a sabotaged pipeline, the kid turns round to me and says:

"Can't you see what I'm doing? I'm filling up a bottle."

As cool as that, just like we'd arranged to meet up under this drainpipe.

"It's Verdun's last bottle, Ben, this year's vintage. He's not going anywhere without it."

The cab starts hooting like a mad thing.

"Get a move on, Jeremy, you'll catch your death!"

His hands are blue and the bottle only half full.

"It's that fat fucker over there's fault. I had to buy a real bottle off of him then empty it out. The bastard wouldn't even lend me a funnel!"

The fat fucker in question is the owner of the dairy over the road. He's got his cashier of a wife and his handful of customers together on his doorstep so they can all have a nice little giggle. The cabby's starting to feel a bit lonely so he winds down his window and puts his oar in:

"Scuse me, ladies and gents, but is that a hospital over there or a loony bin?"

When you've got it in for yourself it's the others that cop it. That's the way it always goes. So I nip round to the other side of the cab in three submarine strides and ram a hundred franc note into his big laughing gob.

The hospital nurses think they're being invaded by two Things from the Blue Lagoon.

"Hey, you two! You can't come in here like that!"

They do their best to catch us, but we're uncatchable. Nothing could stop us now.

"You're making the place filthy!"

"Just be thankful we took our flippers off!" Jeremy barks back.

Then:

"It's this way, Ben, shift your fat arse."

We've got too much of a lead on the nurses, and they give up. Mops and buckets dance before their eyes.

"Turn here, and it's at the end of the corridor," Jeremy announces.

We turn, but in the middle of the corridor we run into a big get-together. The one who's doing the loudest shouting is a little medic in a white coat whose voice sounds familiar to me: a professor's voice which shouts *calmly*.

"You've been drugging that girl for the last ten days, Berthold! You're going to turn her brains into white sauce, believe you me!"

One of his fingers is aimed up towards a long stick of asparagus with a crimson head, then it points inside a room where, on a white bed, a form is lying, bristling with translucent tentacles.

"And I'm telling you that if we wake her up with a jolt, she'll snap. I'm not going to take the risk, Marty."

(Marty! He's the little medic who sewed Jeremy's finger back on for him last year after he'd blown it off while setting fire to his alma mater.)

"You're only being careful so as to protect your fat arse, Berthold, and the golden nest egg it's sitting on! But if that girl ever wakes up, she won't be able to tell your arse from your elbow, what with all that shit you've been pumping into her veins."

A case of big guns scrapping over how far to dope up a patient. The other white coats must be students or underlings. The scene's so tense they don't even dare laugh in their sleeves.

"Go screw yourself, Marty. So far as I know, this isn't even your department."

"So far as I know, my dear Berthold, if this was my department, you wouldn't even get to clean out the toilets."

We've reached this point in their exchange of diagnostic views when, standing in his puddle with his bottle in his hand, Jeremy suddenly yells:

"Hey, you lot, get your arses in gear. We haven't got all day!"

Everyone goes quiet and Marty turns round:

"Oh, it's you!"

He takes hold of the kid's hand, like he'd only seen him yesterday, glances at the finger and says:

"Looks like you've healed up nicely again. What have you got in store for us next? Double pneumonia?"

Oddly enough, Jeremy shows him the bottle.

"We need a label for this, doctor."

He goes on:

"An old friend of ours is dying down the corridor. Do you want to come with us?"

* * *

Louna, Laurent, Half Pint, Clara and the granddads are all there, with Thérèse just by the bedstead, holding Verdun's hand. The first hospital tentacle has already sprouted from his left arm and is linked to a drip dangling above his head. He isn't exactly lying down and he isn't exactly sitting up. He's a Sardanapalus slumped out on the three feathery clouds that Louna's slipped under his back. I whisper to her to head straight off home so as not to leave mum on her own and she slips discreetly out taking Half Pint with her. Jeremy writes out the label, sticks it on the bottle and clambers up onto the bed to wedge it under Verdun's arm. "*Rain Water. Last Winter.*" Without saying a word.

"Go into the bathroom and get undressed. Dry yourself then put on a dressing-gown. There's one in the wardrobe."

Jeremy obediently follows Marty's instructions. There's nothing left but our motionless presence and Thérèse's voice beside Verdun's bed. Thérèse's familiar gesture, smoothing out the old hand with the cutting edge of hers. Thérèse's knitted eyebrows scanning the deep lines that life has gouged out. As for Verdun, he hugs his bottle to one side and, on the other, lets his hand dangle. Verdun is looking at Thérèse. Yes, at the threshold of death, as they say, Verdun is looking at Thérèse with the future blazing in his eyes, that blaze which my sorceress of a sister has been able to light in everyone's eyes since she was a little girl. Then suddenly I understand what her reasoning was on the one occasion when, from the lofty educational heights of my big-brotherdom, I was daft enough to ask her: "For Christ's sake, Thérèse, you don't really believe all that mumbo-jumbo do you?" She'd then lifted her eyes up to mine, untroubled by the tiniest doubt, but also unlit by any revolting flame of conviction. "It isn't a question of believing or of not believing, Ben, it's a question of knowing what you want. And all that anyone really wants is eternity." And I'd said to myself: Here we go. I've set her off this time. I should have kept my big gob shut. But she went on, in her pathetic bony voice: "But what we don't know is that we have got eternity and, in this respect at least, *we have already got what we want.*" And I whispered to myself: Oh we have, have we? But she, who never notices a flicker of laughter in your eyes, who is totally immune to irony, continued: "When we talk about *life expectancy*, you know, the years, months and seconds we still have to live, all we are really doing is expressing our faith in Eternity." "Oh, we are, are we?" "Yes, we are. If I am here now, Ben, tirelessly adding up your life expectancy, if, each second of your life, I add up the number of seconds you have left, and if, in the middle of the *last* second, I'm still here adding up the tenths of a second you have left, then the hundredths, then the thousandths, and if I'm still here in the midst of the infinitesimal, still adding up what you have left in spite of everything, that means that you will always have some expectancy of life, Ben, and Eternity is nothing else but this ever-watchful consciousness." The next day at The Store, I'd told all that to my mate Theo, who ran the DIY department. Theo'd shrugged and announced that my sister was a menace to society. "That's the sort of thinking that makes little buggers do a ton across a junction on their 1000ccs, since at that speed they've got less chance of banging into someone than at a nice easy 30."

We'd had a good giggle at Thérèse's expense and since then I'd let the subject drop.

But we've now been standing here for two hours listening to Thérèse predict Verdun's future for him and, during all that time, we haven't been able to take our eyes off Verdun's delighted gaze, the convinced serenity in his smile has wiped out the passage of time, to such a point that we don't even feel tired from standing there, motionless, even though we're young and fidgety or old and rusty and I, Benjamin, the eldest brother, am just about ready to believe in Thérèse's idea.

"What I can now see in your palm, Granddad Verdun, is a little girl who looks so much like you that she could even be you, and you're going to see her again very soon, because I've got some good news for you, Granddad Verdun, some news that I really must tell you straightaway, because you've been waiting for so long, and that's why this little girl's been waiting for you as well, so she can share the good news with you, listen, Granddad Verdun, listen to me carefully: *Spanish 'flu isn't fatal anymore.*"

It's just then that Marty discreetly taps me on the shoulder. A smile is still lighting up Verdun's face, but Verdun isn't there anymore. Clara walks over and gently lifts Thérèse to her feet, then Marty whispers in my ear:

"Well, that's the first time I've seen a patient die with his future still in front of him."

Someone says:

"We must phone mum."

But the phone rings before we can get to it. Jeremy answers it.

"What?"

And then:

"You're joking!"

He turns round towards us:

"Mum's just come up with a little sister for us."

Then, without asking anyone's opinion:

"We're calling her Verdun."

(That's going to be one hell of a handle for a girl, that is: Verdun Malaussène!)

"And, Ben, there's something else."

"What's that?"

"Julius is better."

Chapter 22

THE RAIN WAS still bucketing down. Lying on his camp-bed with his head propped up on his hands, Pastor listened to it slither down the window panes. He was trying to get that image of a wrecked flat out of his mind. How long had it been since he'd been home, to Boulevard Maillot? What if he'd left a window open? The library window, for example . . . I'll drop by tomorrow. But he knew he wouldn't drop by tomorrow. Just as he hadn't dared go there since the last time. And then he'd only lasted five minutes, just the time to stuff a few clean clothes into a bag, which now slumbered in a metal cupboard he'd commandeered. Sleep at the office, just like Chief Superintendent Coudrier did. A young lad who knew how to make himself useful, who was always on call, at his country's service! And his colleagues certainly didn't mind. They were only too pleased to be replaced on nights by the squad's ever-present member. That way, one copper's ambitions let other coppers go out and get laid . . . Pastor thought about the library. After Gabrielle, books had been the Councillor's second love. Their shared second love. First editions, blind-stamped and signed by their authors on publication. The scent of leather, of old wax with a hint of honey, the rustling of gilded pages in the half-light. And absolutely no music! No gramophone, no stereo, no hi-fi. "Music is for band-stands," the Councillor proclaimed. Nothing but the silence of books which, in Pastor's memories, now harmonized with the drumming of the rain. Their bindings were only opened occasionally. Down in the cellar, there was an exact replica of the library. The same bookcases, same authors, same titles in precisely the same positions as the first editions above them, but in everyday formats. The books in the cellar were the ones that got read. "Jean-Baptiste, please go down to the cellar and bring us up a little something to read." Pastor did so, the choice left up to him, proud of his mission.

"Have I got a surprise for you, kiddo!"

The light snapped on. Thian had just reappeared. Not as widow Ho this time, but as Inspector Van Thian in his service uniform, an ancient long shapeless woollen thing. The final result was the same. Two seconds later, he'd become a matchstick man in long-johns again, his drenched outfit crumpled up in a heap in the corner.

"Here, this is for you."

He casually threw something large and limp, parcelled up in a newspaper, over to Pastor.

"A present for me?" Pastor asked.

"I've been dying to give myself a nice little treat for ages."

Pastor started undoing the string. Thian raised his hand.

"Just a sec, I have to own up to something first."

He had a repentant look. Standing there in his white undies he looked like an ancient child who'd been made to stand in the corner of his dormitory for the last fifty years.

"I'm sorry to say, kiddo, that I've been keeping something a secret from you."

"It doesn't matter, Thian. That's the way you inscrutable Asians are. I read in a book somewhere that you just can't help yourselves."

"Another common fault we've got is having a yellow man's memory. That bit goes with our patience."

As he spoke a spasm of pain zigzagged across his face.

"Fuck this rain. It's set off my lumbago."

He snapped open his drawer and prescribed himself some Valium. Pastor handed him the glass of bourbon.

"Thanks. It's about your Malaussène character. I told you a bit of a porky. By not mentioning, I mean, that even if I'd never laid eyes on him before, his name was not unknown to me."

Pastor couldn't help wondering if there was a single copper in the whole of Paris to whom the name of Malaussène was totally unknown.

"He was a friend of my widow Dolgorouki's."

"The latest victim?"

"Yeah, my neighbour. She used to go round his place every Sunday."

"So what? Belleville's like a village, isn't it?"

"Yeah, but it so happens that Malaussène's dive's on Rue de la Folie-Régnault."

"And what's so important about that?"

Thian put down his glass and took a long pitying look at his team-mate.

"Doesn't Rue de la Folie-Régnault ring any bells?"

"Of course it does. It was a meeting place for hunters until the eighteenth century. What's that got to do with our inquiries?"

Thian shook his head in despair, then added:

"You know what? I rather like the fact you've still got things you can learn off me. As a clever-clogs you were starting to get on my tits. Fix me a hot toddy, then pin back your lugholes."

An old couple fixed in their ways. Pastor put the kettle to heat on the ring.

"Do you at least remember doing the rounds of all the police stations where screaming women had been reported on the night you fished your semi-stiff out the barge?"

"If I try hard enough, I'm sure it'll come back to me."

"Right. And the eleventh was one of the batch, kiddo."

"Oh yes?"

"Oh yeah. A long scream was heard outside number 4, Rue de la Roquette, just where it crosses Rue de la Folie-Régnault."

"And they checked it out?"

"By phone, they did. They called up the old dear who'd tipped them off and she told them that everything had quietened down again. They often do that, ring back before going round. Nine times out of ten it saves them having to go out for nothing."

"And this one was the exception?"

"Spot on, kiddo. Looks like you're waking up a bit at last. I went round to see our fine upstanding old dear and got her to describe exactly what she and her hubby'd heard. 'A woman screaming, tyres screeching, a car-door banging and that's all,' she goes. 'Did you go down for a look?' I ask her. 'Well, we just 'ad a peep through the curtains like.' 'And what did you see?' 'Nuffink, nuffink at all!' they both intone in unison. Now their unison routine was a bit too good to be true. So, you know me, kiddo, I put on my best inscrutable Asian prick look and asked them if they'd like to swear to that in court. (Hey, kiddo, you trying to fry that kettle or what?)"

Three measures of rum for one of boiling water, a slice of lemon and a small pink Tranxene. Thian's grog was ready.

"And then?"

"And then they start squirming around from their scalps to their arses, if you see what I mean. It was hubby who cracked first. It's always the geezer that coughs first in a scenario like this, never the bird, ever noticed that? 'Well, well, mum, maybe we should fill in the Inspector like, if it's to 'elp law and horder 'n everyfink.' 'Fill im in abart what?' she asks, going all defensive. 'Well, abart the bloke what we saw scarpering off.' 'Oh, you mean the bloke what went scarpering off up Folie-Régnault? I'd forgotten all abart 'im.' 'Someone was running away?' I ask politely. 'Yeah, this bloke what was all doubled up like 'e was carrying somefink.' 'And you didn't report this to the police?' That got them. 'Well, it's just that it completely slipped our minds like.' 'Oh, it did, did it? Which way did it slip? You know the scarperer do you?' No, no, no, before almighty God they don't! 'So why were you covering up for him, then?' 'Why would we cover up for a bloke what we don't heven know?' 'That's exactly what I'd like to know.' At that moment, my son, we got to that moment of silence which happens in every well-conducted interrogation. And then, going more and more Cong with my Viet, I whisper: 'You didn't happen to see anything else, did you?' Then, before they get the chance to come up with any more crap: 'WHAT THE FUCK ELSE DID YOU SEE?'"

A long, satisfied pause.

"Great toddy, kiddo. It was a good idea you moving in here."

"And so, what else had they seen?"

Thian flicked his thumb out towards the parcel done up in newspaper.

"You can open it now."

The parcel contained a superb fur-coat of a kind Pastor was incapable of identifying.

"A skunk-skin, my little mate. There's three or four grands' worth of little beasties in that thing. It's a greeny's nightmare. Anyway, that's what our wrinkly had spotted from behind the net curtains. And she must have had a pretty good guess at its value at the same time. So do you reckon she's going to pass that on to the boys in blue? Is she fuck. Nor mention the scarperer neither. Just in case the pigs come round and snuffle out a skunk to wrap round their own sows' shoulders. She just put up a prayer to God Almighty that a motor wouldn't show up, waited for our sprinter to vanish into the night, got into her slippers, slipped downstairs pronto, shot back up again, softly softly, with a nice little wrap-around for the coming winters, which look like they're getting harsher and harsher."

"And she just handed it over to you, like that, without a word of complaint?"

"That's the law for you, kiddo. But she was so down in the mouth that I told her that the entire world's mafiosi were out looking for her wrap-around and, if she ever wore it, it'd be like sticking a target on her back."

"That was good of you, Thian."

"No, but the way I look at it, give me an old wrinkly with a perfectly human desire to lay her hands on a nice coat any day rather than that squeaky-clean fuck we saw this afternoon at The Store, that Human Resources cunt, I mean."

"You were very nice to him, too."

Later that evening, Pastor was on the receiving end of a few ideas about where the coat came from. Thian spoke as he typed out his daily report, which had nothing to do with the matter. His typing was hypnotically regular.

"I'm talking to you while I type so as I won't nod off. If the coat really belongs to La Corrençon, then your Malaussène's in deep shit, isn't he?"

"He is indeed," Pastor nodded.

Later, when they'd finished their respective reports:

"What about you, kiddo? How did you spend your evening while I was doing your job for you?"

"I've been keeping something a secret from you, too."

"We couldn't go on together if there weren't little surprises from time to time. That's what life in a couple's all about."

"I thought I recognized the girl in the photographs that Malaussène dropped."

"A school friend maybe? Someone you got confirmed with? First love? A one-night stand?"

"No, just on drug-squad records. I'd already seen her photo. I asked Caregga to check her out discreetly for me."

"Discreetly?"

"I don't work for Cercaria."

"And?"

"Bull's-eye. She's a pusher who got arrested five years ago outside the gates of the Lycée Henri IV. Her name's Edith Ponthard-Delmaire. She's the architect's daughter. Could you give me a hand with this one, Thian? We'll have to locate her, then tail her for the next few days. Could you do that, in your spare time?"

"Course. A pusher, is she? A hole-punch for kids' arms. This Malaussène really does seem to hang around with a nice crowd."

"Yes, we're going to have to pay him a visit. I'll need your help with that as well, Thian. You keep the family busy downstairs while I take a look around upstairs in the bedroom. He's hiding some photos that I may be in need of."

"How do you know that, kiddo?"

"Hadouch Ben Tayeb, the lad I questioned this afternoon, told me."

Then came the moment when Inspector Van Thian stuck his medicine vouchers on his NHS forms. It was a twice-weekly ritual which he'd practiced since his wife Janine had died. "Thank Christ your dad the Councillor set up the NHS!"

"Didn't *set up* anything," the Councillor grumbled when he came across that sentence in the press. "Just unified several already-existing bodies after the war." But the NHS had been his life's work and this was something which the Councillor couldn't deny. One day, Pastor had asked him why he had become so wrapped up in the Welfare State. Why hadn't he just lived off his personal fortune and lived out his passion for Gabrielle? "Because love is taxable, my boy. Individual happiness must create general well-being, if not, society would turn into a shark pool." And, on another occasion: "Every time Gabrielle and I screw, I like to think that a patient is receiving free health care." "Only one?" Pastor had asked. He often used to wonder if this perfect old couple had adopted him as 'a tax return on love'. But later, when he'd grown up, he realized that that wasn't the reason: he was their *witness*, the Man Friday on their private desert island. Otherwise, who would know that a man and a woman had loved each other in this vale of tears? "What about you?" Gabrielle would ask him. "When are you going to fall in love?" "When I have a vision," Pastor would reply.

Long after Thian had gone, when it was almost dawn, the rain at last stopped and the phone rang. It was Coudrier.

"Pastor?"

"Sir?"

"You weren't asleep?"

"No, Sir."

"What would you say to a spot of breakfast with me next Sunday, just to catch up on our news."

"I'd be delighted, Sir."

"In that case, meet me at nine o'clock in the Saint-Germain Drugstore."

"Just opposite the Deux Magots?"

"That's the place. I break my fast there every Sunday."

"Very good, Sir."

"Till Sunday, then. That gives you a few days to iron out your report."

Chapter 23

MADEMOISELLE VERDUN MALAUSSÈNE, portrait of a baby who's already three days old!

As plump as a large family's Sunday roast, like red beef and fat tied up with string in the thick layers of her swaddling clothes, gleaming, as chubby as anything, a baby, innocence. But watch out: when she's asleep with her eyes and fists tight shut, she's only doing it so that she can wake up again and let everyone know about it. And when she wakes up, it's Verdun. The artillery batteries go straight into action, shrapnel whistles, the air becomes pure noise, the world trembles on its foundations, men tumble onto their neighbours, everyone is ready to be the greatest hero or else the most craven coward if only it will stop, if only sleep may come again, even for a quarter of an hour, so that she will turn once more into that immense eyelid, still as threatening as a grenade, I grant you, but at least silent. If she goes back to sleep, that doesn't mean that we can sleep as well, we're too busy watching her in case she wakes up, but at least our nerves can unwind a little. There's a calm, a ceasefire . . . a breathing space between two phases of combat. We sleep with one eye and one ear open. In his own little trench, the watchman never sleeps. As soon as the first flare flashes in the sky, over the top, damn it! Every man to the bottles and teats! Push back the attack! Nappies, nurses and nappies for Christ's sake! What goes in one end comes streaming straight out the other. And the screams of lost cleanliness are more terrifying than those caused by starvation. More bottles! More nappies!

Phew! Verdun's gone back to sleep again. She's left us standing there, dumbly shaking with shellshock, gazing vaguely at her as she silently digests her feed. Her smile is her hour-glass. It's going to slowly run down, imperceptibly the corners of her mouth are going to draw together and when it becomes a little pink fist, the reveille will sound to call up the reinforcements. Once again, that long hungry scream will burst out across the trenches and fill up the sky. And the sky will answer with a downpour of shells: neighbours hammering on the ceiling, banging on the door, curses exploding in the courtyard . . . Wars are like brush fire: if you don't watch out, they spread. Any little old thing can start them off, a bullet explodes in an archduke's head in Sarajevo and five minutes later the whole world goes and gets its gun.

And it goes on and on . . .

Verdun won't be over by Christmas.

Three days already.

Jeremy, his eyes hanging down his face, sums up the situation nicely by leaning over Verdun's cot and asking in exhaustion:

"Don't babies ever grow up?"

The only person to come unscathed through all this is mum. Mum is sleeping like a baby. The countless legions which Verdun unleashes against our homeland don't come near her! It's the Geneva Convention. Mum's asleep. As far back as I can remember, she's always slept after each birth. She slept for six days after Jeremy was born. That's her record. Then, the complete opposite of God, she woke up on the seventh day and asked me:

"Well, number one son, tell me what the little fellow's like."

And so it came to pass, as they say in flowery books, that none of the Malaussènian offspring can pride themselves on having been breast-fed. Julia reckons that explains my adoration of her own mammaries. "Julie, give us a lend of your mammaries!" Julie laughs and those white dunes surge out of the opening of her double-breasted dress: "Come here, my little darling, make yourself at home." ("My little darling" . . . that's me, that is. Where are you hiding, Julie?)

And so, Verdun sends her starving divisions into the fray, and mum sleeps. It would be quite understandable if we held this against her. Ships' crews have mutinied for less. And yet our only concern when calming down Verdun is not to wake up mum. And when we're at the end of our tethers, it's by contemplating her slumbers that we get our strength back. Mum's not just asleep, she's recreating herself. As the exhausted fighters lean against her door jamb, they can watch her peaceful beauty working its way back.

"She's as beautiful as a coke bottle full of milk," Jeremy whispers, with tears in his eyes. Risson screws up his old eyelids in a heroic attempt to visualize this image. Clara takes a photo. That's right, Jeremy, she is as beautiful as a coke bottle full of milk. I know that beauty well. It's as irresistible as a Sleeping Beauty, as Venus coming out of her Shell, an indescribable guilelessness, the birth of Love. Do you know what happens next, kids? A Prince Charming is in the offing. As soon as she wakes up again, mum will be open and ready for passion. Then if, by any chance, a handsome gypsy (or, for that matter, a nice accountant) happens to pass by . . .

Jeremy, on the same wavelength, suddenly whispers:

"Jesus, Ben, she's not going to get whisked off again, is she?"

Then, after glancing anxiously at the cot, in which the baby is having a short-lived doze:

"Verdun's the One to End All Ones, isn't she?"

Who knows? That's one thing at least that love's got in common with war . . .

So, it's been three days and nights of hell on earth. Despite drawing up a rota, the lads, the lasses and the granddads are all on their knees. Especially Clara, who's taken the brunt of the work. We've all got post-natal depression, which is common enough, apparently. Sweeney's even threatened to go back on his drip.

"I swear to you, Benjamin, if this keeps up, I'm going back on the smack!"

Risson, who certainly doesn't dislike children, leans over the cot, gives his head a long shake and asks:

"I can't help wondering if I didn't prefer the 1914–1918 version."

As for Kidney, I have the impression that he keeps staring ferociously at his butcher's knives. The way times have changed is beyond him. In Kidney's day, a roast was seen and not heard.

Thérèse, Julius and Half Pint are the ones that get off the lightest. Since Verdun's death (the other, quiet one), Thérèse has started putting together a complete horoscope for senior citizens. Something for the newspapers which will tell oldsters all they want to know about their tomorrows. Thérèse is working like crazy on it. The whole house could collapse round her ears and she wouldn't hear a thing. As for Julius the Dog, he spends the entire day sitting with his eyes fixed in deep astonishment on Verdun's cot. But that's only the way things seem. The fact that his head's leaning one way (and his tongue's dangling the other way) is but the after-effect of his latest attack. According to Laurent, Louna's adored quack, he's going to keep that look of profound stupefaction all his life. In fact, like any pooch who knows his job, Julius is delighted to have another sprog around the place. Half Pint behaves, like Julius, in a responsible manner. He's set about trying to rock Verdun to sleep come what may. He's telling New Verdun all the stories that were handed down by Old Verdun. As soon as his little sister opens her eyes, he picks up again his endless litany of the quantities of cloth that were swallowed up by the War to End All Wars. And the louder she yells, the louder he speaks, heroically refusing to let his voice be drowned out by the din of battle . . .

But nothing we come up with calms down Verdun. Until one day, when what can only be called a miracle happened.

It happened just now. Verdun had just woken up. It was seven o'clock (nineteen hundred hours). Time for her umpteenth bottle. As service wasn't as rapid as she would have liked, she let everyone know about it a bit more strenuously than usual. Jeremy, who was on duty, plonked a saucepan down on the gas ring and picked the tocsin up in his arms. Half Pint started up again where he'd left off:

"250,000 mufflers at 1 franc 65 centimes and 100,000 balaclavas, more than 2,400,000 metres of double sheets for uniforms . . ."

It was then that there was a knock at the door. Our first thought was that it was one of the neighbours and we carried on leading our quiet homely existence, but the knocking kept up. Jeremy cussed and went to open the door with Verdun still carrying on in his arms. Verdun and

Jeremy then found themselves confronted by a tiny Vietnamese woman who was standing there in her clogs with a uncertain smile on her face. The Vietnamese woman asked:

"Malotzen?"

Given Verdun, Jeremy said:

"What?"

The Vietnamese woman repeated more loudly:

"Malotzen?"

Jeremy yelled:

"What about Malaussène?"

The Vietnamese woman asked:

"Is tis te Malotzen lesidentz?"

"Yep, this is where the Malaussènes reside," went Jeremy, waggling Verdun like a cocktail shaker.

"Can Hi spik to Bendjameen Malotzen?"

"What?"

Verdun was screaming more and more loudly. With almost legendary patience, she tried to ask her question once more:

"Can Hi spik . . . ?"

Then the milk in the saucepan started boiling over.

"Shit!" said Jeremy. "Here, hold her for a second will you?"

He stuck our vibrant Verdun into the Vietnamese woman's arms. And that's when the miracle happened. Verdun suddenly went quiet. The house woke up with a start. Jeremy dropped the saucepan of milk on to the kitchen tiles. The first thought that crossed our minds was that the Vietnamese woman must have discreetly banged Verdun's head off the wall. But she hadn't. Verdun was lying there beaming angelically in the old woman's arms who, with a crooked finger, was tickling the base of her neck. Verdun was laughing with a new-born baby's gurglings. In return, the Vietnamese woman was giving her a little exotic giggle: "Hi-hi-hi . . .". Then, once again:

"Can Hi spik to Bendjameen Malotzen?"

"That's me, madam." I said. "Come right in."

With Verdun still gurgling in her arms, she closed the door behind her and walked into the room. She was dressed in a long black silk dress, with a Chairman Mao collar, and thick hiker's socks. Shaken out of their daze by the silence of the armistice, Clara and Risson got to their feet together to come over and get a better look at our saviour. There was something ghostly about the way they walked, like the return of the living dead. This must have worried the old lady a bit, as she frowned and stopped uncertainly in the middle of the room. I think the same fear gripped all of us at the same time: that she'd piss off and leave us alone with Verdun. Clara, Risson and I fetched her a chair. That made three chairs. Not knowing which one to take, she stayed standing there. We felt that she was getting ready to leg it at any moment. I rubbed my chin: there was three days' growth on it. I looked at Risson: a war veteran turned into a memorial through exhaustion. I looked at Clara: a wreck. Jeremy's hands were shaking so much that he tipped half the milk over the floor. We were quite a sight. Only Verdun, pink and fresh in our visitor's arms, was bursting with blossoming health.

"Clara," I said. "Go and lie down for a bit. You need it. And you too, Monsieur Risson."

But Risson answered no, he's fine thank you very much. In fact his face had suddenly lit up. He gazed at this little old lady with undisguised admiration.

"Yes, madam?" I said at last. " You wanted to speak to me?"

What she wanted was to see Stojilkovicz. Her name was Madame Ho. She was widow Dolgorouki's neighbour from, she emphasized, the door opposite, just over the landing. Since the death of her friend, she'd started to feel too lonely and now she wanted to take part in the coach outings Stojil organized for the old ladies. She, too, was a widow.

"Nothing could be simpler," I replied. "I'll mention it to him and he'll pick you up on Sunday morning. Be at the junction of Boulevard de Belleville and Rue de Pali-Kao at nine o'clock."

She nodded her head and looked delighted. She got a wad of banknotes out and waggled them under my nose, laughing her exotic laugh as she did so.

"Hi can pay! Hi-hi-hi! Hi got lotsa mohnee!"

Risson and I were totally taken aback. There must have been a good three or four thousand francs in her hand.

"There's no need for that, Madame Ho. Stojilkovicz doesn't do it for the money. It's all free."

Then three things happen simultaneously. Jeremy turns up with the bottle, which is ready at last, and shoves it into Verdun's gob before she's got time to miss the Vietnamese woman's arms; Thérèse, who we'd completely forgotten about, comes out of her corner to take the old lady gently by the hand and lead her away to her table, where she starts telling her about her future; meanwhile the phone rings.

"Malaussène?"

I recognize that cracked rattle. That was all I needed. It's Queen Zabo of the Vendetta Press, my ladyship and mistress in the World of Letters, just to round things off nicely.

"Speaking, your Highness."

"That's enough sitting around on your arse, Malaussène. You're going to have to come back to work. And that means now!"

"Is it that bad?" I ask, just in case it isn't.

"A disaster, the balls-up of the century, the shit's really going to hit the fan, so we are in dire need of your skills as a scapegoat."

"What's happened?"

"It's Ponthard-Delmaire, remember him?"

"Ponthard-Delmaire, the architect? The king of the concrete-coated phrase? How could I ever forget?"

"Well, there's been a fuck-up with that book of his we are supposed to be publishing."

(The penny starts to drop. I'm going to have to go and see that creep to get a bollocking for someone else's balls-up.)

"The driver who was taking the proofs to the printers had an accident. His car is a burnt-out wreck and the book with it."

"What happened to the driver?"

"You're a fan of life's little tragedies, aren't you, Malaussène? He's dead, of course. The post mortem revealed that he was drugged up to the eyeballs. The little prat."

"And what exactly am I supposed to do about it, your Highness? Go and see Ponthard-Delmaire, tell him that our delivery boys drop dead of overdoses at the wheel, that his precious tome has gone up in smoke and therefore it's all my very own fault?"

"I hope for your sake that you'll come up with something better than that."

(At the other end of the line, she's in no laughing mood. To prove it, she starts talking money.)

"Do you have the slightest idea how much dosh has been invested in that book, Malaussène?"

"Ten times more than it will make you, probably."

"Wrong, sonny jim. We've already banked everything that the book's going to earn us. Massive local authority subsidies to promote THE book by THE architect which will reveal the Paris of tomorrow. A nice down payment from the Ministry of Public Works which is adopting a policy of public accountability . . ."

"My arse, it is."

"Shut up, you moron, and do like me. Add it all up! I'll continue. There's a huge advertising account laid down by Ponthard's own Architect's Office. The translation rights have already been sold in fifteen languages, which don't want to get on the bad side of this philanthropist of ours who's been flooding them with building projects."

"And so on and so forth."

"Exactly, Malaussène." (Then, switching to a tone of deep compassion:) "I heard through the grapevine that you've got an epileptic dog, my lad."

This bit cuts me in two. So I shut up. Which allows Queen Zabo to start up again, still in her sweetest tones:

"And rather a large family, aren't I right?"

"You are," I reply. "In fact it's just got considerably larger."

"Ah! A spot of good news! I'm so happy for you!"

Any moment now she'll be bouncing up and down in glee and clapping her eternally-girlish mitts together.

"Do you want to hear the rest of my woes, your Highness?"

Silence. A long, telephone silence. (They're the worst.) Then:

"Listen up, Malaussène. It's going to take us a good month to reset this fucking book. But Ponthard-Delmaire's expecting to see the proofs next Wednesday. And it's due out on the tenth."

"So?"

"So? . . . So, you're going to take your new-born babe in one hand and your epileptic dog in the other, you're going to dress the entirety of your Holy Family in rags and, next Wednesday, you're going to crawl round to Ponthard-Delmaire's place on your knees, once there you're going to be such a convincing scapegoat that he'll grant us the month's reprieve we so badly need. Cry, my old chap. Cry like you mean it. There's a good goat."

(There's no point arguing.) I simply ask:

"What if I fail?"

"If you fail, then we'll have to pay back that mountain of cash, which has already been usefully invested elsewhere, and I'm afraid that the Vendetta Press may have to lose some of its better-paid employees."

"Me, for example?" (Silly question.)

"You especially."

Click. And the call's over. I must be looking a bit under the weather when I hang up in turn, for Thérèse, who's still busily reading the Vietnamese woman's palm, looks over at me and says:

"Trouble, Ben?"

"Yes. Unforeseen trouble."

Chapter 24

THIAN FELT THAT gawky girl take his hand in her icy grip with a sensation of indescribable horror. He almost pulled it back, like he'd put it into a nest of vipers. But the copper in him restrained him just in time. He had to stay as long as he could in this den of druggies – Jesus, just look at the state of them all! Even the little lad of twelve or thirteen was shaking like a leaf. And he had to eavesdrop on that phone call, rake in as much info as he could, even if that did mean having his palm felt by this fortune-teller. Plus he had to keep the family downstairs as long as possible, while Pastor was searching Malaussène's bedroom.

"You aren't a woman. You're a man."

This was the first thing the girl said. She whispered it, fortunately, but with a nasty tone in her voice, like a schoolteacher who's gone sour in spinsterhood. Thian frowned.

"You're a man dressed up as a woman because of your love of the truth," the schoolteacher explained.

Despite himself, Thian felt his eyes widening as far as they would go.

"You've always been passionate about the truth," the young wrinkly went on, still in that left-on-the-shelf voice.

Meanwhile, on the telephone, Malaussène was asking if it was 'that bad'. Thian decided to stop listening to this ultra-lucid skeleton and to concentrate every inch of his lugholes on the phone conversation. 'What's happened?' Malaussène asked. His voice sounded anxious.

"But, all the same, you've been lying to yourself," the teller continued.

"Ponthard-Delmaire, the architect?" Malaussène said into the phone. The copper in Thian gave a start. It was the name of the girl in Malaussène's photos, the same girl that Pastor had found on the drug squad's records: Edith Ponthard-Delmaire. Thian had now been tailing that little bitch for three days. And he'd unearthed enough about her to send her down for a ten-year stretch.

"That's right, you've been lying to yourself by inventing illnesses which you haven't got," Thérèse proclaimed.

Thian's attention drifted away from the phone conversation for a moment. (Which I haven't got? Which I haven't got? What the hell do you know about it?)

"Apart from the damage caused by the incredible quantity of drugs you swallow, you're in perfect health," Miss Future went calmly on.

(I'm not going to sit here being preached at by this silly little smack-head, am I?) The exposed hypochondriac started to rage in the copper's breast. But a snatch of the phone conversation suddenly burst across loud and clear: "*tell him that our delivery boys drop dead of overdoses at the wheel . . .*" Malaussène was saying.

"You've been thinking that you're ill ever since your wife died."

At that moment, the medium's and sceptic's eyes finally met. On his face, she saw a mixture of pain and surprise. Thérèse was perfectly familiar with this "moment of truth", as she called it, when *what is no more* suddenly grafts itself on what now is, that is to say, a face. The rest of the phone call completely passed Thian by. The girl's hand no longer felt icy. She was gently stroking the old man's palm and, for the first time in twelve years, Thian felt his hand open completely.

"It's quite common," said Thérèse, "for people to invent illnesses after a bereavement. It's a way to feel less lonely. It's a sort of doubling of the personality, if you like. You nurse yourself as though you were someone else. There are two of you once more: the person I am and the person I nurse."

Her voice remained dry and unsmiling. But her words settled on Thian as gently as snowflakes, to melt there and "drench him with truth". (I'm acting like a complete twot, thought Thian. I'm going gaga. I should be listening to the bloke on the phone . . .)

"But you're not going to be alone for much longer," said Thérèse. "And I can see a happy life in front of you, a happy family life."

There was no way out. The phone conversation was now a distant rumour for Thian. He felt his entire body dissolve into the girl's hand. It was the same feeling of peace which he had experienced long ago when, coming home from work with his brains tied in knots over some difficult case, he'd abandon his tiny body to Janine's adoring hands. How he'd loved his giantess!

"But before that happens, you're going to have to go through a real illness. Very serious and very real."

Thian awoke from his dream with cold sweat between his shoulder-blades.

"What sort of illness?" he asked, managing to distance himself with just the right dose of irony.

"An illness brought on by your quest for the truth."

"Yes?"

"You're going to contract saturnism."

"What the hell's that?"

"The illness that caused the fall of the Roman Empire."

Thian was now banging his head against the wall of his widow's flat on Rue de Tourtille. The spell had worn off and Thian re-emerged to measure the extent of his mistake. He'd listened to that scarecrow's fortune-telling bullshit while that Malaussène character had been quite openly spilling the beans on the phone. Jesus Christ! How stupid he'd been! How criminally fucking stupid! Because what Malaussène had been talking about was definitely smack, with his ravaged face and all those wrecked kids around him. Take that teenager, the one he'd called Clara, for instance . . . Jesus, the state of her! And she must have been pretty, *once upon a time*! And the worn-out little lad with that baby in his arms! And that baby! That baby! How it had been screaming when Thian knocked on the door. And how it had calmed down in his arms! It broke Thian's heart. Get that baby out of there sharpish, then tip off the social workers. Put the granddad into a home where they can sort out what's left of him. That sweet old fellow, with his hollow eyes and snow-white hair, who'd timidly come over to Thian when he was leaving and had handed him a little pink book: "For you to read, so you won't feel so lonely . . ."

Thian took the book out of his pocket. Stefan Zweig: *The Royal Game*. He looked long and hard at the soft, pink cover. "It's a book about loneliness," the granddad had said. "You'll see . . ."

Thian threw the book down onto the bed. "I'll ask the kiddo to give me a summary of it." And Thian started thinking about Pastor. Pastor hadn't waited for him. Had he found the photos in Malaussène's bedroom? Thian already had a load of things to tell Pastor for the evening report. Malaussène was in cahoots with Edith Ponthard-Delmaire's father and smack was their business, just like it was Edith's business, too. There could be no doubt about that. Pastor could always add that to his report for Coudrier.

But what about Thian? The aging Inspector Van Thian, who'd got his eyes dazzled by a load of crystal balls (what future had he ever had?), what was he going to put in his own evening report? Bugger all, that's what. He'd been on the trail of the old ladykiller for weeks now and for nothing. He had no more of a lead than Cercaria's community coppers had. Inspector Van Thian was a failure. A pathetic old fuck of a failure!

Two images suddenly crossed his mind. He clearly pictured widow Dolgorouki's face. She'd been a beautiful woman. With a special sort of beauty: a solid sweetness that never faded, that the years couldn't wipe out. Thian pictured widow Dolgorouki's face, a piece of game that had been hunted down in Malaussène's place by Stojilkovicz, that Yugoslav coach driver . . . Then he pictured himself waggling that wad of bank-notes under Malaussène's nose. An icy rage gripped him and he heard himself mutter between his teeth:

"If it's you, you little bastard, then come on, come and get the Vietnamese wrinkly's dosh straightaway. Come on. I've been waiting too long, come and pay for that old lady's death, and the other ones' as well. Come on, it's time to settle the score . . ."

It was of course at that precise moment that there was a knock at the door. "Already?" He felt as relieved as he had done, just before, in that girl's hand. "Already?" He almost felt like thanking whoever it was who was knocking so politely on his door. He went and crouched down behind the coffee table, with its bug-eyed marquetry dragons, under which he'd hidden his nice hefty Manhurin. He felt extraordinarily relaxed. He knew that he wouldn't shoot until he saw the razor flash. He rather liked this atmosphere of waiting to save a penalty. Especially since he'd never let in a single goal so far.

"Come hin!" he called out in a welcoming voice.

The door slowly opened. Someone had turned the handle and was now pushing the door open with his foot. Someone seemed to be waiting indecisively on the landing. "Come hin," Thian murmured. "Come hin, now you hare here, come hin . . ." The door opened a little wider and Leila came in, pushing it shut again behind her, her hands full of a tray on which, like every evening at the same time, she brought up the widow's couscous.

Thian was as still as a piece of Chinese porcelain while the girl put the tray down on the coffee table.

"Today, papa's given you some kebabs."

Every evening, old Amar "gave him some kebabs". And every evening the girl announced the news. When she'd put the tray down, she stood there fidgeting indecisively. Thian didn't seem to notice her, so Leila finally said:

"Nourdine's down there, hiding in the staircase."

Nourdine's hiding in the staircase, Thian mechanically repeated to himself, without understanding a word of what the girl was saying.

"It's so he can get a fondle when I'm on the way down," Leila explained in a voice like a morning alarm-call.

Thian jumped.

"Fhondhel?"

Then:

"Ah yes! Fhondhel! Hi-hi-hi! Fhondhel!"

And he did what the girl was waiting for. He got up and opened a large grocer's jar, which was standing on the sideboard in the little room, and took out two pink, cubic lumps of Turkish delight, which he gave the girl with his usual words of advice:

"You share, yes? Share!"

Little Nourdine was still at the age when, if he jumped a girl, he went for her Turkish delight first.

Chapter 25

NEITHER THE CROISSANTS, the hot chocolate nor the lighting were up to what was on offer over the road. After only three sips, Pastor plucked up the courage to ask why Chief Superintendent Coudrier seemed to prefer the Saint-Germain Drugstore to the Café de Flore or the Deux Magots.

"Because it's from here that one has the best view of them," the Chief Superintendent answered.

They went on breaking their fasts in a polite silence, dunking their croissants in the French manner, but, in the English manner, avoiding making any slurping noises. They were both stiff and watchful, their backs hardly brushed against their chairs. Meanwhile, as a ground bass, the Drugstore slowly filled up with its gold-plated clientele. Not so long ago, as Pastor remembered, all that tomfoolery had attracted the bombers. Naive convictions: bomb the reflection of wealth while, on the terraces of the cafés across the street, espressos went for fifteen francs a go to a public of finely-tuned spectators. Pastor recalled how all that play of mirrors had been blown away into bloody shards and how the Drugstore had ended up looking like what it had always really been: an underground warehouse full of perishable goods and humanity.

"A penny for them, Pastor."

Two kids from another planet (dressed in bottle-green duffel coats, mouse-grey shorts, impeccable diamond socks and with Vanini-like cropped blond heads) came in timidly with their pocket money clutched in their little fists topped with freshly scrubbed nails.

"I was here to help the victims after the bomb last year, Sir. I was still in training at the time."

"Were you, indeed?"

Coudrier took his last sip.

They ordered espressos to wash away the taste of the hot chocolate and a jug of water to clean out the lingering smack of the coffee. When they'd picked out the last croissant crumbs from between their teeth, Coudrier asked:

"So, how does it stand?"

"Coming along, Sir."

"You have a suspect?"

"A highly probable one. A certain Malaussène."

"Malaussène?"

Pastor told the story. The girl who had been thrown into the barge had caused Malaussène to be sacked a few months back. "He was employed by The Store, Sir." According to the Human Resources Manager at the above-mentioned establishment, Malaussène was just the sort of person to go out for revenge – someone with a persecution complex, who liked acting as a scapegoat. Now, on the evening when Julie Corrençon had been thrown overboard, Malaussène's neighbours had heard a woman screaming, a car door banging and the screeching of tyres. The victim's coat had been found on the scene. All of which wouldn't have mattered too much if Malaussène hadn't been suspected of drug dealing and even of doing away with Belleville's old ladies.

"Goodness!"

"Chief Superintendent Cercaria has solid evidence regarding the drug business. He practically caught him red-handed. And Julie Corrençon had been drugged prior to being depontated."

"Depontated?"

"A word I've coined, Sir, with reference to the verb to 'defenestrate.'"

"I don't know if I can allow such rash coinages in my squad, Pastor."

"Perhaps you would prefer 'embarged', Sir?"

"And what about the old ladies?"

"Two of the recent victims were regular passengers in the coach belonging to a certain Stojilkovicz, a close friend of Malaussène. They were also regular visitors to his house."

"How do you know that?"

"Van Thian was acquainted with widow Dolgorouki, the most recent victim. She was his neighbour and she told him about her visits to the Malaussènes."

"Which proves what?"

"Nothing, Sir. Except for the way she was killed . . ."

"Which was?"

"That she freely opened her door to her murderer. Apart from Thian and Stojilkovicz, the only other person she saw regularly was Malaussène. Stojilkovicz was driving his coach at the time of the murder and, if we discount Thian . . ."

"That leaves only Malaussène."

" . . ."

" . . ."

"Well, well, well, Pastor, suspicion of attempted murder, drug dealing and serial killing – you haven't got a suspect there but a walking case-book!"

"Apparently so, Sir . . . What is more, Thian paid a visit to this Malaussène and, according to him, the whole family is drugged up to the eyeballs."

"Appearances, Pastor . . ."

Twisting round and planting his elbow firmly on the back of his chair, Chief Superintendent Coudrier let his gaze multiply itself in the mirrors.

"Talking about appearances, do you notice anything particular going on in this hall of mirrors?"

He sounded like a psychologist throwing a Rorschach test at you. Pastor didn't follow the line of his boss's stare. He didn't glance around the Drugstore. He looked this way and that, fixing his eyes on different places for a few seconds at a time. He was a motionless camera. It was up to the Drugstore to move in and out of his frame. Two tight little butts in impeccable blue jeans came into view. This early in the morning? Pastor wondered to himself. Those in need of literature were leaping down the steps of the bookstore four at a time. Others, calmer now, were coming back up with their load for the next week. Demagnetized literature which they would read, sitting comfortably across the street. One of them, as he went up the three steps of the exit, right under Pastor's nose, had Saint-Simon clung to his breast. Despite all his efforts, Pastor couldn't stop the image of the Councillor bursting into frame and Gabrielle's voice drowning out the din: "*The Duke of La Force, who perished at that time, had no regrets . . . notwithstanding his blood and his dignity.*" The tones in Gabrielle's voice, as she read out loud, brought the smile of the old Duc de Saint-Simon to the Councillor's lips. Those evenings spent reading . . . and little Jean-Baptiste's ears pricking up in the half-light . . .

Pastor shook himself, closed his eyes for a second, opened them again and finally saw what he was supposed to be seeing. The two boys who had come in earlier (in shorts, duffel coats and diamond socks) were quite coolly turning over the blonde hi-fi salesgirl. One of them was pinning her down across the gutted shell of a little Sony, while the other one was emptying out a showcase, to which he had obviously stolen the key. Pastor had never seen anything like it. It was as if the lad's body was magnetic. Goods were literally drawn towards him. With one sweep of his hand, he managed to pinch the stuff and put the empty boxes back in place. So fast, no-one had spotted him. Pastor couldn't help smiling in admiration. The glass door closed all by itself and the little key found its way back into the salesgirl's nylon pocket. Not a sound. With their strict little blond heads to cap it all.

"Got it, Sir. Two kids have just totally cleaned out the salesgirl over there."

"Well spotted, my lad."

Meanwhile, the two kids were calmly cruising towards the exit.

"Shouldn't I collar them, Sir?"

Coudrier lifted a world-weary hand.

"Oh, let them go their way."

Like Saint-Simon a moment ago, the two blond heads leapt up the steps to the exit, but they then suddenly angled off and headed for the table where the two coppers were sitting. Pastor glanced in panic at Coudrier, who hadn't noticed the children's approach. But the nearest of the two was already tapping the Chief Superintendent on the shoulder.

"There, grandpa, we did it."

Coudrier turned round. The kid opened his duffel coat. Pastor wondered how such a slight frame could bear such a load of merchandise. Coudrier gravely nodded his head.

"What about you?"

Through the opening of the second coat, Pastor glimpsed a collection of tape recorders, calculators and watches dangling off a number of hooks, which were in turn attached to a sort of harness.

"We're making progress, grandpa, don't you think so?"

"Not that much. Inspector Pastor, sitting here in front of me, spotted you."

Then he turned to Pastor with a weary gesture of presentation:

"My grandsons, Pastor. Paul and Germain Coudrier."

Pastor shook the two boys by the hand, trying not to make them jangle. Then, seeing how disappointed they looked, he thought he'd better apologize:

"I only spotted you because your grandfather told me to keep my eyes open."

"One notices nothing with one's eyes closed," Coudrier remarked.

Then, to the children:

"Go and put that lot back, and try to be a little more discreet this time."

With hunched shoulders, the kids walked away.

"Theft, Pastor . . ."

Coudrier was watching the children as they went.

"Yes, Sir?"

"There's no better way of learning self-control."

At the other end of the shop, the salesgirl was welcoming the kids back with a delighted smile.

"In today's society," the Chief Superintendent concluded, "one needs an extraordinary amount of self-control if one wishes to stand any chance of remaining honest."

There was room only for one image in Pastor's frame right now: Coudrier's face. Coudrier was staring at his inspector with the concentrated weight of the entire planet's police forces.

"I hardly need to tell you," he said slowly, "that those two boys would drop dead on the spot rather than take twenty centimes that didn't belong to them."

"That goes without saying, Sir."

"So, when it comes to what is 'apparently so', as you put it, be careful as regards this Malaussène character."

Announced in ponderous tones, the message was loud and clear.

"I have another important thing to check out, Sir. A certain Edith Ponthard-Delmaire, whom Thian and I have been tailing . . ."

Coudrier cut him off with a gesture.

"Check her out, Pastor, check her out . . ."

Pastor

"TELL ME, PASTOR, HOW DO
YOU MANAGE TO MAKE SUCH
SWINE CONFESS?"
"BY ADOPTING A HUMANE
APPROACH, SIR."

Chapter 26

"Your name is Edith Ponthard-Delmaire, you're twenty-seven years old and you were arrested five years ago for drug possession and dealing. Is that correct?"

Edith listened to the curly-headed inspector question her in a tone of voice that was as warm as the sweater he had apparently been born in. Yes, her name was indeed Edith Ponthard-Delmaire, the estranged daughter of Ponthard-Delmaire the architect and of the great Laurence Ponthard-Delmaire, who had once embodied Chanel, and then Courrèges, but had never embodied a mother – even though she had been one. Yes, that was correct, Edith had been arrested for drug dealing, though not outside some suburban tech, but in front of the prestigious Lycée Henri IV, because there was no reason, according to her, why rich kids shouldn't get off just as much as poor kids did.

Edith answered the young inspector with a gleaming smile, the sort of special girlish smile which one day might make her into a deliciously wicked old lady.

"That's correct. But it's all ancient history."

Pastor returned her smile, but with a more thoughtful edge to it.

"You were inside for a few weeks, then did six months in a detox clinic in Lausanne."

That's right, our fat Ponthard-Delmaire, being who he was and with a public image which wouldn't put up with upsets like this, had managed to haul his daughter out of the can and bundle her away to a highly discreet Swiss clinic.

"Oh yes, a clinic that's as white as the purest heroin."

Edith's comparison made the inspector laugh. It was a genuine,

149

spontaneous, childlike laugh. This brunette, with her bright eyes, seemed to him to be an extraordinarily vivacious beauty. The inspector crossed his amazingly delicate hands across his old corduroy trousers and asked:

"Would you mind if I told you about yourself, young lady?"

"Not at all," she said. "Not at all, I'm my favourite subject."

Then, since that was what she wanted, Inspector Pastor told her about herself. He began by informing her that she wasn't an evil drug pusher but, rather, a philosopher, or a woman of principles. Her idea was ("stop me if I'm wrong") that once anyone had reached the age of reason (about seven or eight years old) then he or she has the right to "get off on" the biggest hit available. So, it would be quite wrong to say that after her first unfortunate love affair (with a famous actor who treated her like actors do) Edith had *resorted* to drugs. On the contrary, drugs had allowed her to reach such a high that illusions could no longer reach her for lack of oxygen. "Because freedom," (as she had declared at the time of her arrest) "above all meant the freedom from having to understand."

"Yes, that sounds like something I would have said at the time."

Inspector Pastor smiled at her, apparently pleased that he and Edith were now on the same wavelength.

"All the same, Chief Superintendent Cercaria sent you off to prison just to see if there wasn't a little something that you had to *understand*."

That was true. On her release, the clinic had given Edith such a good clean-out that she'd completely lost her taste for intravenous ascensions.

"Because you're not on drugs anymore, are you?"

But now the inspector wasn't asking questions, he was stating the case. No, she hadn't done drugs for years, she no longer touched the stuff – except for just the odd line now and again to jolly herself up a bit – no, what she did now was turn other people on. But not the same other people as before. She was no longer to be found outside school gates. When in prison, she'd worked out that the young had the good fortune, no matter how slim their chances were, of being young. But what about the doors of retirement homes? Derby and Joan Clubs? The staircases leading to old people's bed-sits? The doorways into buildings where people lived who were lonely and cold, without even that slim, imaginary chance of being young? The old . . .

This inspector, who'd just told Edith her life story as though she were his own sister, this young Inspector Pastor, with his rosy cheeks, his curly hair, his soft voice and his baggy sweater, was in a state of health which changed as the tale was being told until his skin had become a ghastly white and bottomless black crevasses ran under his eyes. To begin with, Edith had reckoned that he was young – she'd spotted the stitch of his sweater, a hand-knitted job, made by his mum – but as their conversation went on, she was no longer sure how old he was. His voice, too, had become scrambled, like a tape being erased and occasionally jamming, and his eyes sank into their sockets until they were staring out with bleak exhaustion.

That's right, the old . . .

Edith now listened to her own thoughts emerge from that haggard inspector's limp, stammering mouth, she heard herself reciting her theories about the old, how they'd been robbed of their youth twice over, once in 1914, then again in 1940, not to mention Indochina and Algeria, leaving aside inflation, bankruptcies, their little businesses being swept away into the gutter one fine morning, passing in silence over their wives who had died young and their children who had forgotten them . . . If these oldsters' veins didn't deserve a little comfort, and their heads a little enlightenment . . . If their shadowy lives couldn't blaze up in an apotheosis, no matter how illusionary, then there really wasn't any justice in this world.

"How do you know that I think that?"

Edith blurted out the question and the copper looked up at her with his ravaged face.

"It isn't *what you think*, young lady, it's what you *say*."

That was true as well. She'd never been able to live without the reassurance, or the alibi, which a theory gave her.

"So, may we know what I really think, then?"

He took his time answering her, like an old man without much of it left.

"Like most of the psycho-theorists of your generation, you hate your father and you've gone off the straight and narrow in order to destroy his reputation."

He shook his head bitterly.

"But what's really amusing about this whole situation, young lady, is that your father's pulled a fast one on you."

Then Inspector Pastor revealed a fact which froze the young woman's blood in her veins. The image of Ponthard-Delmaire erupting in a huge guffaw flashed in front of her eyes. She reeled under the shock. She had to sit down.

The inspector was touched by her emotions. He sadly shook his head.

"My God," he said, "all of this is so terribly simple."

When Edith had recovered a little, Inspector Pastor (but what on earth had made him get into such an awful state?) cited all the arrondissements in whose Town Halls she'd exercised her skills as an unhealth-visitor. He showed her hard photographic evidence (how happy she looked in the 11th arrondissement's Town Hall with that bag of goodies in her hand!). Then Inspector Pastor listed a good ten possible witnesses and started reciting the names of those who had drawn her into this line of business. Everything emerged so naturally that Edith named all the others of her own accord.

From his pocket, Inspector Pastor then produced a statement which he had already prepared, wrote in the few names that had been missing, then politely asked the young woman to sign it. Far from being afraid, Edith felt enormously relieved. What a shitty society full of job'sworths! Nothing was real in this crap-heap unless it had a signature on it! Obviously, she refused to sign it.

That's right. She calmly lit a cigarette and refused to sign.

But Edith was far from the inspector's thoughts. Pastor's eyes had followed the path of the match towards the tip of her English cigarette, then he'd stopped thinking about the woman in front of him. He was no longer with us, as they say. He was miles away . . . somewhere in the past . . . standing in front of the Councillor who, with his head drooping, was saying: "It's all up this time, Jean-Baptiste. What with her smoking her three packets a day, Gabrielle has finally contracted something terminal. There's a stain on one of her lungs. And metastasis is becoming generalized . . ." Cigarettes were an old point of friction between Gabrielle and the Councillor. "The more you smoke," he would say, "the less I get a hard-on." So she cut down a bit. But only a bit. And now, standing in front of Pastor, the Councillor was murmuring: "So there we are, my boy. You can't imagine Gabrielle falling to pieces in hospital, or me becoming a senile old widower, can you?" The old man was asking for his son's permission. For a double suicide. That's what he wanted. Just don't say no, now, will you! A double suicide . . . in a way, that was how it was always going to end. "Give us three days, then come back. All the papers will be in order. Dig just one hole for the two of us. Nothing fancy. Don't waste your inheritance." Pastor had given his permission.

"I'm certainly not going to sign your bit of paper," Edith announced.

The inspector looked at her with the eyes of the living dead.

"I have a foolproof method to make you sign it, young lady."

Edith could now hear Inspector Pastor going down the stairs. His tread was a heavy one for such a light frame. She'd tried everything she knew in front of that death's head which left her absolutely desperate. And then she'd signed. The inspector's "method" was certainly an effective one. She'd signed. But he hadn't arrested her. "I'll give you forty-eight hours to pack your bags then disappear. It won't be necessary for you to give evidence." She picked up a bag and filled it with the items which seemed most to sum her up: the teddy bear she'd been given when she was born, her adolescent tampons, one of today's dresses and two wads of banknotes for her tomorrows. When her hand was on the doorhandle, she stopped for a second, sat down at her dressing-table, took a large sheet of white paper and wrote: "*My mother never knitted me a sweater.*"

Then, instead of going back to the door, she opened the window and, still holding her bag, climbed up onto the ledge. At the bottom of the abyss, Inspector Pastor was walking along beside a tiny Vietnamese woman. Edith suddenly realized that in Belleville recently she'd bumped into a very old, extremely tiny Vietnamese woman rather too often for comfort. Inspector Pastor was about to turn the corner of the street. Edith suddenly had a vision of a huge Ponthard-Delmaire wobbling his fat guts in a titanic fit of laughter. It was the laugh of an ogre. An ogre who'd been her father. She was an ogre's daughter. She made a last wish: that that copper would hear her hit the pavement loud and clear. Then she threw herself off the ledge.

"Tell me a joke, please, Thian."

When they'd turned the corner of the street, the Vietnamese woman began:

"Well, there's this bloke, a mountain climber, and he takes a dive."

"Very funny, Thian. Please, just get on with it . . ."

"Patience, kiddo, patience. So, anyway, this mountain climber takes a dive and down, down he tumbles, his rope snaps and he grabs hold of an icy ledge of granite. Beneath him, there's a two-thousand metre drop. So he waits a bit, with his legs dangling out in mid-air, then, at last, he whispers: 'Anybody there?' . . . Bugger all. So he asks again, a bit louder this time: 'Anybody there?' Then he hears a deep voice rumbling out from the middle of nowhere: 'Yes,' says the voice, 'God. I am here!' The mountain climber waits a bit longer, with his heart beating and his fingers freezing, then God speaks again: 'Believe in me, then let go of that frigging ledge. I'll send two angels down to catch you as you fall.' The little mountain climber thinks it over for a while then, in the silence of the big void, he asks again: 'Anybody else there?'"

The usual spasm crossed Pastor's face. When the young lad looked like he was more or less in the land of the living again, Thian said:

"Kiddo?"

"Yes?"

"We're going to have to collar that Yugoslav Stojilkovicz."

Chapter 27

JUST AS MALAUSSÈNE had told her to do, widow Ho had been
waiting at nine o'clock sharp at the corner of Boulevard de Belleville
and Rue de Pali-Kao. At that very instant, an ancient coach reminiscent of a horse-bus, full of joyous old ladies, pulled up in front of her.
Without a moment's hesitation, she got in and was welcomed with an
ovation fit for a princess being led to the stud farm. They took her by the
arm, kissed her, petted her and gave her the best seat – an enormous
pouffe, upholstered in cashmere and placed on a kind of raised platform
next to the driver. This driver, Stojilkovicz, an old man with a jet-black
head of hair, boomed out in his basso profundo voice:

"Today, girls, in honour of Madame Ho, we're going to do Paris for
the Asians."

When seen from the inside, the coach looked nothing like a coach.
Little cretonne curtains jollied up the windows, plump sofas replaced the
seating, the sides were covered with velvet, coffee and card-tables were
bolted down onto the floor through the thick shag carpet, a stove made
of Austrian stoneware gave off scented wood-smoke, modern-style
lamps shed a warm yellow light and a broad-bellied samovar gleamed
like something out of a book of adventure stories. All this second-hand
bric-à-brac, which had obviously been picked up off the street, made
Stojilkovicz's coach look like a TransSiberian whorehouse and left widow
Ho feeling decidedly uneasy.

"I swear to you, kiddo, I was worried I was going to end up as a
worn-out prossie in some dive in Ulan Bator."

But Pastor's stare expressed nothing beyond professional curiosity.
A young woman was falling through Pastor's mind. A blood-stained

pavement was pounding in Pastor's mind. Thian handed him a glass of bourbon and two pink pills. Pastor pushed back the pills, but sipped at the amber liquid.

"Go on."

Thian had, in fact, got into the coach in a state of fury, still absolutely convinced ("female intuition, kiddo, every copper has it") that Malaussène was guilty of massacring the old women and that this Yugoslav with a voice like Big Ben was his accomplice. He didn't let the atmosphere inside the coach get to him. Admittedly, it was thanks to this Stojilkovicz that all these old dears seemed happier than most young women are these days; admittedly none of these women looked like they ever suffered from loneliness, poverty or even a twinge of rheumatism; admittedly everyone seemed to love one another dearly; admittedly old Stojilkovicz set about satisfying their every whim like no husband ever would . . . Admittedly . . .

"But if it's to end up like an old goose on the chopping block, kiddo . . ."

So widow Ho kept her eyes peeled. They were peeled while the coach toured round Chinatown to the south of Place d'Italie; they were peeled when she was handed a juicy mango and a highly sought-after mangosteen (widow Ho had never tasted these fruit and obviously didn't know what they were called, so she squealed in delight and hid behind her incomprehensible pidgin) and they stayed peeled, hostile and peeled, until Stojilkovicz unwittingly laid low all her defences with one decisive blow.

"This is modern Chinatown, girls," he announced. "With its fragrance of coriander and ideogrammatic shop-fronts on Avenue de Choisy. But a far older version exists and, as I am the archæologist of your younger days, I shall now show it to you."

At this point in his narrative, Thian hesitated. Then, like a crap player, he snapped up the two pills which Pastor had refused and threw them down his throat. He washed them down with a long pull of bourbon, wiped his lips with the back of his hand and said:

"Now, pin back your lugholes, kiddo. The far-eastern shopping trip's over. We all get back into the coach and Stojilkovicz drives down Rue de

Tolbiac towards the bridge of the same name which, as you probably know, leads out onto the Wine Market, the post 1948 version, anyway."

One of Pastor's eyebrows beetled.

"That's the neighbourhood you were brought up in, isn't it?"

"Spot on, kiddo. Our Yugoslav swerves left along Quai de Bercy, then next right, bombs across the Seine and brakes his ton-load of wrinklies right in front of the new Made-in-Chirac velodrome."

"'Do you see that massive molehill over there, girls?' he booms out. 'That underground upthrust of our modern architectural perceptions? Do you see it?' 'Yessss!' goes the chorus of virgins. 'And do you know what it's for?' 'Noooo!' 'Well, it's for young lunatics to go round in circles in on ultramodern velocipedes, but which still remain antediluvian machines, with pedals!'"

"Does this Stojilkovicz really talk like that?" Pastor asked.

"Even better than that, kiddo, what with his gorgeous Serbo-Croat accent. I don't know whether they cop onto half of what he comes out with, but they never interrupt him. But listen to the rest: 'Ladies, this is a crime!' Stojilkovicz bellows. 'Because do you know what was here before this green boil?' 'Noooo!' 'There was a little wine business. Oh, nothing special. Just a modest little Gamay, with as much alcohol in it as it could muster, but it was owned by the most extraordinarily generous couple it has been my fortune to encounter!'"

Widow Ho's heart stopped beating and Inspector Van Thian's heart had frozen inside the widow's. He was listening to the story of his parents' lives.

"The woman's name was Louise," Stojilkovicz went on. "And everyone called her Tongkinese Louise. She'd made the most of a brief spell as a teacher in Tongkin by realizing that the curtain must be drawn down on the farce of colonialism. In her lap, she brought home a tiny Tongkinese with her, her husband, and the two of them took over Louise's father's little wine business. She'd been born a plonk-pedlar and a plonk-pedlar she'd remain, that's what the wonderful destiny was which had been picked out for her! And the most charitable of plonk-pedlars with it! She was a boon to poor students and various other displaced persons, whom

History had turned into waifs and strays, such as we Yugoslavs. *Chez Louise et Thian* was our refuge, girls, when we were penniless, our paradise when we thought we had lost our souls, our home town when we felt uprooted. And when the post-war period weighed down on us too heavily, when we no longer knew whether we were today's peace-loving students or yesterday's heroic killers, then Louise's husband, old Thian of Mong Cai (that's the name of his home town) used to take us by the hand and lead us towards the visions he kept in his stock room. He would tenderly lay us down on mats, like the sick children we were, hand us long pipes then, between his fingers, roll little lumps of opium which, when set crackling, would send us where even his Gamay could no longer take us."

"And suddenly, kiddo, I could see them all there in front of me, that little gang of Yugoslavs which used to hang around my parents' place after the war. And this Stojilkovicz, he was one of them. No doubt about it. Even though it's forty years back, I recognized him like it was yesterday! With his voice like the pope's . . . and his visionary way with words . . . in fact, he hadn't changed a bit . . . Stojilkovicz, Stamback, Milojevich . . . those were their names. My mum fed and watered them gratis, that's true. Of course, they were boracic. And then sometimes my dad used to tuck them up in bed with a bit of opium. I remember not liking that bit too much. 'They fought against the Nazis,' my mum used to say. 'They defeated Vlasov's armies and now they'll have to watch out for the Russians. Don't you think they deserve a little puff of opium now and then?' I was already in the force at the time, all wrapped up in my cape on my bike, and their stock room used to worry me a bit. It was getting a reputation and rich kids were starting to hang around it. So as not to scare anyone, I used to get out of my uniform before I went home. I jammed it into my bag and turned up in overalls, wheeling my bike, like I'd just got out of the Lumière factory."

Thian chuckled for a moment nostalgically.

"And now I'm disguising myself as a Chink. You see, kiddo, it's like I've had something about being an undercover copper ever since I started out. But there's something else I wanted to tell you . . ."

Thian ran his hand through his sparse brush of hair. It stood up like it was on springs.

"Memories, kiddo . . . when you've got one, then it brings up another . . . it's like imagination backwards . . . crazy like that."

Pastor was now all ears.

"One day," said Thian, "or, rather, one evening, one spring evening, under the wisteria in front of the warehouse – that's right, there was a wisteria, a mauve one – mum's young Serbo-Croat heroes were all sitting round a table. They were pretty pissed up and one of them yelled out (I can't remember if it was Stojilkovicz or one of the others): 'We're poor, we're alone, we're naked, we have no women yet, but we've just written one hell of a page in the history books!' At that moment, a tall bloke, bolt upright, all dressed in whites comes up to their table and goes: 'Writing pages in history books means playing havoc with geography.' It was one of my dad's customers. He used to come round for a smoke at the same time every day. He had a pet name for my dad. He used to call him his 'chemist'. He used to say: 'This old arthritic world is going to need your drugs more and more, Thian.' Do you know who that bloke was, kiddo?"

Pastor shook his head.

"Corrençon. Colonial Governor Corrençon. The father of that little Corrençon who's doing the sleeping beauty bit down at Saint-Louis Hospital. It was him. I'd completely forgotten about him. But now I can see him again, sitting bolt upright in his chair and listening to mum predicting the end of French Indochina and Algeria, then I can hear him answer: 'You're so right, Louise. Geography is going to assert itself once more.'"

The bottle of bourbon in front of Inspector Van Thian was now empty. He kept shaking his head, like he was up against some impossible idea.

"I got into that coach, kiddo, to keep tabs on that Yugoslav, Stojilkovicz, convinced that he was our old ladykiller, or at least an accomplice, and lo and behold he resurrects my mum for me in all her splendour, and my dad in all his wisdom . . ."

Then, after a long silence, he added:

"And yet, being the good coppers that we are, we're still going to have to run him in."

"Why?" Pastor asked.

"And now, girls, what are we going to do next?" Old Stojilkovicz wasn't asking a real question, he was booming out a rallying cry, a ritual exclamation, like a game-show host. And, all in unison, the old dears replied: "ACTIVE RESISTANCE TO ETERNITY!"

Stojilkovicz had just parked his coach near Montrouge, just by the ringroad, beside an abandoned railway station. It was one of those waste lands on the outskirts of Paris, where what has died hasn't yet been swamped over by what is being born. The station had long lost its doors and its shutters, weeds were growing up between the rails, its roof had caved in under the weight of its shattered tiles, all sorts of graffiti told all sorts of stories across its walls, but it still hadn't lost that look of optimism that stations have when they refuse to believe in the death of the train. The old dears started squealing with delight, like kids being taken to the park on Sunday. They happily jumped up and down and the rubble crunched under their crepe-soled shoes. One of them kept watch at the door while Stojilkovicz lifted up a trap door concealed under a worm-eaten dais which, in that tiny room with its high windows, must have been used by the station manager to get a good view over the platforms. Widow Ho, timidly following the rush, was swallowed up along with the other dears in the pit under the trap door. The pit was circular, with iron ladders sunk into it. The old woman in front of widow Ho (she was carrying a large shopping bag and had a hearing aid snugly fitted in the shell of her ear) told her not to worry and said she'd warn her when they reached the last rung. Widow Ho felt like she was going down inside her own soul. It was pitch black. Widow Ho said to herself that life after death was going to be a cold and clammy one.

"Watch out!" said the old lady with the big shopping bag. "We're here."

Widow Ho did her best to step down from the ladder as carefully as possible, but she couldn't stop Inspector Van Thian's hair from standing on end under her wig. Jesus fucking Christ, what the fuck have I got myself into? The ground was supple and yet hard at the same time, unyielding and yet powdery, firm and yet totally inconsistent, it was neither solid, nor liquid, nor muddy, it was dry and soft and it was for some unfathomable reason utterly terrifying, a direct line into the most ancient horror imaginable.

"Don't worry," the old lady with the shopping bag said. "It's only the charnel-house of Montrouge cemetery, the oldest bones from the paupers' graves."

This is no time to throw up, Inspector Van Thian and widow Ho decided together. And what had leapt into their throat had to be glugged back again.

"Have you pulled down the trap door up there?" Stojilkovicz's voice asked.

"Trap door down!" an old woman's youthful voice confirmed. It was like it was coming down the turret of a submarine.

"Good, then switch on your torches."

And widow Ho was enlightened, so to speak. They'd gone down into the catacombs. But not the Denfert-Rochereau catacombs that have been artistically done up for tourists, with the skulls all set out in lines and the tibias arranged in jolly patterns, no, these were the real ghastly messy catacombs, through which our little gang had to tramp for several hundred yards, over a heap of trampled-down bones from which the odd butt of a femur still stuck up with a strangely human aspect. This is fucking disgusting! Inspector Van Thian felt his anger with Stojilkovicz starting to mount again. "Shut you bruddy gob!" widow Ho muttered back at him. "And keep tem peelt!" So he shut it and kept them peeled, particularly since Stojilkovicz had just said:

"Watch out, girls, here we are. Switch off your torches."

They'd just arrived in an enormous opening, which widow Ho had only got the barest glimpse of, but which seemed to be completely lined with sandbags. There was a moment of darkness, then:

"Lights up!" bellowed Stojilkovicz.

A blinding light, as white as an ice-cold shower, suddenly shone down from the ceiling. All the old dears had lined themselves up on either side of widow Ho. Then all of a sudden, she spotted something else. It bounded out in front of her, about ten yards away, leaping off the ground like a jumping jack flash, but she never got to see what it was. A gun went off and the 'thing' immediately exploded. Widow Ho jumped out of her skin. Then her eyes swivelled round towards her neighbour, the lady with the shopping bag and hearing aid. Crouching, with her torso bent and her arms sticking out in front of her, her hands were still clutching a P.38 revolver, which was silently smoking away.

"Well done, Henriette," Stojilkovicz exclaimed. "You'll always be the quickest!"

Most of the other old women also had guns in their hands, but they hadn't had time to aim at the surprise target.

"I'm telling you, kiddo, Stojilkovicz has armed the old dears so as they can defend themselves against the killer and, every Sunday afternoon, he trains them: reflex shooting, target shooting, shooting from a prone position, on the dive, the full works. He isn't stingy with the cartridges and they draw like Jesse James. Believe you me, the young kids in the crime squad would do well to take a leaf out of their book."

"All the same, that hasn't stopped two of them getting their throats cut," Pastor pointed out.

"That's what Stojilkovicz keeps drumming into their heads. And they've decided to up their training sessions."

"So that's what they mean by 'active resistance to eternity'," said Pastor who'd finally got his smile back.

"That's it, kiddo. What do you reckon?"

"The same as you. That we're going to have to put a stop to their little hobby before they gun down the lot of us."

Thian sadly nodded his head.

"We'll do it on Tuesday, if you'll give me a hand. They meet up every Tuesday at the mutt woman's place to clean their weapons, swap them around and make their cartridges. It's like a sewing circle, or a Tupperware party . . ."

There was a moment of silence, then:

"You know what, kiddo? I've just thought of something."

"What?"

"About our Vanini. What if he got popped off by one of these old dears?"

"Quite likely," said Pastor. " That is, at least, what Hadouch Ben Tayeb claims."

Thian gave his head another prolonged shake, then, smiling into space, said:

"You know what, they really are adorable . . ."

Chapter 28

THE OLD DEARS didn't put up the slightest resistance to the three inspectors. It was a bit of a shame, really. Pastor, Thian and Caregga felt like they were taking toys off a group of orphans rather than disarming a gang. The old women just sat there, round the large table on which they'd carefully laid out their scales, their shells, their powder and their shot. (They had been about to make their weekly supply of cartridges.) With their heads drooping, they remained silent. Neither guilty, nor terrified, not even worried, they'd quite simply become old once more, had been handed back their lives of loneliness and indifference. Caregga and Pastor filled up a large bag with the weapons they'd seized while Thian dealt with the ammunition. The entire scene took place in perfect silence under Stojilkovicz's gaze. His stare was so impassive it was almost like he was supervising the operation.

When passing in front of him, Thian was afraid that the Yugoslav would say: "So, little Viet, it was you, was it? Congratulations." But Stojil didn't say a word. He hadn't recognized him. Thian felt even more ashamed of himself. Stop tormenting yourself, for Christ's sake, you must be completely out of your tree, you couldn't just let these women gun down everyone who's about twenty. Isn't Vanini's death enough? It was in vain that Thian reasoned with himself. The sense of shame just wouldn't go away. And since when have you been mourning for that little runt Vanini? That thought didn't cheer him up much either. If this gang of now-disarmed vigilantes had gunned down a regiment of Vaninis, his reaction would have been to give them all a medal. "What's more, they're going to get scared again, just waiting there like trapped geese for their throats to be slit." Thian had to face up to his own failure once again. If that psycho was still out there, then that was his fault! He was taking their weapons off them, but he was absolutely incapable of protecting them. He didn't even have a lead anymore. Since he'd got to know Stojilkovicz, the Malaussène hypothesis was starting to look like a dead duck. Someone like Stojilkovicz could hardly be mates with a serial killer.

The three coppers had finished going round the table. They were now standing nervously on the threshold, like embarrassed guests who can't get out the door. Pastor finally cleared his throat and said:

"We're not going to arrest you, ladies, nor even bother you about this matter again. I give you my word."

He hesitated:

"But we can't let you keep these guns."

He went on, immediately cringing at what he was saying:

"It was dangerous . . ."

Then he turned round to Stojilkovicz:

"Would you mind coming along with us, sir?"

All the weapons they'd seized were pre-war models. Most of them were revolvers and came from a variety of different countries: they ranged from Soviet Tokarevs to German Walthers, from Italian Glisentis to Swiss S.I.G Sauers and Belgian Brownings. But there were also a few automatic weapons: American M3 machine-guns, good old British sten-guns and even a Joss Randal style Winchester whose butt and barrel had been sawn off. Stojilkovicz made no bones about the fact that he'd put together this hand-me-down arsenal during the last months of the war and that it had been meant for his Croatian militia. But, when operations came to an end, he'd decided to bury his weapons as deeply as possible.

"I didn't want the partisans of Tito, Stalin or Michailovicz to get their hands on them and use them in further massacres. I'd had it with warfare. Or, at least, I thought I had. But when the old ladies started to get their throats cut . . ."

He then explained how a man's conscience works in mysterious ways, like a fire you thought had gone out and which suddenly kindles itself again. After what he'd gone through during the war, he would never have resurrected these guns. But times had changed. Thanks to the medium of television he'd witnessed countless examples of injustice which could have been fought against using his arsenal . . . But no, his stash had been hidden for good. And then someone had started murdering old ladies and ("probably because I'm getting old myself") he started having terrible nightmares in which he saw hyped-up youngsters with guns attacking this neighbourhood (he gestured vaguely towards Belleville). They were like wolves bursting into a sheep fold. "And, in my country, we know all about wolves." They were young wolves with a naive love of death – both the deaths they caused and the death they injected into their own veins. He himself had experienced that passion for death. It had been the driving-force behind his own young years. "Do you know how many of the Vlasov prisoners had their throats slit? That's right, we *slit their throats*, with knives, because we were short of ammunition, or because they'd raped our sisters and killed our mothers and so didn't deserve a bullet. How many do you think? With a knife . . . Just think of a number. And if you can't guess the grand total, how many of them did I kill myself? And, among them, how many old men whom history had stranded there? How many of their throats did I slit? Me, the young defrocked seminarist? How many?"

Since no one answered, he finally said:

"That's why I decided to arm these old women, against the young wolf I used to be."

He frowned, then added:

"Yes, I suppose that was why . . ."

"But they wouldn't have hurt a fly! Accidents just couldn't happen. They were too well trained. They drew quickly, but they were to fire only when they saw the razor . . ."

Vanini's green and blond shadow flitted silently before the eyes of the three coppers, who ignored it.

"There we are," said Stojilkovicz at last. "This has been my last battle."

Then he grinned:

"The best causes must come to an end."

Pastor said:

"We're going to have to arrest you, Monsieur Stojilkovicz."

"Naturally."

"But you will be charged only with possession of firearms."

"And roughly how long will I get?"

"In your case, probably only a few months," Pastor answered.

Stojilkovicz thought for a moment, then calmly observed:

"Only a few months in prison isn't long enough. I shall need a full year, at the very least."

The three coppers stared at one another.

"Why?" Pastor asked.

Stojilkovicz thought it over again, carefully estimating how much time he would need, then finally said in his bassoon-like voice:

"I've started translating Virgil into Serbo-Croat and it's a long and rather arduous task."

Caregga drove Stojilkovicz away in the squad car, while Pastor and Thian paced indecisively up and down the pavement. With his fists clenched and his face screwed up, Thian remained silent.

"You're furious," Pastor said at last. "Do you want me to find you a good chemist?"

Thian waved away the suggestion.

"I'll be all right, kiddo. Let's walk for a bit, shall we?"

The cold had taken over the city once more. It was the last cold spell of winter, its dying fall. Pastor said:

"How odd, Belleville doesn't believe in the cold."

This was just about true. Even in minus-fifteen weather Belleville remained vibrant. Belleville always played at being Mediterranean.

"I've got something to show you," Thian said.

He opened his fist right under Pastor's nose. In his palm, Pastor saw a 9mm shell with its lead split open in the shape of a cross.

"I took this one off the old mutt, you know, the lady whose flat it was. She was loading a P.38 with them."

"So?"

"Out of all the ammo we picked up, this is the only bullet which could have blown Vanini's head apart like a melon. When the lead's been split open, it goes inside then separates. Vanini is the result."

Pastor absentmindedly pocketed the bullet. They'd now arrived on

167

Boulevard de Belleville. They were standing like good citizens beside a traffic light, waiting for it to turn red so they could cross.

"Look at those two little fuckers over there," said Thian, indicating them with his chin.

On the pavement across the street, two clean-cut kids, one in a green overcoat and the other in leathers, were checking the papers of a third, much less clean-cut person. This was going on outside a betting-shop in which old Arabs were cracking down their dominoes in time to the beat of the youngsters' pinball machines.

"Cercaria's community coppers on the beat," said Pastor.

"Little fuckers," Thian repeated.

It was thanks to the fact that he was furious with himself, and because neither the driver of the car nor the hit man imagined that an old man like him could move so fast, that Thian saved his own and Pastor's life that afternoon.

"Watch out!" he yelled.

As he drew his gun, he sent Pastor reeling behind a row of dustbins. The first bullet smashed the red light, just where Pastor had been an instant before. The second went straight from Thian's gun into the driver's right temple, where it left a neat round hole. The driver's head shot to the left, bounced back off the side window then landed on the steering wheel, while a dead man's shoe was stepping on the accelerator. The BMW leapt forward, deviating the third bullet, which hit Thian's right shoulder. Thian swivelled round under the impact and his MAC 50 jumped, as though of its own accord, from his right hand to his left. The bonnet of the BMW piled into one of Paris's revolving billboards. A figure leapt out of the right-hand rear door and Thian plugged three 9mm shells into it as it fled. The body flopped onto the pavement like a dummy. Thian stood there for a moment or two with his arm stuck out, then lowered his gun and turned round towards Pastor, who was getting to his feet and feeling a shade vexed at having missed all the action.

"What the fuck was all that about?" asked Thian.

"I am what all that was about," said Pastor.

With their guns drawn, Cercaria's two community policemen were crossing the road and yelling:

"Don't move! Stay perfectly still or we'll fire!"

But Thian had already got his badge out and was waving it casually at them.

"The cavalry's a bit late, I'm afraid."

Then, to Pastor:

"You still on for the chemist's, kiddo?"

"Let's have a look."

Pastor carefully undressed Thian's shoulder. The bullet had torn the material to shreds, then gone through the deltoid, but it hadn't touched either the collar bone or the shoulder-blade. And Pastor had cut his hand on a broken bottle.

"And there isn't that much meat on me," Thian remarked. "What were our two lover-boys after you for?"

Chapter 29

W HAT I, BENJAMIN MALAUSSÈNE, am after is how to
spew all my humanity out of myself, something as sure as
ramming two fingers down your throat, how to look down
on people, or a good bit of bestial hatred, how to chop people up with
your eyes closed. I'd like someone to be pointed out to me one day and
be told: that's him, public fucker number one, shit in his face, Benjamin,
make him swallow your shit, kill him and the others like him. I'd like to
be able to do that. I really would. I'd like to be one of those who
campaign for the reintroduction of the death penalty, and for it to be
public, and for the condemned man to have his feet sliced off first, then
for him to be stitched up so they can start all over again, still from the
wrong side up, cut his tibias off this time, then stitch him up again,
then whoosh! through the knees, straight through the kneecaps, right
there where it hurts most. I'd like to be a member of that big, united
family which cries out for punishment. I'd take the children along to see
the show and say to Jeremy: "You see what's in store for you if you keep
burning schools down?" And I'd tell Half Pint: "Look! Look! He used to
turn blokes into flowers as well!" And as soon as little Verdun became
aware, I'd pick her up in my arms, high above the crowd, so that she
could see the blood running from the blade. That's dissuasion for you!
I'd like to belong to that great big beautiful Soul of Humanity, the one
that firmly believes in punishment as an example, the one that knows
who the goodies are and who the baddies are. I'd like to be the proud
owner of a *personally-held conviction*. Jesus, how I'd like that! Wouldn't
that make my life so nice and fucking simple!

These are the thoughts that go racing through my head in the métro while on my way home from the Vendetta Press where, like the poor stupid bastard I am, I tried to wheedle my way round Queen Zabo, pleading with her in the name of my family, not to fire me if I fail tomorrow with Ponthard-Delmaire.

"Stop your sobbing, Malaussène. Keep your scapegoat act for Ponthard-Delmaire, it's wasted on me."

"But why should I get the sack if I don't get him to agree to postponing publication, for fuck's sake?"

"Watch your tongue. Because you will have failed, that's why. And no publishing house worth its salt can keep trash on its payroll."

"But what about you, your Impeccable Majesty, didn't you fail by letting the proofs of the book go up in smoke in the car?"

"It was the driver of the car who failed, Malaussène, and it was the death of him. Grilled alive in his own self-made inferno."

I stared back at Queen Zabo's unbelievable physique, that huge skinny carcass with a big fat watermelon stuck on top, and her chimpanzee's arms finishing in baby hands, as chubby as mittens. I listened to her voice, as jolly as a spoilt brat's, always on the look-out for signs of its own intelligence and I wondered for the umpteenth time why I didn't detest her.

"Look, Malaussène, let's get this straight. Neither you nor I give a tuppenny fuck about Ponthard-Delmaire the architect. But, in the first place we can't let that mountain of subsidies slip through our hands (other people will only cash in!) and, in the second place . . ."

There's a momentary break in her rattling voice and she stares at me using high persuasion.

"In the second place, you're *the man for the job*. Winning victories by whining is your trademark! It'd be a criminal shame for me not to put you up to it. My poor darling, I'd be taking away the very blood from your veins."

(So there we are. If she's packing me off to the front, it's only for my own good.)

"*You are* a scapegoat, damn you. Just get that into your head once and for all. You're scapegoat to the marrow, and you're as gifted in your job as I am in mine! As far as everyone is concerned, everything is always going to be your fault and you'll quite happily carry on cashing in by making swines cry their eyes out. Just so long as you don't have any doubts about yourself. One moment's doubt and you'll be stoned to death!"

That's when I hit the roof:

"But what the Jesus fucking Christ are you talking about? *You are a scapegoat!* What the fuck's that supposed to mean?"

"It means that all the shit in the world magnetically sticks to you. It means that in this city all sorts of people you don't even know think you're to blame for all sorts of things you haven't done and, in some ways, it really is all your fault, for the sole and unique reason that people *need someone to blame.*"

"What?"

"What me no whats and stop playing the fool. You know perfectly well what I mean. If you didn't, you wouldn't even be here, in the Vendetta Press, doing a filthy goat's job after being sacked from The Store, *where you did the very same job!*"

"That's right, and I got myself fired for the very good reason that I was pissed off always getting bollocked for everybody else's cock-ups!"

"So why did you agree to do the same thing here?"

"I've got a family to feed! I don't spend my life loafing about studying the workings of my navel!"

"Family, my arse! There are endless ways to feed a family. By not feeding it at all for starters. Rousseau managed that one perfectly. And he was at least as barmy as you are!"

Once the conversation had got onto these lines, it could have gone on for ever. But Queen Zabo managed to draw it to a close in her oh-so professional style.

"Tomorrow, being Wednesday, you will pay a call on Ponthard-Delmaire, you will get him to agree to a delay in the publication of his architecture book, or else I'll fire you. An appointment has already been made for you at four p.m. on the dot."

Then she sweetened for a moment and stroked her babyish hand over my several days' growth.

"Don't worry, you'll make it. You've got us out of worse scrapes than this."

So home I come with visions of the guillotine crowding my mind and Clara opens the door. I no sooner glance at my favourite little sister than I sense there's trouble brewing. Before she has time to open her mouth, I put on my most reassuring voice and ask her:

"Yes, sweetheart? Is anything the matter?"

"Uncle Stojil's just phoned."

"So?"

"He's at the police station, Ben. They're going to send him to prison."

"What for?"

"He says it's nothing serious. The police have discovered an arms cache that he'd been keeping in the Montrouge catacombs since the end of the war."

(*What?*)

"He says that whatever we do, we're not to worry. And he'll let us know as soon as he's comfortably settled into his cell."

Comfortably settled into his cell . . . That's Stojil to a tee, that is. The monk in him has woken up now that prison's in the offing. Knowing him, he's probably absolutely thrilled. (There's society for you: Hadouch and Stojil get sent down, while Queen Zabo's been left free to roam the streets!)

"What's the bit about the arms cache in the catacombs all about?"

Before Clara has time to explain, Jeremy starts pulling at my sleeve.

"And that's not all, Ben. There's some more news."

He's got that air about him which I know only too well and which bodes ill. Like he's chuffed with himself for God alone knows what reason.

"What? What other news is there?"

"A surprise, Ben."

With this family, anything that remotely resembles a surprise puts the willies up me. So I glance round the flat. The granddads and the kids all have the same innocent look on their faces, like they're cooking up a surprise party. And then I reckon I've twigged onto what's up: the place is strangely quiet, like the calm after the storm. I ask:

"Where's Verdun?"

"Don't worry, she's asleep," says Kidney.

I don't find his tone at all reassuring, so I press the point:

"You haven't been putting gin in her bottle by any chance?"

"No," says Jeremy. "That's not the surprise."

I look at Julius. With his lopsided head and dangling tongue, he's completely inscrutable.

"Well you haven't given Julius a bath, that's for sure. What a nice surprise that would have been!"

(They're not really going to put Stojil in the hole, are they?)

"The surprise I've got for you is much better than that," says Jeremy, starting to get into a sulk. Then he adds with a pout: "But if you don't want it, I'll take it back to where I found it."

All right, I give up.

"Come on then, Jeremy, what's the surprise? I'd like to know what shit I'm going to be landed in next."

"It's upstairs in your bedroom, Ben. It's lovely and it's warm and if I were you, I'd bomb straight up there for a look."

It's Julia! It's Julie! It's my Corrençon! In my bed! There's one leg in plaster, a drip in her arm, bruising on her face, but it's Julia! Alive! *My very own* Julia, for Christ's sake! She's asleep. She's smiling. Louna's standing to her right and Jeremy's at the foot of the bed, pointing at her with a dramatic gesture and going:

"It's Auntie Julia."

Leaning over the bed, as if it was a cot, all my questions come out in one go:

"What's the matter with her? Where did you find her? Is it serious? Who did this to her? She's lost weight, hasn't she? What are those marks on her face? And what about her leg? What the hell's she doing here? Why isn't she in hospital?"

"That's just it," says Jeremy.

A vaguely pregnant pause then follows.

"That's just it! What's just it, for crying out loud?"

"She *was* in hospital, Ben. That's what. But she wasn't being looked after properly."

174

"What? Which hospital?"

"Saint-Louis. She was in Saint-Louis Hospital but not being looked after properly at all," Jeremy repeats himself, his eyes sending SOS flares across to Louna.

Silence. A silence which, though more dead than alive, I finally manage to break:

"And why doesn't she wake up when you speak to her?"

Then Louna finally comes to Jeremy's assistance:

"She's been drugged, Ben. She won't wake up for a while yet. She'd been drugged when they admitted her and then they went on drugging her so that she wouldn't wake up too suddenly."

"Meaning, if we'd left her in hospital, she'd never have woken up again at all," goes Jeremy. "Anyway, that's what Marty was saying the other day."

This time, I pin him down with a look that makes him come out with the goods sharpish:

"You remember that row between Dr Marty and that other quack called Berthold when we were on our way to see Verdun when he was dying? You remember that, don't you, Ben? Marty was yelling: 'If you keep on drugging her like that, you'll wind up killing her.' On the way back, I had a peek inside the room Dr Marty had been pointing at, and it was Auntie Julia in the bed, Ben. It was her!"

And just to prove it, he points at my Julia in my bed.

So there we are. And this is what Jeremy and Louna have done, without asking a word of advice from anyone: they have quite simply kidnapped Julie. They got her out of the hospital by pretending they were taking her down to be x-rayed. They loaded her onto a trolley, wheeled her down the miles and miles of corridors, with Louna in her nurse's outfit and Jeremy in tears, playing the dutiful family member ("don't worry yourself, mum, you'll see, everything's going to be fine"), then they went outside, as cool as cucumbers, loaded our still slumbering Julie into Louna's motor, drove off then piled her upstairs into my bedroom. And here we are. One of Jeremy's ideas. And how proud of themselves they both are, and how chuffed, waiting there for their big bro's congratulations, because they obviously reckon they deserve a medal for spiriting away a patient from out the hospital . . . On the other hand, they have brought me back my Julie. As ever, I'm wobbling between two extremes: giving them the thrashing of their lives or hugging them to death. All I do is ask them:

"Do you have any idea how the hospital's going to react?"

"The hospital was going to kill her!" Jeremy exclaims.

A big-brotherly silence follows; a long, thoughtful silence. Then the verdict: "You're a pair of angels, you really are. You've just made me the happiest man alive . . . now get the hell out of here before I beat your heads against the wall."

I must have sounded pretty convincing, because they both obeyed me immediately and started backing out of the room.

"You poor devil, it isn't a family you've got there, but a walking disaster area!"

Doctor Marty chuckles at the other end of the line.

"I can just see the expression on Berthold's face! One of his patients has disappeared! You'll see, he'll be getting a self-justificatory press conference together even as we speak!"

I let him enjoy his little moment of professional triumph, then ask him:

"So, what's your opinion, doctor?"

He's always got a ready answer, has Marty.

"I think that from a strictly medical viewpoint, Jeremy's action can easily be defended. As regards the hospital, this business naturally creates an irritating administrative problem. But the real snag is going to be the police."

"The police? Why the police? You're not going to phone the cops, are you?"

"No, I'm not. But your Julie Corrençon was *brought in by* the police. You didn't know that?"

(No, I didn't know that.)

"No, I didn't know that. Was it a long time ago?"

"About a fortnight. A young inspector used to come and sit by her from time to time and talk to her as if she could hear him – a very good thing, in fact – that's why I noticed her in that room."

176

"A fortnight in a coma?"

(My Julie . . . completely out for the last fortnight. Jesus Christ, whatever did they do to you?)

"She's been maintained in a coma, to avoid any shock when she wakes up. Which is ridiculous in her case, I think. She should now be woken up as rapidly as possible."

"Is there any risk? When she wakes up, I mean. Could waking her up put her in danger?"

"Yes. She could have a fit and suffer from hallucinations."

"Could she die?"

"That's where Berthold's opinion differs from mine. I don't think so. She's a tough woman, you know."

(That's right, she is tough. I know that.)

"Will you come by, Doctor? Will you call and see her?"

He answers at once:

"Of course I'll take care of her, Monsieur Malaussène. But to begin with, I'll have to sort out the problem with the hospital and inform the police. We don't want them to think we're trying to hide a suspect or anything of that sort."

"How are we going to deal with the police?"

I'm obviously starting to lose it. I'm putting myself totally in the hands of a character I've only seen twice in my life before: last year when we brought in Jeremy, who'd been cut to ribbons and roasted like a turkey; and the day Verdun died. But that's the way it goes. If you find a human being in the crowd, follow him . . . follow him . . .

"I'll give that Inspector Pastor a ring, Monsieur Malaussène. The one that used to come in and whisper into her ear. That's it, I'll ask Inspector Pastor's advice."

Chapter 30

"COME IN, PASTOR, my lad, come in!"
It was night-time, but Chief Superintendent Cercaria's office was still lit up *a giorno*, just like it was at any time of the day or night, by the same unbroken light, the sort which springs back off the walls and ceiling, wiping out any shadows and making a frigid cut-up of real life's contours.

"Pastor, this is Bertholet, Bertholet, this is Pastor. The bloke that nobbled Chabralle, remember?"

Big Bertholet grinned fleetingly at Inspector Pastor, who was timidly standing there in his ancient woolly, like he was floating in the light. He even looked a bit soft. And yet this latex copy of Rupert Bear had got Chabralle singing. Big Bertholet just couldn't believe it.

"I hear someone tried to whack you, Pastor. Sounds like you were lucky old Thian happened to be there."

There wasn't the slightest hint of irony in Cercaria's voice. He was just summing up the report concerning the two men which was lying in front of him on his desk.

"I didn't even have time to draw," said Pastor. "It was all over in a blink."

"Yes," said Cercaria. "I've already seen Thian in action. He's really something. It's just a-fucking-mazing the way such a little bloke handles the big artillery."

Then, noticing the bandaged hand:

"Cop one, did you?"

"No, I just fell on a broken bottle in a dustbin," said Pastor. "Quite a glorious war wound!"

"Everyone has to start somewhere, lad."

The light in the office also had another effect. Coming as it did from nowhere, it also obliterated time. The Chief Superintendent had learnt how to take advantage of this fact when questioning suspects. Even though it looked like it was made of glass, there wasn't a single window in the room. And no clocks on the walls. And no watches on the wrists of the coppers who came into the room during an interrogation.

"Are you busy?" Pastor asked softly. "I wondered if you might spare me a little of your time."

Big Bertholet grinned. Didn't Pastor speak posh. With his softly softly voice and all.

"For you, lad, I've got all the time in the world."

"It's a personal matter," said Pastor apologetically, staring at Bertholet.

"Bugger off then, Bertholet, my old mate. And don't forget to tell Pasquier to double the men tailing Merlotti. I don't want that frigging wop to be able even to go for a crap without me knowing about it."

The door closed behind Bertholet as he set off with his instructions. It was a thick glass door in an aluminium frame.

"Fancy a tinny, lad?" Cercaria asked. "I bet your little brush with the action scared you shitless."

"It did, rather," Pastor admitted.

Cercaria took two beers out of his mural fridge, opened them and handed one to the young inspector before slumping down into his white leather desk chair.

"Take a seat, lad, then tell me what's up."

"I have something to show you which you should find interesting."

A good beer is always a good beer, especially when drunk in good company. Cercaria liked Pastor. He liked him even more when Pastor had placed in front of him a 9mm bullet, with its lead filed down into a cross.

"This bullet comes from the gun that killed Vanini. It's a home-made job."

The Chief Superintendent nodded sagely, as he turned the bullet round and round between thumb and index finger.

"And have you got the gun?"

"I've got the gun, I've got the murderer and I've got the motive."

179

Cercaria lifted his eyes up towards the young man who was holding out half-a-dozen black and white photographs. They depicted Vanini at his best, beating demonstrators to the ground with a knuckleduster. In one of the photos, a protester's head had been split open. One of his eyes was dangling out of its socket.

"Where did you unearth this lot? I've had warrants to search all of Ben Tayeb's lads' places and I didn't find a thing."

"Malaussène had them," said Pastor. "I did a bit of discreet burglary," he explained. "He won't even have noticed I was there."

"And the gun?"

"There too," said Pastor. "You were right, it's a P.38 and Malaussène had it too."

Cercaria stared across at the youngster sitting in front of him. The one who'd nobbled Chabralle and who was now handing him on a plate what he and all of his squad had been after for such a long time.

"What tipped you off, lad?"

"You did. I realized you were right about Ben Tayeb spinning me a yarn. I don't appreciate that at all. And then, I'm investigating the case of a young woman Malaussène tried to kill, which led me to trespass a little onto your patch."

Cercaria nodded.

"And then?"

Pastor smiled with embarrassment.

"I'm rich, as you no doubt know from my file. I inherited a fortune and so can afford to buy the best informers, that is to say, the ones that have the highest prices."

"Like Berber Simon?"

"For example. And Black Mo."

Cercaria took a long sip from his beer. When the last fleck of foam had evaporated from his moustache, he asked:

"So what's the overall picture, according to you?"

"Simple," said Pastor. "You were right about Ben Tayeb, he's well into the drug business. But the top dog is Malaussène, who's carefully hidden behind his image of being a good family man. He and Tayeb had a novel idea: shift the drug market from the young to the old. They started out with Belleville, with the firm intention of expanding later. But Vanini – and you can say what you want about him, but he certainly wasn't stupid – plus he had his own highly efficient way of making informers' tongues wag – got wind of the affair. So they topped him. That's all. Or, rather, Malaussène topped him. They reckoned you wouldn't make too much fuss about that, so long as you didn't get your hands on the photos, which were highly incriminating for your squad."

Pastor emptied his glass and concluded:

"But now you've got the photos, and the negatives as well."

Time really didn't exist in Chief Superintendent Cercaria's office. Pastor would have been incapable of saying how many seconds had gone by before Cercaria asked:

"And you're handing me all this on a plate, just like that, free, gratis and for nothing?"

"No," said Pastor. "I want something in exchange."

"Go on."

Inspector Pastor smiled in a strangely childish way.

"I want another beer."

Cercaria burst out in his best Cercaria-laugh and went back to the fridge. He turned his back to Pastor. The illuminated inside of the mini-fridge, fixed high up in an aluminium bookcase, set his torso off against a warm yellow light, while the rest of him remained in the vacuous brightness of the office. Cercaria had a beer in each hand, with his back still turned, when Pastor said blandly:

"You shouldn't have tried to kill me, Cercaria."

The man didn't turn round. He stayed there, his hands occupied by the beers, the fridge door now shut, fixed in that timeless light, motionless, with his back to the danger area.

Pastor laughed merrily.

"Turn round! I'm not holding a gun on you! I'm simply telling you that you shouldn't have tried to kill me."

When he turned round, Cercaria glanced at once at Pastor's hands. No, he wasn't pointing a gun at him. He breathed a slow sigh of relief.

"I'm not even annoyed with you for trying. All I'm doing is explaining to you that you made a mistake."

A boyish look flickered across Cercaria's face.

"It wasn't me!" he said.

Children shout loudly when they're lying. And even louder when they're telling the truth. Pastor believed what the man standing in front of him had said.

"So it was Ponthard-Delmaire, then?"

Cercaria nodded.

"His daughter left a note mentioning your name before chucking herself out the window. Ponthard was out for revenge. I told him he was being stupid."

Pastor agreed with a long, slow nod of his head.

"Your Ponthard never stops being stupid. Are we going to drink those beers, or what?"

The beers were at last opened and fizzed with satisfaction as they filled up the glasses.

"In the first place, killing a cop is a pretty stupid thing to do, isn't it?"

As he asked his question, Pastor smiled at Cercaria, who unsmilingly nodded in reply.

"Then, using two cretins to do the job is even stupider."

Cercaria's glass remained full.

"Not to mention the fact that the two of them – and I'd swear it was the same two – had already made a mess of a previous contract."

Pastor clearly saw two ears prick up *inside* Cercaria's head, while that muscular mustachioed mask had recovered its usual impassiveness.

"They missed that journalist, the Corrençon woman, Cercaria. They drugged her and threw her into the Seine. But she fell into a barge and the two of them didn't even notice!"

"Useless wankers!" Cercaria blurted out.

"That's exactly my opinion too. And do you know where they tried to ditch her?"

A shake of the head.

"Off Pont Neuf, just over the road from the station. Someone obviously spotted them. It was the same night Vanini got himself killed."

Pastor spun out his sentences one by one, giving them the time to be soaked up nicely by the brains sitting opposite him, which were obviously working overtime. There are times when men really do look like computers: all sleek and hard on the outside, but with neurons flashing away like mad things inside. When Cercaria had measured the importance of what he'd just heard, he took the only way out:

"Look, Pastor, stop playing silly buggers with me. Just tell me what you know, how you found it out and what you want. OK?"

"OK. It started when I was investigating that young woman who had been thrown into the barge and who, today, is still in a coma. I discovered that she was a journalist and, given the sort of articles she was in the habit of writing, it seemed obvious that she'd stuck her nose into an affair which someone wanted to hush up. Is that clear so far?"

A nod.

"When I went to search her flat, I ran into a certain Malaussène who was making such a rapid getaway that he barged into old Thian and dropped a batch of photographs on impact. They were snaps of Edith Ponthard-Delmaire."

A pause, then Cercaria's head nodded again.

"Being the good copper that I am, I've done a spell in the drug squad and I recognized her face. I looked her up in the records and found that you had indeed arrested her in 1980. So I supposed that she must have started dealing again and that the photos were proof of that fact. Was Malaussène taking them to La Corrençon, or had he pinched them from her flat? That's what I didn't know yet. And that's where you unwittingly helped me out."

A glance which said "Me?" "How's that?"

"By having me grill Hadouch Ben Tayeb. You were obsessed by Vanini's death. You were all out to nail Tayeb. But when I told you that the past-their-sell-by-date drugs, which you nicked him with, had come from a Town Hall and that they'd been given to a little old man by a local health visitor during a medal ceremony, you wouldn't believe me, remember?"

A nod of a head that's starting to cop on.

"You were in too much of a hurry about refusing to believe me. Why won't he listen? What's so unbelievable about it? So I thought I'd check the story out, just from curiosity. And that's what I did."

He paused for a sip. The beer tasted good.

"And I discovered something rather odd. That fifty-years' service medal, which our deserving old man received that morning in the Town Hall of the eleventh arrondissement, had been awarded by Arnaud Le Capelier, the Permanent Secretary for Senior Citizens."

The eyebrows were tensed. They were saying: Where's all this heading? How far is he going to go?

"Now, among the photos Malaussène dropped there was a close-up of Edith Ponthard-Delmaire, with Arnaud Le Capelier behind her, on the dais, follow me? With his lovely smooth hair, and its perfect central parting which tumbles straight down onto the ridge of his nose and the dimple in his chin."

(Get on with it . . . Get on with it . . .)

"The rest then fell into place. I tailed little Edith for a few days. She was there in attendance at all the events which our handsome Arnaud, the Permanent Secretary for Senior Citizens, had organized for old folk. It was all very official, above board and above suspicion. And each time, she used her charms on a group of old men and, each time, a little packet of pills passed from her handbag into their pockets."

Silence. Silence. And the suspension of time in the transparent light of the truth.

"And yet," said Pastor with genuine astonishment, "there was always at least one copper in attendance as well. An officer from the drug squad in a green overcoat, or leathers. Imitations of their boss."

The boss was understanding things better and better. It was like a house of cards collapsing in slow motion.

"I found it odd that they didn't spot her. Especially since she wasn't very subtle about what she was up to. And then the thought occurred to me: what if they're there to *protect her*, to make sure the little lass doesn't run any of the risks of her business . . . What do you reckon, Cercaria?"

"OK, OK, get on with it."

"So I had Edith Ponthard-Delmaire brought in and I presented her with these ideas of mine as though I was sure about them. She confirmed what I thought. She opened up. She confessed everything. Making her sign the confession was a little problematic, but I have a method for doing that. A method whose effectiveness you have been able to judge for yourself in the Chabralle affair."

Cercaria's beer was now totally headless. But the liquid was still there, stagnating, panting for oxygen. Pastor's voice went on:

"Before bringing Edith Ponthard-Delmaire in, I did another piece of run-of-the-mill research. I wanted to know about this charming young lady's father. Ponthard-Delmaire the architect. A fine profession. A fine way with words too: 'The Unity of Mankind and Architectural Space', that's the title of one of his lectures. 'How to make each lodging the rhythmic expression of the body haunting it' (sic). Lovely stuff, don't you think?"

"Go on." (The glass was full, the voice dry.)

"Right. So I phoned up the Town Planning Department and found out what sort of things Ponthard-Delmaire builds in Paris. I discovered that he didn't want to disfigure the capital by putting up new buildings. (We can be thankful for small mercies, seeing what he's done to Brest and Belleville.) No, his architectural approach consists in 'internal modelling'. In other words, he conserves Paris's external appearance by renovating the interiors of flats which have been acquired by a subsidiary of his Architect's Office. I made a list of these flats. There are 2,800 of them (so far). I tried to find out who their previous owners were. 97% of them belonged to lonely old people who died in hospital, without any family for the most part. I phoned round a few hospitals to try and find out what these old people had died of. Almost all of them had senile dementia and were in psychiatric hospitals. Empty flats . . ."

This time the silence was the silence of eternity. Time now belonged to the ageless young man who was sitting there.

"Shall I sum up?" he asked.

Silence, of course. Silence.

"Right, so I'll sum up. Here, then, is the entire business in all its simplicity: among its inhabitants, Paris includes an extraordinarily large number of lonely, hopeless old people. If these old people's flats could be purchased on the cheap, then renovated according to the precepts of that most humane of architects, Ponthard-Delmaire, and if they could then be sold off again at a price worthy of such a master's work, then the profits would be around 500 to 600%. But the flats still have to become vacant. What do old people die of? Of old age. Is hastening on old age, giving them a push down the last slope of senility, really such a great crime? That's arguable. It could even be thought of as being an act of humanity. So consciences become clear and senior citizens' bank accounts can at last be tapped by the drug market. I'm talking a lot. I'd like another beer."

A robot gets to its feet. A robot opens the fridge door. A robot opens the beer. A robot sits down again.

"Turning the drug market away from the young and towards the old can almost be called a moral task and the source of massive profits. The clients are above suspicion, under the protection of Chief Superintendent Cercaria, the head of the Drug Squad, and with the blessing of the Permanent Secretary for Senior Citizens. It's a gold mine. Where to find the pushers? That's easy. It's simply a question of using people who are already on our books and who are in our power. But who are forbidden to go back on drugs themselves. Reliable people. Like Edith Ponthard-Delmaire, for example. They just have to be paid well. And the money's there for that."

Still the same silent light and the truth getting truer and truer.

"Then, lo and behold, a journalist starts sticking her nose into the business . . . the first big snag."

Right. One hell of a snag. The eternal fly in the ointment.

"There we are," said Pastor. "That's all I know. I've finished."

He didn't get up. He just sat there, drinking his third beer, like a rodeo champion contemplating a fine bucking bronco which he's just broken in for good.

"All right, Pastor. So what do you want?"

The answer wasn't immediately forthcoming. First came this additional piece of useful information:

"Coudrier, my boss, knows nothing about all this. He's been fed the Malaussène angle for the attempted murder of La Corrençon, the serial killing of old women and the drug dealing."

A tense face unwinding is a lovely sight to see. There's nothing more relaxing in the world than a vision of relief. That's what Chief

Superintendent Cercaria had to offer young Pastor, who was sitting there in front of him, when he exclaimed:

"My fucking beer's gone warm!"

Another round trip to the fridge.

"Right then, lad, so what do you want?"

"Firstly, that you stop calling me 'lad'. I think I've done some growing up of late."

A dream comes to an end.

"All right, Pastor, what do you want?"

"I want 3% of the total profits. 3%."

"Are you crazy?"

"No, I'm perfectly sane. And, don't forget, I know about money. I manage my own little fortune very nicely, thank you. I want a meeting with Ponthard-Delmaire tomorrow and for the three of us to sort out the terms of my contract."

A regiment of accountants went into action behind the Chief Superintendent's forehead.

"Don't start doing your sums, Cercaria. I'm not coming to you empty-handed. I'm even bringing along a nice little dowry. Firstly, I know the truth and the truth at 3% seems to me to be a pretty good deal. Secondly, and most importantly, I'm bringing you Malaussène, who, as I've explained, fits snugly into the frame for the whole business: Vanini's murder, the serial killing of old ladies and the pushing of drugs to old men. He's the perfect scapegoat. What's more, we'll be making a happy man of him. It's a part he apparently likes playing."

And then the phone rang.

"Who's that?" Cercaria barked into the receiver.

"Yes, he's here."

Then:

"It's for you, Pastor."

The phone passed from hand to hand.

"Yes?" said Pastor the innocent. "Yes, speaking, Doctor. No! Whyever did they do that? Oh, I see, yes, I understand . . . No, she isn't being charged with anything, no, I don't think that's particularly serious. Oh yes, I should be able to sort things out . . . That's all right, Doctor, don't mention it . . . No, no, no, that's perfectly all right, yes, goodbye Doctor."

He slowly hung up and smiled to himself for a while.

"I can now give you a little something extra, Cercaria. Malaussène's had Julie Corrençon kidnapped from Saint-Louis Hospital where, according to him, she wasn't being looked after properly. She's his girl-friend, by the way. She's now in his flat and I think it wouldn't be a bad idea if she died there."

A final smile. This time, he got up.

"But we'll sort that out tomorrow as well, at Ponthard-Delmaire's house. Does around half past three suit you? Oh, and don't forget about the 3%."

Chapter 31

WIDOW HO'S SHOULDER hurt. One of the few scraps of flesh that still wrapped up her bones had been torn open and she saw that as a great piece of injustice from the hand of fate. If the hit man's bullet had been a few inches lower, in towards her body, then widow Ho wouldn't have existed anymore, which would have been a great relief to her. But instead of that happening, widow Ho was still there, alive and kicking, with a hole in her shoulder, watching Belleville collapse around her ears, smelling the stench of piss and rat shit as it rose up the stair-well to fight it out with her perfume, The Thousand Flowers of Asia. Widow Ho had lost her appetite and she stared at old Amar's kebabs and couscous going cold on their plate. Widow Ho hated little Leila, who'd come back with her last piece of Turkish delight. Widow Ho knew that she was being unfair to the little girl, but her hatred helped her bear the pain in her shoulder. Widow Ho had had enough of being an old, lonely, widower and a failed copper. What particularly annoyed her was that this business of cross-dressing had been her own idea which she'd put up for her admired boss's approval. "As bait, Thian? That's not a bad idea," Chief Superintendent Coudrier had said. "I'll have a bank account opened for you at once, in the name of . . . ? of . . . ?" "Ho Chi Minh." Thian knew nothing about Vietnam, his Indochinese fatherland, and this was the first name that came into his head, along with General Giap. But widow Ho hadn't wanted to be widow Giap. Widow Ho had then buried herself at the top of her block and waited for someone to be kind enough to come along and slit her throat. Half the flats in the block were empty and derelict, and the killer hadn't come. Drugged up to the eyeballs with Palfium (and with a piece of chemical cotton holding a vague lump of lint over her pain), widow Ho's head was clearer than ever. She was disappointed with herself, had probably disappointed her boss and, worst of all, she'd failed to give a good example of efficiency to that young curly-headed inspector who shared her office during the hours of the night, when she became Inspector Van Thian once more. More than anything else, widow Ho would like to have won Pastor's respect because she liked his old-fashioned gentleness and admired his rectitude. She'd also failed to achieve that. And, that evening, she suddenly found herself alone with herself. Along with the memory of the person whom she'd betrayed. For the only thing widow Ho had recently managed to do was to betray a good man, a Serbo-Croat with a heart of gold, who had defended Belleville's old women with more self-denial than she had and, probably, with more efficiency. Widow Ho had let her friend and neighbour, widow Dolgorouki, get herself murdered. Widow Ho was nothing but a Judas in a Thai dress.

Widow Ho started to snooze. Soon, between the links of an agitated dream, which was being torn to shreds by the splinters of her pain, she glimpsed the image of her mother, whom the Serbo-Croat had resurrected, and of her father, tiny and smiling, floating on a honey-scented cloud. Then she saw a pallid face topped off by a central parting which led straight down to a dimple in a chubby chin. This face was giving evidence against her parents at their trial. It was the brightly polished face of the Permanent Secretary for War Veterans, a young fast-laner who knew what he was talking about when he said that this illegal opium den was an insult to the veterans of Indochina . . . he was called . . . what was he called? There was something like a chapel in his name, or a cap. He was now Permanent Secretary for Senior Citizens . . . Widow Ho's parents had been sent to prison and Inspector Van Thian had been incapable of getting them out of the mess they were in. The father, that old Tongkinese from Mong Cai, had withered away in his cell. When Thian had gone to embrace him for the last time in the prison infirmary, his body was so light that it was like a huge dead butterfly. And it was certainly true that, when he'd been alive, his hands had had the fluttering lightness of touch of a butterfly. Then the mother, widow Louise as she now was, had been released and packed off, with what was left of her brains, to repose for ever in a psychiatric hospital. She'd died there from an overdose of drugs that she'd managed to filch from the medicine cabinet, "but it's always kept padlocked, sir, as you can see for yourself." Thian had then sold off the wine business and, many years later, they'd built over it that golf course which had been left in the oven too long, that massive green boil hiding an all-round, epicyclic sports centre. Widow Ho went on weeping for the misfortunes of widower Thian, whose every secret she kept in her heart and who, apart from his parents, had also lost his wife, Janine the Giantess, whose hands had been skilled at making the tiniest part of him grow to a huge size. Janine was dead. How could that have happened to a Giantess? "You've still got Gervaise left." There had been an uncertain smile in Janine's last words. That was true, there was still Gervaise, the daughter whom the Giantess had mothered on earth. She wasn't Thian's, but may just as well have been. They'd given her a radical name, from a supposedly radical book. But that hadn't stopped Gervaise from finding Jesus. She had now smoothed out her curls behind a veil. A Little Sister of the Poor. How could anyone find Jesus in this world? The end result for Thian had been worse than his Giantess's terminal illness. No more Gervaise. Entirely devoted to the cause. Heroes don't have parents. Putting whores back on the straight and narrow in a home in Nanterre. Janine had been a whore, before Thian had fallen at her feet in admiration and chucked her whole family of Toulon pimps into prison. Brothers-in-law and cousins swearing in Corsican that they'd skin that little yellow cop alive. Not a bit of it: down they went. How did things stand now? Some of them were dead, others were still inside, Gervaise was with God and widow Ho was all on her own with that failure of a widower cop inside her, who was so lonely himself that he was incapable of keeping her company. Widow Ho surprised herself by starting to pray. She was all in. She murmured a prayer between her burning lips. My God, send me the old ladykiller and stop playing the fool. Send him to me and I promise to put that old cop Thian asleep inside me. I'll unplug him. I'll switch off his incredible reflexes. You don't believe me? Just a second, God, watch, I'm getting out his Manhurin from its hiding place and I'm unloading it. I'm throwing the magazine way over that way and the gun way over this way. Now, my God, I beg you, send round my liberator.

And so she murmured on, in a state of virtual levitation, for the first time in her long life. And since, as everyone knows, faith can move mountains, when she opened her eyes again, there he was standing in front of her, the killer of Belleville, pointing a Llama 27 at her, the same one he'd found in widow Dolgorouki's bag. He'd come in through the door, which widow Ho always left open ready for his visit, he'd watched her muttering gibberish for a while, patiently waiting for her to open her eyes again so that he could relish his triumph to the full. When she'd finally half opened her eyelids, which were red with fever, he said:

"Good evening, inspector."

Suddenly, Inspector Van Thian woke up. Sitting cross-legged behind the coffee table, his first instinct was to locate his Manhurin with his knee. No Manhurin. And there the awaited guest stood in front of him, training on him a Llama, complete with its silencer.

"Do please keep your hands on the table."

No fucking Manhurin. Thian suddenly had a vision of widow Ho, in her mystical carry-on, unloading the gun, throwing the magazine that way – yes, there it was, it had slid under the sideboard – and the gun the other way. Jesus fucking Christ, what a silly old bitch! Thian had never hated anyone as much as he hated widow Ho just then. He'd never have time to put his piece back together again before the guest pressed his trigger. That old fucking cow of a bitch of a widow! Fucked. He was fucked. It was only when he'd realized that fact that he bothered to see who the guest was. So it was him? It was unbeliev-able . . . He was standing there in front of Thian, straight-backed, ancient, with his luxurious halo of white hair surrounding his sainted head, like an image of God the Father Himself, who had been brought down by the prayers of that stupid old cunt widow Ho. But it wasn't God the Father, it was the most junked-out of his fallen angels, it was old Risson, the former bookseller who widow Ho had met round at Malaussène's place.

"I've come to get my book back, inspector."

Old Risson had a friendly smile on his face. The way he was holding the revolver, clamped tightly in the palm of his hand, showed that he was no stranger to pieces like that.

"Did you read it?"

He brandished the little pink book: Stefan Zweig's *The Royal Game*, which was lying at the foot of the bed, where Thian had dropped it without even opening it.

"You haven't read it, have you?"

The old man shook his head sadly.

"I have also come to take possession of the three or four thousand francs which you waggled under my nose the other day, while you were playing at being widow Ho round at the Malaussènes'."

His smile was truly charming.

"Did you know that you've been the favourite pastime of the youth of Belleville these last few weeks? An old bobby dragged up as a Vietnamese widow, all the youngsters wanted to see you, at least once, so that they could tell their grandchildren about it."

He went on talking, but the Llama 27 remained silent, aimed by a confident old hand.

"But the greatest moment was when you gunned down those two hit men this afternoon. When you did that, my dear inspector, you became a living legend."

He took the safety catch off with his thumb. Thian saw the cylinder rotate in its casing.

"And that is why you must die now, inspector. Those street arabs adore you the way they saw you this afternoon. If you were allowed to live any longer, you would only wind up disappointing them. You must now become a part of legend."

The bullets were perfectly visible in their cylinder, like a set of little penises in their sheathes. They reminded Thian of widow Ho's tube of lipstick.

"In fact, I'm doing you a favour. Because, between you and me, you're not much of a copper, are you?"

Thian thought that present circumstances quite justified this view of things.

"You really thought that Malaussène was capable of slitting old ladies' throats?"

Yes, he had really thought that.

"What an absurd mistake! Malaussène is a veritable saint, inspector. Perhaps the only one in this entire city. Shall I tell you his life story?"

He told it. He had the gun, so he had the time. He explained why Malaussène had been lodging them, he, old Risson, and three other old boys who'd been turned into drug-addicted wrecks so that they would vacate their flats. He explained how Malaussène and the children had taken care of them, had cured them, how that extraordinary family had given them back a taste for life, a reason to go on, how he himself, Risson, had felt resurrected by Thérèse, how he had found happiness in that house and how delighted he had been each evening by the children's joy when he narrated a novel to them.

"And that's another reason why I'm going to have to kill you, inspector."

I'm going to get myself blown away because this old loony narrates novels to kiddies? Thian didn't get it.

"Those novels are sleeping in my memory. You see, I was a bookseller all my life, I've read a lot, but my memory is not what it was. Those novels are sleeping and, each time, I have to wake them up. That's when I need a shot. That's how I use those ignorant old widows' money: to purchase the necessary for reawakening literature in my veins and thus to enlighten those children's minds. Do you understand the pleasure I have in doing that? Can you at least comprehend that?"

No, Thian couldn't understand why old women got their throats cut so that some kiddies could be told bedtime stories. But what he quite perfectly understood was that this man, with his white fleece, whose eyes were beginning to glisten and whose hands were beginning to shake, was the most dangerous loony he'd ever come across in all his long years on the force. "And if I don't come up with something sharpish, he's going to pop me out of my clogs, that much is crystal."

"This evening, for example," old Risson went on, "I'm going to give them Joyce. Do you know of James Joyce, inspector? No, never heard of him?"

The Manhurin's magazine was under the sideboard and the Manhurin itself was lying out of sight behind the bed . . .

"That's right, I'm going to give them Joyce! Dublin and Joyce's children!"

Risson's voice had gone up a semitone, he was now intoning like a preacher . . .

"They're going to meet Flynn, the priest that broke the chalice, they're going to play by the Vitriol Works with Mahony, I'm going to make them smell the heavy odour in the dead-room of the priest, they're going to discover Eveline and her fear of drowning in all the seas of the world, I'm going to give them Dublin in all its glory and, with me, they're going to hear Villona the Hungarian stand on the deck of the boat and exclaim: 'Daybreak, gentlemen!'"

Sweat glistened under his white hair. Clasping the stock of his gun, his hands were shaking more and more.

"But to bring all that back to life with the full force of its existence I need the Enlightenment which your money, inspector, will set coursing in my veins!"

Thian didn't hear the 'pop', but he felt the force that threw him back against the wall. He was aware of his head bouncing back and realized that he was on his feet again and rushing forwards with the ridiculous idea of disarming the old loon. A second shock wave hit him and he was back against the wall, his already wounded shoulder screamed out and then the darkness came . . . With just one lingering image: a baby babbling in the arms of an ageless Vietnamese woman.

Chapter 32

As soon as he'd seen the tall white-haired man go upstairs, little Nourdine came out of his hiding place. He burst out of the stairwell and started running, running a hundred times faster than he did even when playing kiss-chase with Leila and her mates. He stopped at Koutoubia, at Chez Loula, at the Lumières de Belleville, at Chez Saf-Saf, at Goulette and everywhere he asked for Berber Sim. Have you seen Berber Sim? I have to find Simon the Berber.

He ran through the sizzling of merguez sausages, he crossed fields of fresh mint, he ran on without even thinking of stealing dates from the shop displays, he played a couple of rounds of Where's the Lady? down corridors where the Blacks faded into the gloom, and it was in this darkness that he ran into Black Mo's stomach muscles.

"And what you want Sim for?"

"He didn't believe me," little Nourdine yelled. "He didn't believe me when I told him that the Razor was an old boy. He didn't believe me, but now he can see for himself. It's the same oldster, with his white hair, and he's just gone up to widow Ho's place."

"Who, the drag queen?"

"Yeah, the copper who's doing the pantomime dame. The old killer's just gone up there. He's the Razor, go and see for yourself, it's him! It's the same one who went up to widow Dolgorouki's."

Black Mo turned back into the darkness:

"Mahmoud, take my place for a bit. I'll be straight back."

Then he took the kid by his elbow.

"Let's go, Nourdine. We'll fetch Sim and if you're telling us porkies then you'll be frying your bangers on your arse by the time we've

196

finished with you."

"Leave my arse out of it! I've been hiding there in that staircase for the last two weeks waiting to cop him! The Razor's that oldster! I'm telling you, it's him!"

They ran into the old man with his fleecy white hair just when he was coming out of the building. His eyes were lit-up, his skin was on fire and his face a mirror of sweat. There was no doubt about it. The old boy was hurting. While Black Mo leapt upstairs to check widow Ho's blood pressure, Simon relieved the old boy of his Llama 27 and dragged him down into the cellar. Nourdine went back on guard duty under the stair-well.

The old boy's first thought was that he was being hustled by a couple of dealers. He showed them his money and held out his other hand. The exchange normally took only a couple of seconds. This time, it took much longer. Almost politely, Simon the Berber pushed back the money. The cellar stank of ancient piss and mouldy leather. A beaten-up old chair stretched its arms into the night. Simon sat the old man down in it.

"You want to score, my old lad? Don't worry. That's just what you're going to do."

From his jacket, he produced a syringe as long as a nightmare, a couscous spoon and a small packet of white powder.

"And this one's on me."

A shadow fell across the middle of the cellar. It was Mo who'd come back down from upstairs.

"He's whacked the drag queen."

The Berber bit open the packet and emptied it. He was shaking his head.

"When a copper buys it in Belleville, my old lad, then our youngsters are in for a beating. Why do that to us?"

The answer swam up to the two young men, who were as flabbergasted as if the armchair had started talking all on its own.

"To save Literature!"

The Berber didn't bat an eyelid. A long rivulet of saliva ran from his grinning incisors to the little mound of white powder which rose up from the bottom of the spoon. The powder had started to spit like a wild cat.

"And all the old dears you cut up, that was to save literature and all, was it?"

From Père Lachaise to the Goutte d'Or, Black Mo thought he'd heard it all.

"For all the world's literature, for yours, just as much as mine!"

The old boy was doing his pieces, but he didn't try to escape. He frantically hiked up his sleeve. His voice had shot up a register, too, but he stayed sitting there like a good boy in his armchair, with his pallid arm shining in the darkness.

"Those ignorant old bags' money has saved masterpieces from oblivion, they now live on in those children's hearts. Thanks to me! Baron Corvo . . . Have you heard of Baron Corvo?"

"Don't know no Barons," Black Mo admitted honestly.

Simon had sunk the needle into the molten white volcano. He didn't need daylight to work with precision.

"And have you at least heard of Imru al Qays, the prince of the Tribe of Kinda, young man? That one's part of your culture. Part of your most ancient culture, from before the time of Islam!"

"Don't know any Princes either," Black Mo confessed.

But the old boy had suddenly started to intone:

"*Qifa, nabki min dikra habibin wa manzili . . .*"

Simon translated for Mo, while gently pushing back the valve of the syringe. He was smiling.

"*Stop and weep for the memory of a lover and of a dwelling-place . . .*"

"Yes!" the old man yelled with an excited laugh. "That's one possible translation. So, tell me, do you know Mutanabbi's poetry? His dithyramb for the mother of Saif al Dawla, do you know that one?"

"Yes, I do," said Simon, leaning over the old man. "But, please, do let me hear it again."

He'd just strapped up the old boy's biceps with a length of inner tubing. He felt the veins pop up under his fingers. His voice was soft and gentle.

"*Nwidu l-mashrafiatawa l-awali . . .*" the old boy recited.

While translating, Simon stuck in the needle:

"*We are preparing our broad-swords and our lances . . .*"

198

Then, while emptying the syringe, he recited the next line:

"*Wa taqtuluna l-manunubilla qitali.*"

The mixture of saliva and white powder leapt into the vein. When it reached the old man's heart, he sprang out of the chair and jerked up into the air. He landed at the two lads' feet, his bones broken, crumpled in a heap like a dead spider.

"Which means?" Mo asked.

"*And then Death slaughters us without a fight,*" the Berber recited.

Lying on his camp-bed and staring at the ceiling, Pastor had let the night settle in his office. I'll sell Boulevard Maillot, he decided. He said Boulevard Maillot, like he was playing Monopoly, but what he meant was Gabrielle and the Councillor's house. Anyway, I don't dare set foot in the place. I'll sell Boulevard Maillot and buy myself a little pad on Rue Guynemer, just by the Luxembourg gardens, or in the new buildings near Canal Saint-Martin . . .

He wouldn't even have to go back to the house, he'd do it all through an agency. Don't load yourself down with the sentimental side to your inheritance, Jean-Baptiste. Sell things off, wipe the slate clean and start all over again . . . Pastor was going to fulfil one of the Councillor's last wishes. As restarts go, this is going to be one hell of a restart! And find yourself a Gabrielle. That, Councillor, is quite a different ball game.

Pastor wondered for a moment if he'd really enjoyed his victory over Cercaria. No, he hadn't. What pleasure was there in that? Then the Councillor came into his thoughts once again. The Councillor was sitting in a diagonal shaft of light in the library. He was knitting Pastor's last pullover. While counting the stitches, he was making pronouncements: "It's in the very nature of my Health Service for it to lose money, Jean-Baptiste. But a group of so-and-sos seems to be pushing its nature a little too far." "And how are they managing to do that?" Pastor had asked. "There is any number of ways to do that, my boy. By unnecessarily putting people, and especially old people, away in homes for example. Do you have any idea how much locking someone up in a lunatic asylum costs the taxpayer?" "But, Councillor, how do they go about sending away perfectly sane old people to finish their lives in asylums?" "By tormenting them, by turning them into alcoholics, by giving them too many pills to take, by drugging them, those swine aren't short of ideas, you know . . ." Then, this observation: "A study should be made of the matter." The stitches had been counted and the two long needles had returned to their calm doggedness. "I raised this issue a few months ago at the Inspection Committee and, if Gabrielle and I hadn't decided to commit suicide, I would have liked to have seen it through to its conclusion." Gabrielle had just walked into the library. "In fact, I'm saving him from quite a chore," she said. She hadn't yet been outwardly marked by her illness. But a cigarette no longer dangled from between her lips. "All the same, I have made a few notes," the Councillor went on. "You'll find them in my desk." Then: "Give me your arm, please." Pastor had done as he was asked and the Councillor had covered it with the sleeve of a pullover which still needed a few more rows of stitches. "To be perfectly frank with you, Jean-Baptiste, that young Capelier fellow – you know, the son of my friend Le Capelier, the sub-prefect – well, there's something not quite *clear cut* about him, as Gabrielle would put it." Pastor and the Councillor had then laughed at their recollections of Arnaud Le Capelier, with his dimple, his straight nose, his central parting, his Lord-High-Something stiffness and his profound respect for the Councillor. "He's a top-level dunce," the Councillor had said. "In the fast lane, but at the bottom of his class. As such, the first job they gave him was to look after the war veterans, where he contracted an incurable disease: the hatred of old people. And now his political pals have had him made Permanent Secretary for Senior Citizens . . ." The Councillor gave a long shake of his bald head. "No, if anyone's going to speak up against old people being put away in homes like that, then it certainly isn't going to be our little Capelier."

While the Councillor was speaking, Gabrielle had armed herself with a thin piece of shammy and had started polishing her husband's head. "It must be nice and gleaming; it, at least, is going to be absolutely *clear cut*." His skull was pointed. It started to shine in the light of the setting sun like a saltlick after the attentions of a herd of goats. "Setting up structures is one thing," the Councillor said. "But no matter how solid they are, they still require trust. And when it comes to money, whom can you trust?"

"No-one, Councillor, no-one . . ." Pastor murmured in the darkness of his office. He was now sitting doubled up on the end of his camp-bed. His chin was resting on his knees. Above them, he'd pulled the Councillor's last pullover down as far as his ankles, its stitching stretched out, like he was a young girl in a day-dream, or a scrawny child.

As often happened when Pastor was having a posthumous conversation with the Councillor, his office telephone rang:

"Pastor? It's Cercaria. Someone's whacked Van Thian. The anonymous caller who just tipped me off says we'll find our ladykiller down in the cellar of the same building. He's bought it as well."

Inspector Van Thian wasn't dead. In his bloodied widow's weeds, Inspector Van Thian was as good as dead, but he was still breathing. He was babbling strangely. It sounded like an ancient nanny playing with a baby. When he was being put into the brightly shining innards of the ambulance, Inspector Van Thian recognized Inspector Pastor and asked him a question of medical import:

"Tell me, kiddo, do you know what *saturnism* is? What sort of illness is *saturnism* exactly?"

"Exactly what you've got," Pastor answered. "Lead poisoning."

But the old ladykiller was definitely dead. They found him in a cellar which reeked of fermented urine. Quite unexpectedly, he wasn't young, but an old man with a fleece of white hair. His face had gone horribly blotchy. He lay hunched up, as though a spasm had shrivelled his whole body. They found nearly three thousand francs in his pocket, a Llama 27 and one of those old-fashioned razors which barbers used to use when they shaved their customers. It gave a perfect finish, you sharpened it on a leather strop and it was called a cut-throat. As to determining how the killer had died, Cercaria came up with the following diagnosis:

"A good shot of Vim. Where's the needle?"

A big copper, answering to the name of Bertholet, said: "There it is, it's over there," and then his voice became strangled with uncontrollable terror. Everybody turned round to look where the big copper was pointing and they all thought that they were suffering from a mass hallucination. A large broken glass syringe, of the sort that was once used to take massive blood samples, had been thrown onto the ground. And it was *moving*. It was moving all on its own. It suddenly stood up, swivelled round and shot off, needle first, towards the coppers. Everyone legged it out the door with the exception of young Pastor and big Cercaria, who trod his heel down onto that knight-at-arms rising up from a nightmare to fight his last tournament. Attracted by the blood, a small grey mouse had quite simply crept into the syringe. Driven crazy by the Vim, it had then started dashing around on its hind legs.

Chapter 33

A ND THE GREAT day arrived. I mean that famous Wednesday round at Ponthard-Delmaire's place, the day I met two police men who wanted to fit me up. We'd obviously been converging for some time and a collision had become inevitable. We were made for each other, as they say. And, from this enriching experience, I've formed one of my few convictions: *it's better not to be made for things like that.*

I'd spent the night with Julia. I'd slid into bed beside her with a simple plan of action in mind: resurrecting her. The bastards who had got hold of her had burned her with cigarettes. The marks were still visible. She looked like a huge sleeping leopard. She's fine as a leopard, so long as she's still my Julia. They hadn't managed to change the scent of her skin or the warmth of her body. They must have given her face a good beating, but my Corrençon has a solid, mountain-woman's skull and, if her cheeks were still bruised, the bones hadn't cracked under the blows and the beautiful cliff of her forehead was still intact. They hadn't knocked out any of her teeth. Her lips had been split open, but they had now healed up and, in her sleep, they were now giving me a fleshy smile (in Spanish slang *comer* means 'to love'). They'd broken one of her legs, which had been turned into a plaster statue up to her hip, and her other ankle was surrounded by a bracelet of scars, as though she'd been put in irons. But her smile was still mockingly sure of itself. She'd won, they hadn't got anything out of her. (I'd stake my life on that!) She must have finished her article and stashed it somewhere. That was what the demolition men had been looking for in her flat. But her smile was telling those little bastards that she wasn't some daft hackette who left rough drafts about such a filthy business lying round the place. So where are they? Where did you hide your papers, Julia? In fact, I wasn't in that much of a hurry to find out. The truth would lead to a trial, a trial would lead to the amassing of evidence, amassing evidence would lead to a regiment of boys in blue, solicitors and barristers turning my granddads onto their heads and making them cough up what the kids and I had spent so long getting them to forget. But, on the other hand, the longer this business went on, the more those shit-heads were going to junk-out other granddads and neither my flat nor my vocation is large enough to take in every smack-head in town. One ancestor per offspring that mum downloads on us seems to me to be the perfect proportion.

So I was lying next to Julia, hesitating between these contradictory positions, when I decided to chase them away by making the simple resolution to bring Julia back to the land of the living. And I knew, knowing her like I do, that there was only one way to achieve this. The Prince Charming act. All right, all right, I know this does sound like I was taking unfair advantage of the situation, but Julia and I love taking unfair advantage of each other, though without being unfair to ourselves. If she'd been in my shoes, with me laid out like a dummy in a coma for the last fortnight, she would have taken the appropriate steps (as officialdom puts it) ages ago to give me back, if nothing else, the awareness of her wonderful body. Oh yes, I know what she's like. So I decided to make love to her as she slept, since, when she's awake, she's so lovable. Her breasts recognized me first. Then the rest of her followed (in that slow but sure opening out to pleasure that she practices to perfection) and when I realized that the way home was open to me, well, in I went.

We played, then snoozed together until this morning, when there was a frantic banging on my door and Jeremy's voice started yelling:

"Ben! Ben! Mum's woken up!"

That's the story of my life, that is. I kiss my Sleeping Beauty and it's my mother who wakes up . . . For Julia is still asleep by my side, no doubt about it. Oh, I could of course point to her internal awakening, but her beautiful face remains shut off, with the same wicked grin on her lips which I so thoroughly analyzed last night.

"And there's something else as well, Ben!"

"What's that?"

"Old Risson didn't come home last night."

(Shit. I don't like the sound of that.)

"What do you mean, didn't come home?"

"What I said, he hasn't come home. His bed's still made and every-thing, plus we didn't get our story last night."

My arse rolls out of bed and tumbles into its trousers. My feet go inching out after their shoes and my arms wriggle into their sleeves. There we are, only half-awake and already *thinking*. Risson didn't come home. It's the first time one of the granddads has slept out since we started putting them up. While they used to spend their nights trying to score and their days on a high, not one of them's ever run away from home before. Not one. But now Risson has. What to do? Wait for him, or go out looking for him? And how to set about finding him? We obviously can't report him missing to the police. Shit, Risson, shit. What's got into you?

"Hey, Ben, you gone back to sleep or what?"

The banging on my door gets louder. Though I didn't manage to wake her up, Jeremy is soon going to.

"I'm getting dressed, Jeremy, I'm getting dressed and I'm thinking. Go and get Verdun's bottle ready, then ask Sweeney to come and give me a shave."

The task of the Police Force Clinic on Boulevard Saint-Marcel, with its grimy exterior but brightly lit interior, is to put coppers back on their feet after they've been shot, knifed, burnt in fires, injured in car accidents or, in general terms, been victims of leading a copper's life, nervous breakdowns included. Within the walls of the Police Force Clinic, lay an old depressive sieve, Inspector Van Thian, and Pastor felt unsure whether he was fighting for his life or struggling to expel the little bit of life he had left and which still kept him lying on that bed.

"Can I do anything for you, Thian?"

With all those tubes rammed into his body, Thian looked like a Saint Sebastian who'd spent the whole of his long life tied to his tree. All that Pastor could see in Thian's eyes was the satisfaction of having finally reached the end of the line. He got to his feet and, when he reached the door, was astonished to hear the old inspector's voice once more:

"Kiddo?"

"Thian?"

"There is something, yes. I'd like to see that girl again, Thérèse Malaussène."

Thian's voice had become a whistle. Pastor nodded, closed the door behind him, went down a corridor of ether, then out onto the steps, at the bottom of which Chief Superintendent Cercaria was waiting for him in his personal Jag.

"So?"

"It's not looking good," said Pastor.

The collector's piece swished off and glided down the boulevard towards the Bastille. It was only when it had crossed Pont d'Austerlitz that Pastor decided to break the silence of its engine.

"I've got another little something for you," he said.

Cercaria glanced rapidly round at him. Since yesterday, he'd learnt not to try and second guess his new partner's surprises. Pastor laughed for a second, then fell silent.

Cercaria was now waiting at the red light which seals off the top of Rue de la Roquette.

"Our old ladykiller lived in Malaussène's house," Pastor declared.

The light went green, but Cercaria didn't pull away. The surprise had stalled his normally unflappable motor. Horns began to blare out behind him. Under his neighbour's amused stare, Cercaria started to wrench at his starter.

"I see that you grasp just how advantageous this can be for us," said Pastor.

The Jag leapt forwards, leaving the horns standing.

"Christ on a bike," said Cercaria. "You're sure about that?"

He realized that, faced with a bloke like Pastor, he was now going to spend his life asking pointless questions.

"Thian just told me. Malaussène used to put the killer up, along with three other old junkies."

Pastor was smiling. Cercaria couldn't get over the fact that he'd once thought this smile was angelic. His mind was divided between dumb admiration, he, the Great Cercaria, like he was sitting at some Grand Guru's feet, and utter hatred, bred on fear. There was something decidedly dangerous about going into partnership with a box of brains like that . . . On Place Voltaire, Pastor started chuckling again.

"Just fancy that! La Corrençon and the old junkies are all there under the same roof. It's as if this Malaussène character was working for us!"

He paused:

"And doing a far better job of it than you, eh, Cercaria?"

(I'll kill you one of these days, you little fucker. You're bound to wind up making a false move sooner or later. And then you're a dead man.) The violence of Cercaria's thoughts took his breath away, then it dissolved into a delicious feeling of relief. Cercaria smiled at Pastor.

"How's your hand?"

"A little painful."

They were shooting along towards Père Lachaise cemetery's gates. The Jag screeched round the very corner where, a few weeks before, Julie Corrençon's coat had fluttered away in the breeze. An ancient crone at a window was tapping her index finger against the side of her head, which was bedecked with rollers. Perhaps the same one that Thian grilled, Pastor thought to himself.

"By the way, just how much does Thian know about all this?" Cercaria suddenly asked.

"Bits and pieces, the odd scrap of information," Pastor answered.

Then he added:

"Anyway, he won't last through the night."

(You really are as cold as a razor blade, Cercaria thought to himself. I'm going to enjoy killing you, sonny jim, when the time's ripe. And no messing.)

From Place Gambetta, the Jag turned into Rue des Pyrénées, which it stormed up before taking a sharp right into Rue de la Mare and gliding into an empty parking space, just in front of the architect Ponthard-Delmaire's house.

* * *

We had to find Risson. At midday, I sent the family out to lunch, this way and that, some to Chez Saf-Saf, others to the Lumières de Belleville and me to Chez Amar. Our mission: not to ask any questions, but to listen to Belleville. Why Belleville, for that matter? Why should such a distinguished personage as Risson run away from home to hang out in my patch? Because you're supposed to be able to score there? I could hardly imagine old Risson going round the local dealers to pick up his stuff. And yet, and yet, I can't get that idea out of my mind. Sussing out why an old smack-head does a runner isn't exactly complicated. Unless, for old times' sake, Risson got himself locked up for the night in some big bookshop, the Terrasse de Gutenberg for instance, and spent it worming his way through the shelves. He's got to top himself up sooner or later, hasn't he? His knowledge of novels isn't a bottomless pit. Maybe he's sniffing out that new one everybody's talking about, Süskind's *Perfume*, so he can tell it to the kids this evening. Stop bullshitting, Ben, just stop it. What if old Risson's found himself a girlfriend? That Vietnamese lullaby-lady for instance? I couldn't help noticing that he fancied her. Risson and the Vietnamese lady . . . Benjamin, I told you to stop bullshitting, so can it, will you? All right, so I obeyed myself, I stopped and starting listening. And I heard that the old Vietnamese woman had got herself topped last night. That shook me up a bit. But my grief was purely selfish, as my first thought was to wonder where else we were going to find someone who could make Verdun shut up. And then I learnt that the Vietnamese woman was a Vietnamese man (nothing very surprising about that in Belleville) and that this Vietnamese person was not only a man, but also a copper, and that he'd blown away two authentic hit men a few hours before, even though they'd fired first. Apparently, he'd even got one of them in full flight. It was Jeremy who picked up all the details. After he'd got hit in the shoulder, this Viet cop had chucked his shooter from his right to his left hand then peppered the hit man while he was winging it away like a clay pigeon. Jeremy was speechless with admiration! And to think that, only a few days ago, our marksman was twittering away with Verdun in his arms and getting his future sorted by Thérèse . . . Then a funny idea crossed my mind. What if Risson had really taken a fancy to what was in his mind a genuine South-East Asian Babe, that he'd turned up round at her place, all of a quiver, only to discover that his true love had falsies? Old Risson was enough of a romantic to murder someone for that. (Shut it, Benjamin, once and for all, just shut it!) So, all in all, nothing at all. No news of Risson. We went back home with our heads drooping. Verdun was asleep. So was Julia. But the phone wasn't.

"Is that you, Malaussène? You haven't forgotten about your little appointment, now, have you?"

"Permission to insult you, your Highness."

"If it's to get you in the right frame of mind, fill your boots."

She's like that, is Queen Zabo. All I said was:

"No, I haven't forgotten about your darling Ponthard-Delmaire. I'm going straight round there."

"You killed my daughter."

Pastor was bearing the weight of a stare he knew only too well. This fat old Ponthard-Delmaire, who made houses spring up across the face of the planet, was not just an architect. Nor was he a bereaved father – he wasn't even trying to look like one. That fat man sitting behind his huge oak desk, which, for some obscure reason, he'd had made into the enveloping shape of a womb, was a killer.

"You killed her," Ponthard-Delmaire repeated.

"Maybe I did. But you missed me."

This conversation was certainly 'clear cut' (for a second, Pastor glimpsed Gabrielle's curly head). The opening exchange of words left Cercaria speechless.

"I won't miss you next time."

The fat man's voice remained neutral. Then he added, with a hint of a grin:

"And I have the means to make sure that there'll be plenty of 'next times'."

Pastor looked wearily round at Cercaria.

"Cercaria, would you be so good as to explain to this grief-stricken father that he no longer has the means to do anything whatsoever."

Cercaria nodded briefly.

"He's right, Ponthard, this innocent-looking lad here has got us by the short and curlies. You'd better get that straight into your bonce and save us all a lot of time."

The stare aimed at Pastor became tinged with curiosity and disbelief.

"Oh, he has, has he? Well, he certainly can't have learnt much from grilling Edith. She didn't even know I was part of the set-up."

"That's right," said Pastor. "And she had quite a nasty turn when she found out . . ."

The fat trembled. Blink and you'd miss it. But there had definitely been a wobble.

"In her way, your daughter was an idealist, Monsieur Ponthard-Delmaire. By selling drugs to old people, she thought she was rebelling in a big way against her father's image, as they put it nowadays. So when I told her that she was working for you . . ."

"Jesus Christ."

This time he'd gone white. Pastor drove home the dagger.

"That's right, Ponthard, you killed your daughter. I was only the messenger boy."

A pause.

"So, now we've got that one sorted out, we'll get down to the serious business, shall we?"

The house was wooden. There was nothing to be seen in the entire place that wasn't made of wood. All the scents, all the shades, all the warmth of wood in a city of stone. One of those abstract ideas architects have which, when made concrete, produce abstract houses.

"Pastor has a proposition to make us," Cercaria explained. "And I think we're in no position to refuse."

At that moment there were two discreet knocks at the office door, which opened to reveal the old flunkey in his bumble-bee waistcoat. He, too, was wood-coloured.

"A certain Monsieur Malaussène is here, sir. He says he has an appointment with you, sir."

"Tell him to go and fuck himself."

"No!" Pastor blurted out. Then (overcoming his astonishment) he added: "Tell him to wait."

And, with a broad smile at the flunkey:

"As a matter of fact, why don't you take the afternoon off? It'd do you the world of good. Don't you think so, Ponthard?"

The servant looked quizzically at his master. The master gave a rapid nod of agreement and a wave of his hand to send the bumble bee off to sup Parisian nectar.

"We'll be in need of this Malaussène later," Pastor explained briefly. "Now, as I don't like having to repeat myself, you're going to listen to this."

He produced a tiny box from the folds of his pullover and placed it on the desk. The minuscule tape-recorder faithfully played back yesterday's Pastor-Cercaria conversation for Ponthard-Delmaire's benefit.

Chapter 34

MEANWHILE, BEING THE silly sod that I am, instead of taking to my heels, grabbing my family then legging it straight off to the furthest outback of Australia, I just stand there twiddling my thumbs in the next room. What's more, I'm even burning with impatience. With Risson out to lunch somewhere, Julia out of it altogether and Verdun out to start her next assault, my time would be better spent at home. Apart from all that, I've had it up to here with important fat fuckers who make you wait so that you can work out just how fat and important they are. In any case, I'm here for a bollocking, aren't I? So the sooner we get it over with the better. It's like waiting for a jab, the longer the wait, the more it hurts. A bit of advice for all wannabe scapegoats: the good goat gallops *straight into* any bollocking, starts berating himself even before anyone's accused him of anything. This is the basic principle. Always get there before the firing squad, then lay on the eyewash in buckets so it rusts up their rifles. (You need to be gifted to do that. And I am.)

So, instead of heading for the hills, I get to my feet and, with my back suitably bent, my jowls slightly adroop, my eyes aslant, my lower lip limp and my fingers at sixes and sevens, I sidle towards Ponthard-Delmaire's office with a view to owning up to the fact that his wonderful masterwork will not be coming out on the date we'd agreed on, that it's my fault, all my very own fault, that no-one will ever forgive me, but then I am still my family's breadwinner and, if he kicks up a stink, then I'll be out on my ear and my loved ones out on the street . . . and if, instead of calming down, he rather likes this idea, then I'll professionally turn the tables on him by yelling: "Yes, yes, push me over the edge, that's right! I'm useless, always have been, hit me, hit me where it hurts, that's it, right here in the balls, yes, yes, do it again!" Generally speaking, when the first approach doesn't work, then the second one gets you out of your enemy's clutches, because he doesn't like to think you're enjoying him laying into you. Either way, the final result is something like pity: the charitable variety – "My goodness, how miserable that poor soul is, and how trivial my own problems are compared with his"; or the clinical variety – "What have I done to deserve a masochist like this? I'll say and do anything just to get him out of my hair. He's far too depressing." And if, one way or the other, I manage to convince our mountainous Ponthard that the Vendetta Press is still best placed to rush his book into print, since we all know it off by heart (loving it as we do), if I finally manage to do that, then I'll have won the day. Strictly speaking, Queen Zabo was right. Things aren't looking that bad after all.

That's exactly what I'm saying to myself as I grab hold of the handle of the door, which is just ajar: *things aren't looking that bad after all!* And, as I brace myself to shove this frigging door wide open, a highly dissuasive interrogation glues me to the spot:

"And these old smack-heads are round at Malaussène's place?"

"Two of them are already dead," a voice I vaguely recognize answers. "Which means there are two of them left."

"One of the two dead ones was the Belleville ladykiller. A certain Risson. He killed them in order to buy himself smack."

(What? My Risson? Jesus fucking Christ, whatever will the kids say when they hear that?)

"Well blow me. I've been looking for them everywhere!"

This voice belongs to the architect. It goes on:

"I knew that journalist woman had got hold of them, but we couldn't make her tell us where she was hiding them!"

Then a third voice that I don't know:

"And you had her kidnapped to ask her that?"

"Yes, and even though my boys were specialists, they just couldn't make her crack. She was some tough cookie."

"Your boys were useless idiots. They failed to kill the girl, they missed me and the way they searched her flat made it obvious that they were in the building trade. That was a serious mistake, Ponthard."

What a funny piece of work is Man. Even then, there was still time for me to scarper thanking my Lucky All-Stars. But one of the many things that makes mankind different from the beasts of the field is that we always want more. And even when we have the right quantity, we start worrying about the quality. Good old facts aren't enough for us, we also want the 'whys', the 'wherefores' and the 'how fars'. So, with the shit about to hit my pants, I push the door slightly more open so I can get a good look at the scene. There are three characters sitting there. Two of them I know: Cercaria the big leathery copper, with his sabre-scabbard moustache, and fat old Ponthard-Delmaire behind his baked-bean-shaped desk. But I don't know the third one: a young lad, in a baggy woollen sweater, who looks like a bit of a sixties' leftover, and a wreck of a one with it, from what I can see of his ruined face. (I can only see him in profile, and his right eye has sunk so deeply into its death-like socket that I can't even see what colour it is.)

"Look, Pastor," Ponthard-Delmaire suddenly says. (Pastor? Pastor? Pastor the copper? The one Marty phoned up?) "You have us, as Cercaria put it, by the short and curlies. There's no arguing about that. We have no choice but to do business with you, but that doesn't mean you can come round here telling me how to do my job."

Leather-tache then tries to make the peace:

"Ponthard . . ."

The fat man cuts him off dead:

"Shut it! Our business has been working very nicely all across the country for years now, Pastor. If you hadn't just stumbled across that woman's body in the barge, then you'd still be none the wiser, no matter how much of a smartarse you are. So tone it down a bit, will you? Don't forget you're just starting out in your new career and you've still got plenty of things to learn. You want 3% and you'll get 3%. That's a fair cut for a new partner of your standing, but don't push your luck too far, my son, if you want to be still around tomorrow."

"I don't want 3% anymore."

It's hard to describe how much these simple words flabbergasted the other two. The big leather copper is the first one to react, with this exclamation among exclamations:

"What? You want more?!"

"In a way I do, yes," the old woolly replies in his drained voice.

While the tiny tape-recorder was crisply playing back its cassette of truth and lies, another scene was being acted out before Pastor's eyes. God, how many more times am I going to have to live through this? A flat that had been ripped to pieces with the same methodical brutality as had been used on the journalist Julie Corrençon's. A library full of first editions which had been scattered, spread-eagled across the floor. The same professional way in which every hollow in the place had been sounded out . . . a machine-like pigheadedness. But it must have been wild beasts that had savaged the bodies of Gabrielle and the Councillor. Pastor had stood there in front of their bedroom door for more than an hour. They had been so cruelly tortured that death had brought no relief to their motionless bodies. They were lying there, petrified with pain and fear. Pastor hadn't even recognized them to begin with. They'll be unrecognizable for ever now. He'd stayed standing there in a vain attempt to bring his memories back together again, but they had been dead for three days and nothing he could do would lessen the horror. They wanted to commit suicide, Pastor kept on repeating. Gabrielle was ill, she was going to die, they wanted to commit suicide together and someone did *that* to them. Other words followed on: They've taken their lives, they've robbed them of their death and they've killed their love. Pastor was young at the time. He still thought that words could lessen the weight of what cannot be named. Standing there in that doorway, he drunk himself stupid on words, on rhythms, like a teenager after a first failed love affair. One of these ineffectual sentences became stuck in his mind: THEY'VE MURDERED LOVE. It was a strange sentence, coming from some outdated romantic era or from a heart-shaped book. THEY'VE MURDERED LOVE. But it sank into his flesh like a thorn. It woke him up at night, when he screamed it out on the camp-bed in his office: THEY'VE MURDERED LOVE! He'd then see the corpses of Gabrielle and the Councillor as though he was still standing at their bedroom door. He *saw* their bodies, which he no longer recognized, and he had to fight back the idea that love cannot resist everything, that their love had not been able to resist *that*. THEY'VE MURDERED LOVE! He'd get up, sit at his desk, look through a report or go out into the night. The night air by the river sometimes chased the sentence away. But on other occasions the two tortured bodies walked along side him, then he stopped walking and started to run.

Pastor's colleagues had dealt with the case. Since Gabrielle's jewels had gone, along with all the cash the Councillor used to keep in his wall safe, Pastor had rapidly agreed to the idea that it had been a burglary. Yes, of course, a burglary. The two old people had only been tortured to make them talk. But Pastor knew that they had been eliminated. And he knew why. And, one day, he'd know who. The notes the Councillor had taken concerning people being unnecessarily sent to homes had also disappeared. They were technical notes, incomprehensible to anyone but a specialist. Pastor had kept that point to himself. It was his secret garden. A garden that was being swamped over by one massive thorn bush: THEY'VE MURDERED LOVE! One day he'd tear those thorns up by the roots. He'd find the people who had done *that*.

That day had finally arrived.

"What the fuck, Pastor? 3%'s not good enough for you now?"

"No. I don't want 3% anymore and I'm not going to hand Malaussène over to you."

The aforementioned Malaussène (me), who's crouching behind the half-open door, feels greatly relieved.

"What the hell are you on about, Pastor? So what *do* you want, then?"

A worried tone has crept into Cercaria's voice.

And rightly so. Pastor gets out a small packet of typed pages, which he puts on the desk.

"I want you to sign these confessions. In them, you admit your guilt of, or your involvement in, a variety of crimes including drug-dealing, murder aggravated by torture, attempted murder, corruption and so on and so forth. What I want are your two signatures on each of the five copies. That's all."

(I'm a chatty bloke, but I like talking about silence. When the Silence of Silences suddenly falls when you're least expecting it, it's like Mankind is being rethought from top to bottom. It's really something.)

"Oh yes?" Cercaria says at last, *mezza voce*, so as not to chase away all that silence. "You just want us to sign that? And what are you going to do to make us sign?"

"I have a method."

Pastor wearily trots the sentence out, like he's said it a hundred times before.

"That's right!" Cercaria exclaims. "Your famous method! Come on then, lad, show us what your method is and then, if we like it, we'll sign. Cross my heart we will, ain't that right, Ponthard?"

"Cross my heart," says Ponthard settling himself confidently back into his chair.

"All right," says Pastor. "Whenever I'm up against hard-line bastards like you, I work myself up into the state I'm now in and tell them: 'I've got cancer. I've only got three months at the most to live, so I don't have any future either in the force or out of it. The problem then becomes perfectly simple: either you sign, or I kill you.'"

Silence again.

"And it works, does it?" Ponthard asks at last, glancing across knowingly at Cercaria.

"It worked very well with your daughter, Ponthard."

(Some silences wash whiter than white. Ponthard-Delmaire's face has just been through a machine with that bleach.)

"Well, it ain't going to work with me," declares Cercaria with a broad grin.

A bit too broad. Pastor has just produced a gun from God knows where and shoved it into the grin. There was a strange sound as it went inside. It must have broken a couple of teeth on the way. Cercaria's head is now nailed to the back of his chair. From within.

"Let's try again," says Pastor calmly. "Listen to me carefully, Cercaria. Look at my face. I've got cancer, I've only got three months at the most to live, so I don't have any future either in the force or out of it. The problem then becomes perfectly simple: either you sign, or I kill you."

(In my opinion, this guy's really got cancer. Just look at the state of him.) Apparently, Cercaria doesn't share my medical opinion. After a moment's hesitation, his answer comes in the shape of a raised middle finger, which he brandishes under Pastor's nose. So Pastor presses the trigger and the Chief Superintendent's head explodes. Another bloke who's been turned into a flower. There's no big bang, just a red carpet rolled out over every available surface. All that's left on Cercaria's shoulders is his lower jaw which, as far as I can see, is looking slightly surprised at having escaped the slaughter.

When Pastor gets up and drops his blood-stained gun on Ponthard-Delmaire's desk, he looks more dead than alive. No exaggeration. But Ponthard is still definitely alive and kicking. With all the vivacity that his huge bulk allows him, he grabs hold of the gun and starts emptying the magazine at Pastor. The only thing is, that emptying an already empty magazine never did anyone much harm. Pastor then opens Cercaria's jacket, takes the service revolver out of his holster – a beautiful Chief-Superintendent special, all covered in chrome and mother-of-pearl and what have you – and points it at the architect's ample frame.

"Thank you, Ponthard. I needed your fingerprints on the P.38."

"You've left yours too," the fat man stammers.

Pastor shows him his bandaged hand, with its carefully plastered index finger.

"Thanks to your hit men, I haven't left any fingerprints anywhere since last night. So, Ponthard: do you want to sign the confession, or do you want me to kill you?"

(Well, how can I say it? On the one hand, he'd love to sign, while on the other . . .)

"Look, Ponthard, there's no point racking your brains about this. The situation is perfectly clear. If I kill you, it will be with Cercaria's gun. I'll push it up somewhere near your heart and, that way, you two will have ended up shooting each other during a rather violent brawl. If you sign, then Cercaria will simply have committed suicide. Follow me?"

(Real problems are always posed by those who understand them only too well.) The chair which Ponthard-Delmaire finally slumps down into seems to have been specially designed to carry obese despair: it stands up bravely to the impact. After a good minute's thought, Ponthard-Delmaire at last puts out a resigned hand towards the confession. While he signs it, Pastor carefully wipes clean the barrel and the stock of the P.38, slips the missing rounds back into the magazine and puts the gun in Cercaria's hand, whose middle finger at last folds itself back into place.

The rest is pure routine admin. Pastor phones up someone called Caregga and asks him to go and arrest Arnaud Le Capelier, either at his home or at the Department of Senior Citizens.

"Caregga, tell Arnaud that Edith Ponthard-Delmaire has fingered him, that the lady's father, the architect, has signed a confession and that Chief Superintendent Cercaria has committed suicide. Yes, that's right, Caregga, he's committed suicide . . . Oh! and I was forgetting, tell him that I'll be questioning him myself this evening. And if my name doesn't ring a bell, tell him that I'm the adopted son of Councillor Pastor and of his wife, Gabrielle. That should jog his memory a little. He had them both killed."

He paused, then went on in the gentlest of voices:

"Don't let him jump out of the window, or swallow cyanide, now, will you Caregga? I want him alive, as they say in the westerns. Please, Caregga, I want him alive . . ."

(The sweet tones of that voice . . . And poor Arnaud with his lovely central parting cutting his blond crop in two, poor Arnaud, the gobbler-up of granddads . . .)

"And Caregga? Send me round an ambulance and a Black Maria, then inform Chief Superintendent Coudrier of Cercaria's demise, will you?"

Click. He's hung up. Then, without even turning round towards the door, behind which I haven't missed out on a moment of the murder and the rest:

"Are you still there, Monsieur Malaussène? Don't go, I have something I ought to give you back."

(Give something back! Him? To me?)

"Here."

Still without looking at me, he hands me a large brown envelope. On it, is written INSPECTOR VANINI!

"I had to borrow these photos from you to serve as bait for these gentlemen here. Take them back. Your friend Ben Tayeb may well find them useful. He's about to be released."

I take back the photos in the tips of my fingers and then creep straight off on the tips of my toes. But:

"No, don't go. I still have to go round to your place to tie up a few loose ends."

Chapter 35

"So THERE WE are, lovely lady, it's all over."

Kneeling by the side of the bed, Pastor is talking to Julia as though she was just lying there with her eyes closed.

"The baddies are all dead or in prison."

Julia, of course, doesn't bat an eyelid. (If she did, that really would be the icing on the cake!)

"I promised you that I'd arrest them, remember?"

His voice sounds gentle. (A genuine gentleness now.) It's like he's holding out his hand to a child who's fallen to the bottom of a nightmare.

"As you can see, I've kept my word."

The entire family, grouped together there, is practically melting in adoration in front of this angelic inspector, who's so young, whose voice is so soothing . . .

"Tell me, lovely lady, they made so many mistakes, you really must have put the wind up them!"

Right now, he does indeed have an angelic look. His face has put itself back together again. It's rather a pink, chubby face, with no black caverns around his eyes, and it's topped off by a head of curly hair which is as light as toddlers' locks. How old must he be?

"And so you have won your battle."

(Hang about a bit though. Not even an hour ago, I saw him turn a bloke into a flower. Before my very eyes!)

"Thanks to you, they will now think twice before packing any more old folk off to homes!"

The two of them are obviously out to have quite a long chat. With her playing the Sphinx and hiding behind her inscrutable grin, and him patiently nattering away to himself, but just as if she was all there instead of being in a coma and was in complete agreement with him. There's a sweet harmony about them that chills me to the bone.

"That's right, there's going to be a trial. The victims that you saved will give evidence . . ."

Doctor Marty, who's making a house-call on Julia, pulls a strange face. He must be wondering whether lecturing the dying and comatose is a family tradition.

"But there's a vital part of the evidence that's still missing, lovely lady . . ."

(Between you and me, this urbane killer's starting to get right on my tits, the way he keeps whispering his "lovely lady" routine into my Julia's defenceless ear hole.)

"I need your article," Pastor whispers, leaning even further over her.

Julius the Dog, with his lopsided head and dangling tongue, looks like he's attending a lecture which is a bit beyond him. As he tries to concentrate, you can *see* the stench rising up around him.

"I'd like to be able to compare my own investigations with your article. You wouldn't object to that, I hope?"

And the two of them start talking shop.

"It goes without saying that I wouldn't communicate its contents to any other journalist. You have my word on that."

Just look at mum and the girls: ecstasy! And the boys: blind worship! And the old lads: the adoration of the Wise Men! (Hey, you lot, buck your ideas up a bit. This geezer's just blown someone's head off like he was popping at a watermelon!)

"And then there's something else I'd like to know as well."

He's now snuggling right up against my Julia.

"Why did you take so many risks? You knew they were onto you, you knew what they were going to do to you, so why didn't you just let it drop? What made you go on? It wasn't just professional curiosity this time, was it? What made you want to defend those old men?"

Standing there stiffly on her stiff pair of legs, Thérèse has a frown of professional interest on her face. Judging by her expression, she reckons that this lad knows what he's about. And what happens next bears her out.

"Come on now," says Pastor slightly louder, with a truly persuasive sweetness in his voice. "I *really* need to know. Where did you hide your article?"

"In my car," Julia answers.

(Yes, that's right. You've just read what I just heard. "In my car," *Julia answers!*) "She's said something!" "She's said something!" There are shouts of joy and people jumping up and down left, right and centre. But I'm so relieved, so happy and so riddled with jealousy that I just stay standing there, as though all this jubilation had nothing to do with me. I can hardly hear Doctor Marty's voice when he says to me:

"Malaussène, when I need to lay on a genuine miracle at the hospital, be a good chap and send round someone from your family."

She's now been talking for a long time. Her voice was a little out of sync with us, like she was speaking from somewhere else, somewhere far distant, way above us. But it was her familiar way of speaking. When Pastor asked her where he'd find her car, she answered in a strange, hesitant, fairy-like voice:

"You're in the force, aren't you? You should know. In the police pound, of course, as usual . . ."

Then she started to explain why she'd fought so hard in this struggle. Pastor had been right: it wasn't just from professional stubbornness. Julia's desire to investigate old drug addicts came from way back. And no, she didn't know any of the leaders of the gang, not the architect, nor the Chief Superintendent, nor our handsome Arnaud Le Capelier. She had no personal grudge against any one of them, only against The Lord High Opium. Quite simply against The Lord High Opium and all his incarnations.

This grudge between Julie and opium was a very old one. They had once fought over the same man. It had started in her childhood (and the little girl's voice she told her story in, coming as it did from that strong leopard-woman's body, brought tears to our eyes).

Julie saw herself once more in the mountains of the Vercors, with her father, ex-Colonial Governor Corrençon, the Independence Man, as some of the newspapers put it at the time, or else The Gravedigger of the Empire, one or the other. The father and daughter had an old hastily-renovated farmhouse there, called *Les Rochas*, where they would take refuge as often as possible. Julie had planted some strawberry bushes there. Hollyhocks flourished everywhere else. Independence Man or The Gravedigger of the Empire, Corrençon had been the first to negotiate with the Viet Minh, when it still hadn't been too late to avoid a massacre. Under Mendès-France, he'd worked out a self-governing status for Tunisia, then he'd worked under De Gaulle when it was necessary to give Black Africa back its freedom. But, as far as his little girl was concerned, he was the Great Geographer.

(Lying on the bed, surrounded by a family that's not her own, Julie now tells her story in the voice she'd had as a little girl.)

She recited the names of all those who had spent time in that farmhouse and who had won their nations independence. Her little girl's voice pronounced the names of Farhat Abbas, Messali Hadj, Ho Chi Minh and Vo Nguyen Giap, Ibn Yusuf and Bourguiba, Leopold Sedar Senghor and Kwame Nkrumah, Sihanouk and Tsiranana. Other names, with a Latin-American lilt, joined the list, dating from the time when Corrençon had been sent to play the Consul on Africa's sister continent: Vargas, Arrães, Allende, Castro and Che (Che! a bearded charismatic, whose portrait was to be found a few years later pinned up in every adolescent girl's bedroom).

At one time or another during their careers, most of these men had stayed at *Les Rochas*, that farmhouse lost in the Vercors, and Julie could remember word for word the animated conversations they had had when arguing with her father.

"Don't try to write History, just let Geography have its say!"

"Geography," Che had answered in a burst of laughter, "is just a collection of movable facts."

These men were mostly in exile. Some of them had the police on their tails. But in her father's company they had all the hearty joviality of a gang of building workers. They would start by speaking seriously, then begin playing around.

"What is a colony, student Giap?" Corrençon asked in a colonial schoolmaster's voice.

And, just to make Julie laugh, Vo Nguyen Giap, he who was later to become the victor of the battle of Dien Bien Phu, replied in a schoolboy's chant:

"A colony is a country whose civil service belongs to another country. For example: Indochina is a French colony and France is a Corsican colony."

One night there was a thunderstorm and a bolt of lightning struck just beside *Les Rochas*. The light bulb in the kitchen exploded in a shower of fiery stars, like it was an artillery shell. The rain started to fall as though the heavens were emptying themselves. Farhat Abbas was there, along with two other Algerians whose names Julie couldn't remember. Farhat Abbas had suddenly stood up and rushed outside where, in the apocalyptic storm, he yelled out:

"I shall no longer speak in French to the people around me, I shall speak in Arabic! I shall no longer call them 'comrades', I shall call them my 'brothers'!"

Curled up by the fireside, Julie would listen to these men talking all night long.

"Go to bed, Julie," Corrençon would say. "The secrets of states that don't exist yet are the closest secrets of all."

But she would beg to be allowed to stay, and there was always someone there to speak up for her:

"Let your daughter listen to us, Corrençon. You're not going to live for ever, you know."

All these visitors were friends of her father. There was an incredible sense of exultation during those nights. But, when they left the house, Governor Corrençon would suddenly shrink back inside himself. He'd withdraw into his bedroom and the house would start to smell of that sickly odour of grilled honey. Julie would do the washing-up during that lonely opium ceremony, then go to bed. She'd see her father again much later the following day, his pupils dilated, lighter than air and looking sadder.

"I'm leading a peculiar life, my girl. I'm preaching freedom and unmaking our colonial empire. It's as thrilling as opening a cage and as depressing as unpicking an old pullover. In the name of freedom, I'm sending whole families into exile. I'm frog-marching the empire to the firing squad."

In Paris, he was a regular customer of an opium den which has now been replaced by the Velodrome. The den was run by an ex-colonial schoolmistress, called Louise, and a tiny Tongkinese who Corrençon used to call his chemist. The wine business, which the couple used as a front, was closed down and the case went to court. Corrençon had wanted to testify on behalf of Louise and her Tongkinese husband. He raged against those "Indochina Veterans" who were behind the accusations.

"Souls of criminals with the consciences of plaster saints."

Then he became prophetic:

"Their children will become drug addicts to forget the fact that their fathers didn't make anything new."

But by that time he was so marked by drugs himself that the defence lawyers turned down his offer.

"Your appearance would only testify against the points you want to make, Monsieur Corrençon. You'd damage our clients' case."

He'd now gone from using opium to heroin, from the long pipe to the cold syringe. It was no longer his own contradictions that he was chasing in his veins, it was those of the world he'd helped to create. No sooner had countries been given their independence, than Geography had started making History again, as though it were an incurable disease. An epidemic with a high death count. Lumumba was executed by Mobutu, Ben Barka's throat was cut by Oufkir, Farhat Abbas was exiled, Ben Bella imprisoned, Ibn Yusuf eliminated by his own men, Vietnam was forcing its own History onto a Cambodia which had been bled dry. Friends from the Vercors farmhouse were being hunted down by friends from the Vercors farmhouse. Che himself had been shot in Bolivia, with, so it was whispered, Castro's tacit agreement. Geography endlessly tortured by History . . . Corrençon was now no more than a shadow punched full of lethal holes. He was lost in his old Colonial Governor's uniform which, in mockery, he still wore to do his gardening. He grew strawberry bushes at *Les Rochas* so that Julie would find the fruit of her girlhood when she came to stay there in July. He let the hollyhocks overrun the rest. He gardened there amid those massive weeds, taller than he was, his white uniform fluttering against his skeleton, like a flag carelessly wrapped around its pole.

Then, one summer, Julie had had the ridiculous idea that she was going to save her father. Since neither loving him nor reasoning with him had achieved anything, she decided to terrify him. She could still see the needle which she'd stuck into the crook of her arm that evening, knowing that he would soon be back home and that the syringe would already be half empty when the front door opened. And she could still hear the howl of rage which burst out of him as he threw himself onto her. He'd snatched away the needle and the syringe and started to beat her. He beat her like a man punishing a horse, with all the strength in his body. She was no longer a child. She was a tall, powerful woman, a journalist, a firebrand who'd got herself out of any number of scrapes. She didn't put up any resistance. Not from daughterly devotion, but because an unexpected terror had gripped her. *The blows he was raining on her face didn't hurt at all!* He had no strength left. His hands were as light as feathers. It was like a ghost grappling with a living person in the hope of re-entering a body. He beat her as much as he could. He beat her in silence, with a sort of conscientious fury.

Then he died.

He died.

His arm froze in mid-air like he was waving goodbye and he died. He fell to his daughter's feet without a sound.

And now, in her little girl's voice, she's calling to him. She says "Daddy . . ." over and over again. Doctor Marty, who can take policemen only up to a certain point, pushes young Inspector Pastor to one side and gives that huge hallucinating child a knock-out jab.

"She'll sleep now. Then tomorrow she'll wake up properly and you are all kindly requested to give her a fucking break."

The Fairy Gunmother

IT WAS WINTER OVER PARIS'S
BELLEVILLE QUARTER AND
THERE WERE FIVE
CHARACTERS. SIX,
INCLUDING A SHEET
OF BLACK ICE

Chapter 36

THE CITY'S VOLUME had been turned down low and Chief Superintendent Coudrier's curtains were open to the night. The last pot of coffee which Elisabeth had left there was still warm. Sitting upright on a Napoleonic chair, Inspector Pastor had just finished going through the second version of his oral report. It was completely identical to the first one. But, that evening, Chief Superintendent Coudrier's mind seemed clouded over. The overall picture of the business was clear enough, but as soon as he started to focus on any of its details, his vision became blurred, as though he was staring into a perfectly limpid lake into which a trickster had poured one single drop of incredibly condensed implausibility.

Coudrier: Pastor, would you be so good as to take me for an idiot?
    Pastor: I beg your pardon, Sir?
    Coudrier: Explain it all to me. I just don't understand it.
    Pastor: You can't understand why an architect should want to buy up property at a low price, renovate it, then sell it to the highest bidder, Sir?
    Coudrier: That I can understand, yes.
    Pastor: You can't understand why a Permanent Secretary for Senior Citizens should become involved in having old people put away in homes unnecessarily, if the price was right?
    Coudrier: That is within the bounds of possibility.
    Pastor: You can't understand why a Chief Superintendent, who specializes in narcotics, should start dealing in order to lay aside a nice little nest-egg for his retirement?
    Coudrier: Such things happen.

Pastor: And that the three of them (the Chief Superintendent, the Permanent Secretary and the architect) should put their heads together, then split the profits. Does that really sound so implausible?

Coudrier: No.

Pastor: . . .

Coudrier: That's not the problem. It's all those little details . . .

Pastor: For example?

Coudrier: . . .

Pastor: . . .

Coudrier: Why did that old lady kill Vanini?

Pastor: Because she was too quick for him, Sir. A certain number of our fellow officers go the same way every year. That's why I suggest we let her be, now she's been disarmed.

Coudrier: . . .

Pastor: . . .

Coudrier: And what about that young lady, Edith Ponthard-Delmaire? Why did she commit suicide? I can quite understand why Cercaria committed suicide when faced with defeat. I even find that preferable. But I have never heard of a drug pusher who jumps out of the window after being arrested!

Pastor: She wasn't your typical sort of pusher, Sir. Her reason for dealing was to undermine the reputation of a father who she thought was irreproachable. But she quite suddenly found out that her father was her paymaster and that undermining the reputation of such a foul specimen certainly wasn't going to be child's play. So she killed herself to show him her daughterly disgust. Young people have been doing that sort of thing ever since psychoanalysis invented the father figure.

Coudrier: That's right. These days, there are two sorts of delinquents: those with families and those without.

Pastor: . . .

Coudrier: . . .

Pastor: . . .

Coudrier: What's more, Pastor, it would seem that you got to the bottom of this shady affair thanks to a photograph you found quite by chance.

Pastor: That's correct, Sir. A photograph of Edith Ponthard-Delmaire giving amphetamines to an old man. If you add to this coincidence the fact that four cases which apparently had nothing to do with one another (Vanini's murder, the attempted murder of Julie Corrençon, the serial-killing of old women in Belleville and the selling of drugs to old men) turned out to be closely connected, then you can really say that luck was on our side.

Coudrier: Indeed, and with even more efficiency than a computer.

Pastor: That's what makes our work so novelistic, Sir.

Coudrier: . . .

Pastor: . . .

Coudrier: Another drop of coffee?

Pastor: With pleasure.

Coudrier: . . .

Pastor: . . .

Coudrier: Pastor, there is something I've been meaning to ask you for a long time now.

Pastor: . . .

Coudrier: I had a great deal of esteem for your father, the Councillor.

Pastor: You knew him, Sir?

Coudrier: He taught me constitutional law.

Pastor: . . .

Coudrier: He used to knit while he was teaching.

Pastor: Yes, and my mother used to polish his scalp with a shammy every time he went out.

Coudrier: That's right. The Councillor's scalp used to shine like a mirror. He would show it to us sometimes and say: *When in doubt, gentlemen, come here and examine the reflection of your consciences.*

Pastor: . . .

Coudrier: . . .

Pastor: . . .

Coudrier: All the same . . . a world in which Serbo-Croatian latinists teach old ladies how to shoot in the catacombs, in which these old ladies start gunning down policemen who have been sent out to protect them, in which retired booksellers start cutting throats to propagate the glory of literature, in which a wicked young woman defenestrates herself because her father is more wicked than she is . . . it is high time I retired, my lad, and consecrated myself exclusively to the upbringing of my grandsons. Someone is going to have to replace me, Pastor. And I must say that you do seem better equipped than I am when it comes to understanding such turn-of-the-century paradoxes.

Pastor: But I'm afraid that this turn of the century is going to have to do without my perspicacity, Sir. I am here to give you my resignation.

Coudrier: Come now, Pastor. You surely can't be bored already?

Pastor: That's not the reason.

Coudrier: May I ask what is?

Pastor: I've fallen in love, Sir. And I can't do more than one thing at the same time.

Chapter 37

"THEY'VE GONE, Benjamin."

Thérèse announces the news to me in the iciest tone of voice imaginable. Thérèse, my clinical little sister, has just sliced my heart in two with a single stroke of her scalpel.

"They left an hour ago."

Clara and I have stayed standing there on the doorstep.

"They left a letter."

(Great! A letter telling me they've gone. Just perfect . . .) Clara whispers in my ear:

"You're not saying you didn't expect it, now, are you Ben?"

(Of course I was expecting it! But, Clarinette, what makes you think that expected sorrows are easier to bear than unexpected ones?)

"Come on inside. We're standing in a draught!"

And there's the letter, lying there on the dining-room table. How many letters, in how many films, on how many chests-of-drawers, tables and mantelpieces can I have seen in my life? And, every time, I used to say: What a cliché! What a lousy cliché!

But today, the cliché's waiting for me. A rectangular, snowy-white one, lying right there on the dining-room table. Once more, in my mind's eye, I can see Pastor kneeling beside Julia's bed . . . How dare he take advantage of a sleeping woman! All the pretty lies he must have poured into her ears while she was lying there, defenceless . . . The filthy bugger!

"My heart's bleeding, Thérèse. You haven't got an elastoplast on you, by any chance?"

(I'll never have the guts to open that letter . . .)

Clara obviously senses this, because she goes over to the table, picks up the envelope, opens it (they didn't even stick it down), unfolds the letter, glances through it, lets her arm droop limply by her side, then her young girl's eyes glaze over with cheap romantic glitter.

"He's taken her to Venice. To the Danieli!"

"Did she take her plaster off specially for the occasion?"

That's all I can come up with to plug the gap. ('Did she take her plaster off?' Pretty cool reaction, I reckon.) Maybe it is . . . But if I judge by the way my two sisters are gawping at me, it isn't very clear to them. They obviously just don't get it. Then Clara suddenly twigs. She bursts out laughing:

"But Pastor hasn't gone off with Julia, he's gone off with mum!"

"What? Say that again, will you?"

"You thought he'd gone off with Julie?"

This last question comes from Thérèse. It doesn't sound like she's in a laughing mood. She goes on:

"And that's the way you react? A man goes off with the love of your life and you just stand there on the doorstep without even lifting a finger!"

(Jesus, I'm in for a bollocking!)

"And that's how much you trust Julie? What sort of a lover are you, Ben? And what sort of a man?"

Thérèse carries on telling off her litany of cutting questions, but I'm already on the stairs, taking them four at a time on my way to my Julie, bounding up towards my Corrençon, like a child who's already been forgiven. That's right, Thérèse my darling, I am a doubting lover, my ticker has a doubtful beat. Why should anyone love me? Why me and not someone else? Can you answer that, Thérèse? Every time I realize that it's me, it seems like a miracle! Do you prefer muscle-bound hearts, Thérèse? Big, cock-sure thumpers?

Many hours later, when Clara'd brought us an omelette in bed, many hours later, when Julius had licked his bowl clean, and Julie and I our plates, many hours later, when our second bottle of Veuve Clicquot had rolled dead under the bed, many hours later, when our bodies and souls had been fulfilled, remoulded, cleaned out and emptied, my Julie (my very own Julie, sod it!) asks me:

"So, what about your visit to Stojil?"

And I hear myself answer, with the little breath left in my body:

"He chucked us both out."

That was quite true . . . Our old Stojil chucked us out, Clara and me. Since Pastor had pulled a few strings for us, we got to see him in his cell, instead of in the visiting room. It was a tiny pit, crammed with dictionaries and carpeted with crisp sheets of screwed-up paper.

"Now, kids, will you be good enough to put the word round: no visits to old Stojilkovicz."

There was an odour of fresh ink, gitanes and the two-fold sweat of feet and brain-cells. It smelt of fine intellectual effort.

"I haven't a moment to myself, kids. Publius Vergilius Maro is not going to let himself be translated into Serbo-Croat just like that. And they've only sent me down for eight months."

He pushed us towards the door.

"Even the trees out there are putting me off . . ."

It was springtime outside. Buds were popping out at Stojil's window.

"In eight months' time, I won't even have finished starting."

So there was Stojil in his cell, with rough drafts up to his knees, dreaming of a life sentence so that he could translate Virgil's complete works . . .

He chucked us out.

Then he locked himself in.

Much later still, after a second omelette, a third bottle of Veuve and finding each other all over again, I was the one who asked:

"Why do you reckon Pastor went off with mum?"

"Because that's what he's always been waiting for."

"'That?' What do you mean 'that'?"

"A vision. From what he told me while I was out of it, he could only fall in love with a vision."

"That's what he talked to you about?"

"He told me his life story. He told me a lot about a woman called Gabrielle, who was the vision his father, Councillor Pastor, had."

* * *

"And what about today? What else has happened apart from Pastor and mum going off?"

"Thérèse has gone to the Police Force Clinic."

"Again?"

"I think she's decided to resurrect old Thian."

Chapter 38

A T THE POLICE Force Clinic on Boulevard Saint-Marcel, nurse Magloire sensed that Inspector Van Thian's condition was beyond her professional capabilities. Policemen never made for easy patients. They always held the fact of being hospitalized against the force. With gunshot or knife wounds, most of them dreamed of getting a revenge which the uniform they wore made impossible. They knew it. They hated the force and that made them worse. Until, that is, they came under nurse Magloire's supervision. With her bushels of maternal care, her huge tenderness and her purring wisdom, nurse Magloire was a new force to be reckoned with. The policemen recovered their strength and got better. When they didn't get better, when they died despite of all she did, they still died cradled in her mighty arms. Nurse Magloire would rock them until they had gone cold.

But this Inspector Van Thian was altogether a different kettle of fish. To start with, he should normally have been DOA. Such a frail, bullet-ridden body shouldn't have lasted five minutes. But a strange force was keeping Inspector Van Thian alive. Nurse Magloire was soon to understand that this force was pure, undiluted hatred. Inspector Van Thian wasn't alone in his bed. He was sharing it with a Vietnamese woman, called widow Ho. Imprisoned inside the same body, the widow and the inspector seemed to have been in the throes of a divorce since the year dot. Each of them yearned for the other to die; that was what kept them alive.

Nurse Magloire had never seen anything like the horrible things they did to each other.

Among other things, widow Ho hated Inspector Van Thian for the long winter nights she'd had to spend with her arms in the gaping jaws of cash points. From listening to her, this sounded as dangerous as trying to fish back a wedding ring that had been swallowed by a shark. But the old copper only chuckled and reminded the widow how much she'd enjoyed waving wads of banknotes around under paupers' noses.

"Hit hisn't tlue!" the widow yelled out. "You riar!"

"Get out of my face and piss off back to Cholon with your spling lolls."

They also had a good few rows about their respective nationalities. Inspector Van Thian went on at her about her origins, and she went on at him about his total lack of roots.

"Whallabout yooou? Where yooou come flom? No where! And hi ham flom Tchoaleun!" (That's her pronunciation of Cholon, the Chinese suburb of Saigon; while he made it sound like the French town of Cholon sur Marne.)

"I was born in the plonk trade and you can go fuck yourself."

But this answer left Thian dissatisfied. The widow's attack had hit him hard. The inspector would then go off in a depression for a few hours, which gave nurse Magloire a break. Then suddenly the row would heat up again.

"Don't try and wriggle out of it, you definitely tried to get me blown away."

"Bah! Phooey!"

Who had been the one who'd put widow Ho out onto those dangerous streets for weeks on end? Who'd left the front door open day and night, just waiting for the killer to turn up? Who'd forced her to stand and have a chat with the most boracic smack-heads in town? Whose idea had it been to put her out as bait on a hook when he hadn't even been capable of defending his own neighbour? Who? People don't even treat dogs like that!

"And who unloaded the Manhurin? It was me, was it? Who went down on her knees and prayed for the killer to come round and do me? Who threw the magazine one way and the gun the other way?"

Their slightest exchange of words led them down a blind alley. She hated couscous and, for weeks on end, he'd rammed couscous and kebabs down her throat. He replied that the stench of her perfume, The Thousand Flowers of Asia, had upped his dose of tranquillizers.

"Your lirrel tabrets haren't my fault, tat was Dzanine!"

He groaned:

"Leave Janine out of this."

"Dzanine the dziantess, hit was her wid your lirrel tabrets!"

He repeated:

"Leave Janine out of this!"

But she knew she'd got him there.

"She dead!"

Then Inspector Van Thian threw himself onto widow Ho, yelling at her to shut up and finally tearing out handfuls of those countless tentacles that kept sprouting from her body, chucking them up high among the bottles, or down over the machines with their flashing lights.

"Now you're going to die!"

Blood spurted out. Scraps of flesh flew into the air. The emergency alarm bell went off automatically and nurse Magloire threw the whole weight of her Sumo body onto the widow and the inspector's double incarnation. Then she called for help. The damage got repaired. The blood was mopped up. New drips and drains were installed. Life was plugged back in again. And the frail body was strapped down as thoroughly as if there really had been two of them. Reduced to a state of physical immobility, Inspector Van Thian and widow Ho went quiet. They became a model, dying patient. They didn't row anymore, not even mentally. They went sweetly off to sleep. Calm, calm . . . To such a point that the straps were loosened then totally removed. Freedom of movement was given back to that body which was weakening hourly and which looked incapable of making the slightest gesture. But, in the half-light of the room, a nasty grin spread across Inspector Van Thian's lips. A grin that was full of hidden intent. A naked desire to hurt. When nurse Magloire had left the room, he whispered:

"Just look at your tits!"

Widow Ho didn't catch on at once. She stayed on the defensive.

"Like a pair of fried eggs."

Still no reaction.

"And what about your arse? If you can call that an arse!"

She stayed mum. He went on whispering:

"Like jelly. You've got a jelly arse."

In the half-light, the tension was mounting.

"There's one thing I've always wanted to know . . ."

Silence.

"Where are your shoulders? You got any shoulders?"

She kept mum. And he kept at her, while she started to hunch her back.

"Janine had tits and an arse and shoulders. Janine didn't live in a perfume bottle. Janine smelt like a woman. Janine had her feet firmly planted on the ground, she didn't blow away in the breeze. Janine was a tree. Janine bore fruit!"

She hadn't been expecting that one. She could put up with insults but, like any woman, the rival woman's name was as unbearable to her as the rival man's name is to any man.

"Janine . . ."

One of the machines they were plugged into started blinking dangerously, its needle wobbling at the border of the red zone. Then a gasket blew and the widow's shrill voice nagged back at him:

"Ten go hand dzoin your Dzanine!"

In her little clenched fist, the tubes she'd ripped out looked like a soya harvest. The alarm bell went off and nurse Magloire burst into the room with a porter. They threw their combined weight onto the invalid, who immediately calmed down again. It felt like they were strapping up a stiff.

Nurse Magloire just couldn't understand it. It was proof that, even after forty years' service, she still had things to learn. But who could teach her how to soothe such pain?

A tall gawky girl could.

One afternoon of spring drizzle, she walked into the old Asian copper's room. She sat down stiffly beside the patient's bed, without having any more effect on him than any other of his visitors – a young curly-headed inspector, awash in a huge pullover; or a discreet bigwig,

Chief Superintendent Coudrier. But Inspector Van Thian didn't greet his visitors. He answered none of their questions, he didn't even make eye contact with them. When this tall adolescent with her graveyard looks bent over him, he didn't bat an eyelid either. Nurse Magloire couldn't work out what sort of authority radiated from that dry-skinned girl. The girl undid the leather straps, as though God the Father had ordained her so to do, and nurse Magloire let her get on with it. When she'd freed Inspector Van Thian's body, the girl rubbed his wrists for a while, then massaged his arms up to his elbows, allowing some mysterious current to flow once more. And the old policeman's eyes, which had been staring at the ceiling, did at last swivel round and look back at that tall, silent girl. She didn't smile at his miraculous stare and didn't ask the wounded man the slightest question. She simply took hold of his hand, which she ironed out with the side of her own hand with a sort of professional brutality. When the hand was totally relaxed, the girl stared down into it, then spoke at last:

"The first part of what was to happen has now taken place. You have been struck down with saturnism: an overdose of lead in your body."

Her voice matched her body. It was stiff and dry. Even though she herself had rather a round voice, this fact rather surprised nurse Magloire. The girl went on:

"I told you that this disease brought about the fall of the Roman Empire. This is true. From insanity. Saturnism makes people insane. Just as you are now insane. The last generations of the Caesars spent their lives killing one another, husbands and wives, brothers and sisters, fathers and sons, just as you are killing each other now. But the bullets have been removed from your body and you're going to pull through."

That's all she said. Without a word of goodbye, she got up and left the room. On the threshold, she turned back towards nurse Magloire.

"Tie him up again."

The next day, she came back. Once again, she unstrapped the old inspector, massaged him, ironed out the palm of his hand, sunk her gaze into it and spoke. The patient had spent a relatively peaceful night. Nurse Magloire had heard the germs of arguments sprouting, but this interior

243

fighting had been immediately crushed by some mysterious authority.

"I can see that we now understand each other," the tall bony girl said without a word of explanation. "Today, you have started your convalescence."

She spoke without looking at him. She was addressing his hand. With her two thumbs she stroked its hills and valleys, meanwhile the inspector's face became as smooth as a baby's bottom. Nurse Magloire had never seen anything like it. And yet the girl was speaking without the slightest tenderness in her voice:

"But you haven't gone far enough yet. We'll be able to speak seriously when you've stopped feeling sorry for yourself."

There ended her second visit. She left without asking for the patient to be tied up again. The next day, she came back.

"Your Janine is dead," she said straightaway to the open hand. "As for widow Ho, she doesn't exist."

The patient made no reaction to these two shocks. For the first time since his admission, nurse Magloire saw him concentrate on something being said *outside* his own body.

"But my mother has gone off with your team-mate, Pastor, and I've got a baby on my hands who desperately needs you," the visitor went on. "That little idiot Jeremy called her Verdun. She starts screaming as soon as she wakes up. She's carrying all the memories of the Great War inside her; a time when people thought they were German, French, Serb, British or Bulgarian but they all ended up in the same mincer, as my brother Benjamin would put it. That's what our little Verdun has before her eyes as soon as she opens them: the sight of a mass suicide in the name of national pride. Only you can calm her down. I have no idea why, but that's the way it is. When you hold her in your arms, she stops crying."

She then vanished once more, only to reappear the following morning. She didn't respect the official visiting hours.

"What is more," she said, "we need you to replace Risson and tell the children stories. After Risson's performances, my brother Benjamin is no longer up to the task. But you would fit the bill perfectly. You don't spend twelve years of your life spinning yourself yarns, then invent someone like widow Ho without becoming an excellent story teller. And your jokes have often brought Inspector Pastor back to the land of the living. So now it's up to you: you either die or tell stories. I'll be back in a week's time. Oh, and I think it's only fair to warn you that my family is quite a handful!"

What nurse Magloire witnessed during the next seven days was quite simply a miracle. The wounds seemed to be visibly healing up before her very eyes. When the drains had been removed, he started eating everything in sight. Famous consultants lined up by his bedside. Students took frantic notes.

At daybreak of the seventh day, he got dressed then sat on his bed with his suitcase in his lap and waited for that tall skinny girl. She arrived at six o'clock in the evening. Standing in the door frame, she said:

"The taxi's waiting for us."

He went out without even leaning on her arm.

Chapter 39

"IT WAS WINTER over Paris's Belleville quarter and there were five characters. Six, including the sheet of black ice. Or even seven, if you count the dog that had gone along with Half Pint to the baker's. An epileptic dog, with its tongue dangling out the corner of its mouth."

And it's night in our flat. Clara's just put her cashmere over the little lamp, which is now shedding its smooth yellow light in the children's bedroom. The pyjamas and night-dresses smell of fresh apples. Pairs of slippers are dangling in mid-air. Sitting on Risson's stool, Van Thian is telling a story. Little Verdun is sleeping peacefully in his arms. The children's eyes have already started out on their voyage. They'd been peering suspiciously at the old copper, waiting to pounce on him. Who was this jerk who reckoned he was going to replace Risson? They took turns staring him out. But old Thian isn't someone who gets flurried easily. Plus he's got a film cop's gravelly voice, which helps.

"I'm going to tell you the story of the Fairy Gunmother," he announced.

"Is she the old fairy who turns blokes into flowers?" Half Pint asked.

"Spot on," old Thian said. Then he added: "But watch out now, because in this story, you all have your parts to play."

"I'm too old for fairy stories," Jeremy said.

"No-one's ever too old for them," Thian answered.

Then he started his story.

Julie's head is pressing down onto my lap with the full weight of re-togetherness.

The kids' eyes have finally drifted away from Thian and taken wing.

And when, at the end of the first chapter, the old lady with the hearing-aid turns round to blow that blond head off its shoulders, everyone jumps. A beautiful moment of silence follows, surprise gently melting away.

But Jeremy has decided to be awkward. When everyone's settled down again, he says:

"Something's wrong with it."

"And what's that?" Thian asks.

"Your blond copper there, Vanini, he's a fucking racist, isn't he?"

"Yes."

"He smashes Arabs' heads in with a knuckleduster, doesn't he?"

"That's right."

"So why give him all the funny lines?"

"What funny lines?"

"When he thinks that the sheet of black ice is shaped like Africa, when he thinks that the old dear's just got to the middle of the Sahara, that she could take a short cut through Eritrea and Somalia, except that the Red Sea's frozen solid in the gutter, he's being a bit of a comedian, isn't he?"

"A bit of a one, yes."

"That's what's wrong. A shit-head like him isn't allowed to be funny."

"Oh, isn't he? And whyever not?"

(Oh dear, oh dear . . . looks like we've got a heated debate coming on . . .)

"Just because!"

Faced with such a forceful argument, Thian has pause for thought. Knowing how to tell stories is one thing, but making Jeremy change his mind is quite another.

Silence.

What's he going to come up with? A subtle speech concerning mankind's ambivalent nature, showing how even the biggest bastards can still have a sense of humour?

Silence.

Or else a defence of creative licence, a licence which consists, among other things, in shoving the thoughts of your choice into whichever heads you fancy . . .

Not a bit of it. Like all great strategists, old Thian goes for the third approach: the unexpected. He stares blankly over at Jeremy, measures him up and down with his eyes, then, in his best gravelly voice, he calmly says:

"Listen up, shit-for-brains, if you keep fucking me around, I'll let Verdun do the talking."

And, in the pale light of the bedroom, he lifts Verdun up in his arms, right in front of Jeremy. Verdun opens her fiery eyes and the volcano's crater of her mouth, and Jeremy yells:

"Noooo! Go on, uncle Thian, tell us what happens next! For Christ's sake, what happens next?"